A Diamond in My Heart

The Unaltered Series: Book Two

Lorena Angell

Special Thanks

Special thanks to my daughter, Luna, for encouraging the expansion of The Unaltered universe. Luna, I highly doubt I could have developed such an intricate back-story to the diamond or come up with future ideas necessary for crafting an engaging storyline without your help.

Thanks for being my sounding board, my voice of reason, and for putting up with my inconsistencies. I admire your creative mind and am grateful for your help in expanding the series.

--Love, Mom

Books by Lorena Angell

<u>The Unaltered Series</u>

A Diamond in My Pocket, Book 1
A Diamond in My Heart, Book 2
The Diamond of Freedom, Book 3
The Diamond Bearers' Destiny, Book 4
The Diamond Bearer's Secret, Book 5
The Diamond Bearers' Rising, Book 6
Books 7-10 coming soon!

<u>The Lost Crown Series</u>

Royal Refugee
Royal Resistance
Royal Redemption

Contents

Chapter 1 - Freedom...1

Chapter 2 -- Nyctophobia...8

Chapter 3 -- Bad vs. Evil, Good vs. Right.................21

Chapter 4 -- Brand New Power.................................38

Chapter 5 -- Do Over...55

Chapter 6 -- Deadly Shadows.................................78

Chapter 7 -- A Kiss for Good Luck.........................101

Chapter 8 -- Matchmaker Calli.............................113

Chapter 9 -- Freedom to Choose.............................135

Chapter 10 -- Project T19.................................154

Chapter 11 -- Missing Persons.............................174

Chapter 12 -- The Amulet Thief.............................196

Chapter 13 -- Revelations.................................216

Chapter 14 -- Relinquishment.............................234

Chapter 15 -- The Diamond Bearers.........................252

Chapter 1 - Freedom

I used to scoff at magical powers and abilities, used to have this amazing focused direction in life and didn't allow my time to be wasted on silly conspiracy theories or gossip. I certainly didn't believe in the existence of any superpowers or unnatural abilities—until I became the first person on earth to display all the known powers and abilities.

A few months ago, I learned first-hand that cosmic energy rays exist and have always existed, and that nearly everyone on the planet has been affected by them in one way or another.

My mother, Dr. Charlotte Courtnae, and I belong to a rare bloodline of purity that exempts us from the effects of those cosmic energy rays. Something about our DNA protected us while we were in the womb, and we were never "altered." We are unchanged, unaffected. Unlike me, she doesn't *know* she's an Unaltered.

Living on a planet where I'm a member of this minority isn't so bad, really. Those with powers and abilities who think they can rule the world have no control over me. My mind cannot be read by the Readers. My future remains unseen by the Seers. Healers cannot manipulate my body, and I'm untraceable to a Hunter, for I have no scent. Runners would technically have the advantage over me if I were a regular Unaltered like my mother. But I'm not regular. I'm not ordinary.

I'm an Unaltered Diamond Bearer.

I carry a piece of the Sanguine Diamond within my heart, which gives me every known power and ability plus a couple bonus powers. Maetha, my mentor and the person responsible for the jewel in my heart, hasn't admitted anything, but I suspect she bears a diamond shard in her heart as well. I plan on asking more questions when she comes to visit.

Five months have passed since I returned from the Runner's Compound in Montana. It feels like an eternity ago. I finished up my junior year in high school and welcomed the summer months as a time I could develop my powers. I've had to be more careful when using my abilities. When I healed my neighbor's broken hip right after I returned, I didn't think he would tell my parents— or the whole neighborhood, for that matter. My parents, being the doctors that they are, suspected dementia rather than believe I might have the ability to heal using my mind. Lesson learned. Now I only try to use my healing power when I'm in large crowds.

The last couple of weeks, I've been helping at my mother's counseling clinic while her regular receptionist, Evelyn, is on vacation. Today I'm supposed to take a couple files over to the Behavioral Health Center two blocks away. I could easily walk, but I figure I'll hit the Coffee Shack on the way back as an excuse to drive my new cherry-red Mini Cooper.

My parents bought me the car when I came home from Clara Winter's "Olympic" training camp. They were told I'd been in an automobile accident that resulted in injuries which had disqualified me for this go around of competition. I think they assumed I'd be bummed about being sent home and thought the Cooper would cheer me up . . . and they were right. I know I'm fortunate to be the only child of two doctors and that most kids my age would be lucky to get a rusted-out, dented, twenty-year-old car, so I try not to brag. Needless to say, any opportunity to get behind the wheel excites me to no end.

I take the files to be delivered and leave the building. I climb into my vanilla-scented car and start the engine. After making sure the mirrors are in the correct position, I carefully back the car out of the parking spot. Turning back around to put the car in drive, I see a man leaning against the building I'd just exited.

Strange. I hadn't noticed him before.

He stands around six-feet tall, with well-trimmed black hair, and I guess his age to be mid-forties. He has a square jaw line, straight nose, and his eyes are hidden behind black sunglasses. His long, black trench coat is open in front, revealing a lanky frame dressed in a T-shirt and faded blue jeans. Square-toed motorcycle boots peek out below the hemline of his jeans, hinting at the possibility he owns a Harley. His trench coat reminds me of what cowboys wear in the old Western movies my father loves to watch.

This man doesn't fit the profile of the normal patrons of the clinic. I decide to use my Hunter ability to smell the air around me, searching for his scent. Perhaps I'll be able to determine if he has a cosmic power. The smell of his leather duster, jeans and T-shirt fills my nose. However, this man has no personal scent, which raises alarms.

My attention is pulled away by an approaching car. I move my car out of the way and look back for the scent-less man, but he's gone. I drive away to deliver the files, realizing I haven't met anyone other than Maetha and my mother who doesn't have a scent.

When I arrive at the Coffee Shack after delivering the

files, I see him again. This time he's leaning up against a pick-up truck with his thumbs hooked in the front pockets of his jeans. My first thought is he must be a Runner, but the fact he doesn't have a scent cancels that out. This man is clearly an Unaltered. I'll be waiting for a few minutes until the two cars in front of me have their orders filled, so I decide to exercise my ability to probe his mind—one more opportunity to practice the powers of the diamond on unsuspecting subjects. I reach out with my mind to penetrate his thoughts, but find it hard to feel any kind of mind or thought process. Then, without warning I'm hit with a mental force so strong the wind is knocked out of my lungs. My fingers death-grip the steering wheel while I try to regain my breath.

A smooth, deep voice enters my head. *How is it a young girl like you is able to read minds?*

My lungs burn with the need for air as my mind swims around the realization this man is projecting his thoughts into my head. Maetha told me this type of projection died out over the years and the power only exists inside the complete Sanguine Diamond. I only have a piece of the diamond now, and cannot communicate telepathically anymore. I put my thoughts at the front of my mind, figuring if he has this power he must have other powers too—he must possess a diamond.

Did Maetha send you? I ask with my mind.

Maetha? So she's behind this?

Bingo! He knows about Maetha, so he *must* have a diamond.

Behind what? I question. My lungs finally relax and I am able to inflate them properly.

He readjusts his stance and takes off his sunglasses, revealing heavy eyebrows hovering above squinted eyes. I wonder why he removed his shades. Is he trying to get a better look at me? He must be reading my mind because he puts them back on.

Who died for you? he asks, assuming I'll know what he means.

I don't know what you're talking about.

The car behind me honks to alert me to pull forward one spot. I do so.

Maetha still operates with the same deception, I see. You should take my advice, little girl. Get as far away from her as you can.

Why should I listen to you?

Because I know her better than just about anyone else!

His statement makes my hair stand on end. *What's your name?* I ask.

I don't go by one. Names are mere labels that inhibit progression. I prefer to be recognized by what I offer. Today I offer freedom. You may think of me as your freedom.

Ooh-kaaay. I am officially freaked out. *Oh, I won't be thinking of you at all, bucko!"*

The car in front of me pulls forward and I follow— only I don't stop at the window. I press the gas pedal to the floor, leaving tread marks on the pavement.

My heart races and my eyes check the rear-view mirror repeatedly as I speed through traffic on my way back to the office. My compact Mini slices through tight spots with the ease of a bobsled. The further I travel away from the creepy man, the more my clenched jaw begins to relax . . . until I arrive back at the office, where I discover "Mr. Freedom" leaning against the building in the same spot as before. I should have realized his diamond would afford him the running ability, but I'm still surprised to see him.

Calli, when you decide to utilize my help, all you'll have to do is ask. His lips part in an almost evil smile, revealing perfectly straight white teeth. Then he turns and walks away.

A couple of days have passed since I saw him, and I can't help but frequently look over my shoulder. I still experience the same panic when I think about the man I've come to refer to as "Freedom." His whole demeanor left me feeling uneasy. It's just fine with me if I never meet him again.

I wonder how he found me. Did he seek me out, or was he passing through and detected a difference in me compared to other people? I also ponder what he said.

More than anything, I wonder how many other Unaltereds have diamonds in their hearts.

Maetha said she'd come and train me to visualize auras, like my roommate, Beth, from the Runner's compound. But I haven't heard from her yet. Now that I understand all unaltered humans have identifiable auras, whether or not they have a diamond, I'm excited to learn how to spot other people like me. I certainly don't want to go around smelling everyone, trying to find those without a scent. Being able to view auras would make things so much easier.

An important date is fast approaching: the day Chris Harding resigns as a spy.

I would love to go see him . . . to get my "Chris fix." I could watch him from a distance and he wouldn't need to know I was present. But what if he saw me? What would that do to him? He'd be reminded of the pain we suffered because of Maetha. Not only would he be tortured further, it would also be painful for me. I was several years older in the vision than I am now.

I know I will see him again, but I also know now is not that time. He, on the other hand, doesn't—and shouldn't—know I have powers. From his perspective, the whole chain of events was manipulated, just as he and I were. Not to mention the fact that in his vision I was a Healer, not the ordinary human he now believes I am.

If I were present at his resignation, he would come to the conclusion I have Seer or Reader abilities, which I would need in order to know his plans. Even though I discard the idea of showing up to see him, the longing to do so doesn't leave me.

Chapter 2 - Nyctophobia

I can't help but feel somewhat uncomfortable while working the reception desk at my mother's psychiatric clinic. Compared to the age of most of her patients, I'm just a "whipper-snapper" —which they're fond of telling me. Well, only one patient did, and he was eighty-nine years old. Imagine that, a man so old, yet deathly afraid of the dark.

Most of my mother's patients suffer from the same phobia.

I never realized what my mother went through in the course of one day at the office. Take today, for instance. Her patient line-up begins with a middle-aged man who tapes black garbage bags together and plasters them all over his windows to protect himself from the light. Another patient won't go anywhere at night because his fear of the dark is so severe. Yet another won't even leave the house in the daylight because she's afraid of cloudy days, afraid even of the shade cast by big leafy trees. The final patient of the day is a young girl around eight-years-old who suffers panic attacks whenever her mother tries to take her outside after dark.

When my mother exits her office with the young girl, Sasha, she hands me her chart. A yellow sticky with a phone number and name is attached to the front.

"Calli, would you please call and set up an appointment for Sasha?" my mother asks.

The name on the sticky is Charles Rhondell. My eyes shoot up to my mother, who doesn't seem to understand what I'm thinking. I've met a man with that same name before—the leader of the Mind Readers. Is this the same man? Does that mean . . . I look at Sasha, who's eyeing me curiously, angling her head from side to side.

She speaks in her quiet whisper of a voice. "You're different."

"How do you know I'm different when you've never met me before?"

"No, you're different than most, but just like the doctor."

"Honey, it's impolite to talk to people like that." Her mother nervously tries to suppress her daughter's innocent comment.

Without even looking into the mother's mind I can see she's embarrassed about her daughter's behavior, and she doesn't want to believe her daughter might be able to read minds. I enter the mother's mind and find a couple instances where she thought Sasha might be accessing her thoughts. I can feel how logical reasoning fought with indisputable facts. She feels Sasha has read her mind before, but she doesn't want to admit her suspicions to anyone for fear of ridicule.

"But Mommy, she doesn't have a brain," Sasha insists, only to be quickly ushered across the room and given a sharp reprimand.

I pick up the phone and dial the number for Mr. Rhondell. He's out of the office, but a receptionist lines up an appointment for the following week. He will come to my mother's office to meet with Sasha.

Sasha's mother comes back over to the desk. "I

apologize for my daughter's behavior. Sometimes she says things like that and leaves me horrified. I'm really sorry."

I glance across the room to the couch where Sasha sits with her arms folded and her ankles crossed. I hand the woman an appointment card with the date and time Mr. Rhondell's receptionist lined up. "Don't worry about it. Most of the time I feel like I don't have a brain. The doctor will meet with you in one week."

"*One week?* What am I supposed to do with her until then?"

I look around for my mom so she can rescue me, but she's already gone back into her office. So I say, "Well, don't try to force her outside, and she won't have a panic attack." The woman seems frustrated with my response. She drops the card in her purse, then walks over, snatches her daughter's hand, and briskly leaves the office.

Later that night at dinner, I try to read my mother's mind, hoping this time I'll get in. I'd really like to know how much she knows about Charles Rhondell. Over the past few months I've tried repeatedly to reach out for her mind only to find there's nothing there. When I look at my father, I feel a connection to his mind. If I focus on him, I'm able to read his thoughts. But concerning my mother, when I see her, I don't feel the same connection. I'm reminded of how I felt when I was a regular human. There were no minds attached to people, just people . . . and my wishing I could read their minds.

I'm unsuccessful connecting with my mother's mind, so I decide to ask her about Charles Rhondell. "Who is the man you had me call for your last patient? Is he a doctor too?"

"No. He's a behavioral specialist who works miracles with kids who are afraid of the dark and who think they can read minds."

"Do you get many kids like her?"

"I've seen several patients with nyctophobia, but they weren't as young as Sasha. Sometimes nyctophobia is accompanied with delusions of future sight."

"Future sight?"

"Yes. One mother was so upset because her teenage daughter was predicting the future with surprising accuracy. It took a long time to convince her they were mere coincidences."

"Do you remember what the girl predicted?" I ask, admittedly curious.

"Yes, she claimed to have foreseen the destruction of their entire town of Kalapana on the big island of Hawaii in 1990. I didn't meet the girl until several years later. I tried to explain to her that such 'premonitions' are usually based on facts we observe around us. The fact is their town was in a potential lava path and sooner or later the town would be affected by the volcano. I told her our brains are quite powerful and can formulate possible future outcomes based on the facts at hand, but she defended herself to no end, saying she'd seen the same images in her mind prior to the event happening. The mother was torn between believing her daughter and wanting to help her believe she imagined it."

My father puts his fork down and wipes his mouth with his napkin. "Well, that's completely understandable. If Calli came to us with information that our town was going to be destroyed, I'd listen. I might be a little hesitant, but I know her well enough to know she would never lie about something like that."

"I feel the same, Allen," my mother says.

"Thanks, Dad." I smile and he raises his glass to me. My thoughts travel back to Charles Rhondell and what might happen when he arrives at the office next week. I look at my mother and wonder if she will be blown away when Charles refers to my "injuries." I deduce I should tell her right now that I know the man.

"Mom, I think I met this guy while I was in Montana. One of the athletes was having the same symptoms as your patient, and Mr. Rhondell was brought in to help." A little white lie. *Sorry Dad, but I'm a seasoned liar.*

"Well, he is the best in the nation. I don't doubt they would be anxious for him to help a potential Olympic candidate," my mother says.

"Mom, just out of curiosity, what type of premonition *would* you believe to be of the paranormal variety?"

"It would take something earth-shattering, something unpredictable, so out of the norm that heads are scratched."

"Like predicting the winning lottery numbers?"

"No, that's just dumb luck. I mean something like, 'On such and such a date, at such and such a time, aliens will land at a particular place.' Something like that isn't predictable and is highly unlikely to happen. If someone foresaw that happening, it would certainly catch my attention."

"Calli," my father interjects, "what do you want for your birthday?"

Oh yeah, my birthday is next week—the big seventeen! "I don't know."

"See, I can predict the future. I knew you'd say that." He smiles at me and says, "We'll surprise you. How about that?"

Charles Rhondell enters the office, and right off the bat his eyes meet mine.

"Calli?"

"Hi, Mr. Rhondell."

"What are you doing here? How do you know Charlotte?" My presence has clearly caught him off guard.

"Dr. Courtnae is my mother, Charles. How's your wife?" I ask, knowing they were reunited following the eradication of the Death Clan.

"Good. She's good."

My eyes are drawn to his neck and to the peculiar necklace he wears. The leather cord around his neck is attached to a glass encasement shaped like a teardrop. A piece of the Sanguine Diamond floats gently inside, suspended in a way that defies gravity.

"I'll let my mother know you've arrived." I lift the phone and press button number one. After announcing his arrival, my mother asks he be shown in. "She can see you now, Charles." I stand and walk him to the office door.

"Calli, how are you doing since . . . well, since what happened?"

"All back to normal, Charles. Thanks for asking."

He leans close and whispers kindly in my ear. "It's too bad you lost all your abilities."

As he does this, I experience a sharp pain within my heart, almost as if my shard moved. I keep calm.

"I don't feel that way at all, sir. By the way, my mother doesn't know anything about what happened to me or about the world of powers and abilities." I smile and open the door.

"Well, Calli, I'll keep my tongue in check." He walks past me and closes the door behind him.

I walk back to the front desk, rubbing my chest, trying to heal it with the willpower of my mind. The pain subsides almost instantly. I sit in heavy contemplation in the not-so-comfortable chair at the desk. Did Charles's shard react like mine? Did it move also? I don't have the answer.

The door to the clinic opens, and Sasha and her mother enter. Sasha skips over to my desk and smiles.

"Hello Sasha, do I have a brain today?" I ask, smiling.

"Nope," she says as she fidgets with the cup holding assorted pens on my desk.

"Leave those alone, Sasha." Her mother directs her daughter's shoulders toward the couch and sits her down.

I pick up the phone and speak to my mother, informing her Sasha has arrived. Soon, my mother comes to the waiting room and invites them back to her office. I wonder what will happen to Sasha. Will Charles drop a bombshell on the mother, or will he skirt around the issue for now?

I keep myself busy for the next hour until everyone exits the back office and enters the reception area.

Sasha bounces her way into the waiting room like a jackrabbit.

Mr. Rhondell hands Sasha's mother a packet of information and explains his treatment plan, which, not surprisingly, includes sending Sasha off to his therapy clinic for two months.

The mother isn't very excited, but she's obviously at her wit's end on how to deal with her daughter.

Sasha approaches me. "Mr. Charles has a brain, but he won't let me see it."

"What's the difference? Maybe I have one too and won't let you see it, just like Mr. Charles."

"Nope, your head is empty like the lady doctor." She points to Charles. "I can feel his brain, but it's wrapped up like a present and I don't know what's inside."

I smile at her and realize her mother will gladly hand

off her daughter to Charles in the hope of taming her thought processes.

"That's enough, Sasha! How many times have I told you not to talk to people like that?"

Charles intervenes. "Sasha, would you like to come to my office and meet other kids who can see brains too?" He winks at the mother.

"Yes, but not at night."

"You know Sasha, I don't like the dark either. It makes me feel unsafe."

Sasha's eyes open wide in agreement. "My mom says there's nothing to be afraid of in the dark, but she's wrong."

Before Sasha's mother can scold her, Charles interjects again. "Sasha, not everyone is afraid of the dark. My mom wasn't afraid of the dark either, and she didn't understand why I was. At my clinic, I'll help you understand why, all right?"

"Okay. Why won't you let me see your brain, Mr. Charles?"

"Sasha!" her mother scolds.

"It's all right, Sasha, you are not the first person to ask me that. What if another girl your age came up to you and asked why you wouldn't let her see *your* mind? What would you say?"

"I'd say it's right there," she thumps her fingertip on her temple. "If you can't see it, then you're not looking hard enough."

Mr. Rhondell smiles and thumps his fingertip on his temple. "Sasha, it's right there. If you can't see it, then you're not looking hard enough."

I must say, Charles certainly knows how to downplay the emergence of powers.

♡ ♡ ♡

The whole Sasha/Charles Rhondell episode raises my curiosity about the Shadow Demons, and I decide to conduct a few experiments. What I know so far is the Demons were Healers and are now stuck in our world, preying on people with powers, or at least that's all Ms. Winter knew about them. I could see them when I had the whole diamond in my possession, but come to think of it, I haven't seen any since arriving back home here in Ohio. Do I need the entire diamond in order to see Demons?

I decide I'll venture out into the night and try to find them. I'll have to do it tonight because tomorrow night is my birthday party.

My cell phone rings and the display shows Suz calling.

"Hey Suz."

"You want to go to the mall? I hear Brand will be there tonight."

"Who?"

"Brand Safferson! Where have you been, girl? He's only the hottest guy ever!"

"Oh, right, Mr. All-star quarterback. I don't think he's all that good looking, Suz."

After being around the Runners Clan, no guy in my high school can compare to the looks of those fine specimens, especially when compared to Chris.

"That's just fine. One less girl I have to compete with. Will you come with me, please, and um, would you drive?"

"Sure, I'll pick you up around seven." I'm excited to have an opportunity to hunt for Demons, and I haven't hung out with Suz in quite a while. The sun won't be down until around ten, so we'll have to kill some time till the Demons come out.

♡ ♡ ♡

My experiences of a few months ago have changed me. The diamond inside my heart has altered my perceptions, and not just because I can see into every person around me at will, but because I see intentions, both honest and deplorable. I see the rising generation's low self-esteem and the current generation's frustration.

It doesn't take long to realize Suz asked me to take her to the mall because her other friends were there with Brand, and she hadn't been invited. I normally don't like entering Suz's mind, and I make it a practice not to, but something is bothering her, and I can't tell what it is . . . well, besides being left out of the circle.

I look for her current thoughts and find she's extremely attracted to Brand, but he won't give her the time of day anymore. Just two months ago, they were good friends, even to the point that they'd hang out together—alone. But then something unexpected happened and their relationship ceased. From Suz's perspective, I can't determine what happened. All I can see in her memory is Brand and Suz were in his room getting a little hot and heavy, and then suddenly Brand pulled back and pushed her away both physically and emotionally. He never got close to her again after that, and Suz has been heartbroken and desperate to find out why.

I pull out of her mind and turn my focus across the food court to Brand.

This boy couldn't be more average looking. His height is probably five-feet-eight inches, and he's neither fat nor muscular. His hair is reddish brown, short and wavy, and his eyes are hazel. His eyelids seem a bit inflamed, and he has a few noticeable acne splotches. His one redeeming trait is, at least in my opinion, his dimples when he smiles. Apparently he knows how powerful his dimples are because he smiles all the time. Brand has always been a mystery to me. Girls seem to flock to him for no apparent reason other than his sports talent. Well, now I have the ability to see what's going on in his head. Maybe I'll be able to figure out why he dumped Suz and also figure out why so many girls like him.

Entering Brand's mind is an assault on my senses, sending me this way and that. I can't focus on the images, thoughts, and emotions that are screaming through my mind, but I know every one of them belongs to Brand. I pull out of his mind, shake my head, and try again. This time I only look for the outermost edges of his current thoughts, but again, I am bombarded with confusion—it's like turning on fifty different radios to fifty different stations. What in the world is going on? I decide to simply read his lips and leave the powers of the diamond alone. The conversation is difficult at best to watch because of all the passing bodies, so I give up.

I look over at Suz and enter her mind with ease. I turn my attention to one of the other girls by Brand—Deb is her name—and enter her mind with ease. Eww, I have to get out of that one quick. Her mind is filled with designs on Brand—well, designs on any breathing male who will take her. Still, I easily entered her mind, and Suz's mind, but Brand's mind is different.

A sudden thought occurs to me: I wonder what Sasha would say about Brand's mind. She'd probably say he has a crazy mind, or maybe that he has too many brains, and I'd agree with her.

The girls surrounding Brand are pathetically falling on their faces trying to catch his attention. He seems more interested in the time, as he checks his watch often. Maybe he has someone to meet?

He stands, says goodbye, and leaves, much to the dismay of his adoring fans.

"What? He's leaving?" Suz asks, scooting to the edge of her seat. "At least he didn't take anyone with him. Let's follow him, Calli."

"No. I'm not doing that."

She jumps up and grabs my arm. "Come on, your Cooper is perfect for tailing someone. Pleeease?"

"All right." I cave, not merely to satisfy Suz's curiosity, but to satisfy mine as well.

We hurry out the large doors and spot Brand walking at a fast pace through the parking lot to his vehicle. My car is located nearby, fortunately, and following him is made easier because of that. We tail him straight to his home and watch him park his car inside the garage.

"That's it? He was going home?" Suz asks, exasperated.

"I guess so." I drive past his house to the next main road. "Suz, do you want to walk around town with me?"

"Walk? It's almost dark. Why not drive around town?"

Good point. "Yeah, all right."

With darkness setting in, we drive all over town, up to the heights where all the rich people live and down to the tracks, but not beyond. *No sense placing ourselves in danger.* Suz chats the whole time, and I search for Demons. All I have to do is utter an "Uh-huh" or "Really?" every now and then to satisfy her need to be heard. Not once do I spot a Shadow Demon in the dark. What a let-down.

Later, I drop her off at her house and remind her of my birthday party. She says she wouldn't miss it for anything. I enter her mind, almost accidentally, and find a most disturbing fact: Suz is the one who set off the firecracker in the girl's bathroom in middle school. When she realized how badly she'd hurt me, she became my friend out of guilt, and she still holds onto our friendship because of her remorse.

Well, that sucks!

I drive home to my house in a state of shock, memories rushing through my head. Suz was the least likely person to have befriended me while at the hospital. That should have been my first clue. I remembered feeling thrilled I had made a friend—a popular girl to boot—but it was all a lie.

♡ ♡ ♡

Today, August seventh, is my birthday. The day comes and goes without much of the over-the-top cheesy ridiculousness that so often accompanies a birthday.

My parents give me a new laptop to help with my studies, plus a few other smaller gifts. Suz gives me a gift card that is good for any merchant in the mall, which is nice, but most likely given out of her perpetual guilt. A bouquet of roses arrives late in the afternoon from an "anonymous friend."

Suz excitedly suggests maybe they're from a boy. I have to admit, a small part of me hopes Chris has sent them, but I dismiss the notion upon reading the message in the card: *You are perfect, Unaltered in any way.*

I figure this is Maetha's way of announcing her arrival. Finally, I can ask her some burning questions. The first on the docket will be about Freedom.

Chapter 3 - Bad vs. Evil, Good vs. Right

Three long days have passed without contact or even a message from Maetha. I am beginning to think she isn't coming at all.

After my parents leave for work, I fill a glass with lemonade I made from scratch, then stretch out on a chaise lounge on the stone patio in the backyard, enjoying the warmth of the morning sun. Evelyn is back from vacation, so I don't need to help at my mother's office anymore. Relaxing and soaking up some valuable vitamin D seems like a good way to enjoy my first day off in two weeks.

I close my eyes and listen to the sounds of nature around me using the Hunter's power of intensified senses. A meadowlark sings its beautiful song not far away, a bumblebee bounces from flower to flower near my head, and the leaves of the maple tree rustle from a gentle gust of breeze.

"Hello, Calli."

I bolt upright, knocking over my glass of lemonade. Maetha stands next to me with a pleasant smile on her face. "Maetha! You startled me . . . sorry, I've got to clean this up." I am glad I'd used a plastic cup, or I'd have an even bigger mess to clear.

"When you refill your glass, bring one out for me, dear."

I nod my head and enter the house. My heart is still thumping with the adrenaline from Maetha's arrival. Even with my Hunter's senses, I still couldn't hear Maetha sneak up on me. I pour her a glass of lemonade and refill my own, then gather my thoughts. There's so much I want to talk about.

Maetha positions herself in the shade of our umbrella-topped table. I place her drink in front of her and set mine down. She looks the same as the day I met her in Harold Bates's office—immaculate, with modest clothing, perfectly in-place short brown hair, smooth olive-toned skin, beautiful nails, and a body that's in excellent condition for a fiftyish-looking woman. She'd told me she's actually lived several thousand years, so I guess she looks amazing for a multi-thousand-fifty-year-old.

I know my mother will throw a fit if I don't clean up the spilled lemonade, so I turn on the hose and spray-clean the pation.

"Thanks for the flowers, Maetha." I angle the spray of water toward the grass line.

"I thought you'd like them. How are you feeling?"

"Fine." I finish my clean-up and turn off the water, then walk over to Maetha and sit adjacent to her in the shade. "Maetha, I've had a run-in with a man who calls himself Freedom."

I watch her expression for any sign of recognition, but see none. I continue, "He spoke into my mind."

Still nothing from Maetha to indicate recollection. *Boy, she's a tough nut to crack.*

I continue, this time letting all my questions out at once. "He advised me to stay away from *you*. Does Freedom have a diamond shard as well? Do you have a diamond, Maetha? Should I trust you? Why doesn't he trust you?"

Maetha takes a long drink of lemonade and inhales

deeply. "You'll have to come to your own decision about whether or not you can trust me. Just remember, not everything bad in this world is evil, and just because something's good doesn't make it right." She pauses for a moment, then continues. "I wasn't planning on going into this much detail with you, but seeing how he has forced my hand, so to speak, I suppose now is the time for you to learn the history of the Sanguine Diamond.

"As you know, I've been alive for several millennia. I was born sometime around the twenty-fifth century BCE in the land of Kemet, which you now know as Egypt, during the latter part of King Menkaura's reign. The great Pyramid of Giza was completed only about eighty years before I was born, and the Sphinx was new then—such a beautiful time to be alive.

"It was common knowledge and generally accepted that the kings, as well as various high priests, possessed the powers of gods. These were the mortal gods of this world, delivering the will of the great immortal gods and goddesses, and the people bowed down and revered them. However, the mortal gods were essentially no different than the clans of today, with similar powers and abilities.

"The previous king before Menkaura, King Khufu, had the great pyramid built as his burial place. His high priests claimed to have received divine instruction, stating if they placed a special milky-white stone on the top of the pyramid, the powers of the gods would be funneled into the pyramid for King Khufu's afterlife. He would become all powerful, and through the stone, he would be able to view the land . . . or at least that's what he thought.

"Like the people with powers today, the ancients only had one power each. The thought of being able to possess all the divine powers in the afterlife was tantalizing for Khufu. After his death, his loyal priests placed the stone atop the pyramid. Several years passed by with many attempts made by thieves to steal the diamond. All resulted in the death of anyone touching the stone, which only strengthened the belief that the stone held divine powers. The people of the land firmly believed King Khufu protected the stone.

"In my day, King Menkaura's high priest tried everything to get the stone. He was an evil man, a Healer. He claimed to have had a vision of me being able to pick up the stone and not die. When I was brought before the priest, I was labeled as soulless because he could use his powers on me. Other Healers were unsuccessful as well

"I was considered a threat by some—a threat that should be eliminated.

"Of course, I didn't know at the time that I was an Unaltered. I was able to hold the stone and not die. The priests ordered me to take the large diamond to the king, which I did. I thought delivering the treasure to the altar they had prepared would end my involvement, but sadly I was wrong.

"The order for my death came quickly, as I was a danger to the safety of the powerful stone. I escaped and hid to protect my life, thinking that was the best course of action, but hiding only resulted in my family being executed during the search for me. Out of anger and desperation, I stole the diamond and ran away.

"The stone was large, much larger than the one you carried. The powers emanating from it infused my body the same as the powers from your diamond infused you. I felt invincible.

"The priests found me after a few years and tried to physically remove the stone from my possession. They died and I ran once more. It took several years for more priests to locate me again. This time I knew they were coming, and

I knew I would die because I'd witnessed my death in a vision, and yet, I allowed myself to be caught. I felt dying was the only way to stop the endless pursuit. Plus, I'd seen in the vision the stone would be destroyed.

"The priests arrived and attempted to withdraw the powers of the stone without touching it. The scene was almost identical to what happened with you and the Death Clan. The priests died, the stone exploded, a piece entered my chest, and I died."

I lean forward. "You died?"

"Yes, the same as you. I was revived in the same manner as you, too."

"Who healed *your* heart and brought *you* back to life?"

"I didn't know who she was or where she came from, but she had far greater powers than I had ever seen. My beliefs of the time identified her as the goddess Isis. Isn't it interesting how our culture and belief systems can influence our minds? She gathered the pieces of the stone and divided them into twenty equal-sized pieces and instructed me on the will of nature, charging me to maintain a balance forever. She instructed me to seek out candidates who would also respect the will of nature and empower them with one of the Sanguine Diamonds. The man who refers to himself as Freedom was one of my choices. He and I do not see eye to eye. Freedom lost the desire to continue being an agent of nature and has gone rogue."

"What about the mysterious woman who revived you? Have you seen her since?"

"Yes. I've seen her a few times in my lifetime."

"Does she have a diamond too?"

"I don't know much about her."

"Oh. She divided the stone into twenty pieces, twenty-one pieces all together, right? You have one, Freedom has one, and I do, but where are the others?"

"The rest are in other Unattereds around the globe. Each has a duty or responsibility, and we are all interconnected mentally because all our diamonds came from the same stone."

"I'm connected to other Unattereds?"

"Not yet. You'll need the remaining pieces of the stone you carried before you're connected."

"How is that going to happen?"

She only smiles.

I rephrase my question. "Are you saying I will eventually have the orange-sized diamond inside my heart?"

"Yes. I mentioned this after the Death Clan's destruction. I told you once the splintering takes place, no one can halt or change the future of the diamond."

"I'm sorry, but you didn't tell me I'd get the whole stone eventually." My heart thuds.

"It's what I meant to say. Sometimes I forget you can't read my mind. It's probably for the best that I didn't give too much detail then, judging by how you're reacting to the news now."

"How am I supposed to get the other pieces? You gave them to the clan leaders."

"That is something I cannot foresee. But I know it will happen because it has always happened. On that subject, I want to explain a little about the amulets. The diamond you carried is now in six pieces. One piece is in you, the other five in glass amulets that can be worn by people with powers. So long as the diamond piece is never released from the glass, it doesn't pose any threat. However, if two or more diamond shards are brought together in too close proximity, they will try to hook together. Think of how two magnets will jump toward each other if they get close enough. If that happens with two amulets, the shards will break their casings and become deadly to the touch. The shard in your heart is protected by your body. Others can touch you and not die, but if you get too close to too many of the shards, then some fireworks will go off. Remember that."

I think Maetha is trying to give me a hint about what to expect in the future. I say nothing.

She takes a long sip of her lemonade. "Calli, do you remember what I told you following the Death Clan's destruction about how the diamond had to be delivered by an unaltered human?"

"Yes."

"The reason was because you could not be killed by Healers. However, there was another factor to why the Death Clan died. An even more significant reason why their plan failed: I had relinquished the stone's ownership to *you* in Harold Bates's office, giving the diamond an even stronger power, and *that* was what ultimately destroyed the Death Clan. They tried to forcefully extract the powers from an owned diamond. The Death Clan was always going to be destroyed, one way or another, but I coupled their end with your beginning by relinquishing the diamond to you."

"My beginning? What do you mean?"

"You are a Diamond Bearer, Calli. You were chosen long ago. I wasn't completely sure how you'd receive your diamond. I just knew you would eventually."

"How I'd receive one? You handed it to me. Wait. Are you saying there's another way for someone to get a diamond?"

"Yes. When the diamond on your chest exploded and forced a shard into your heart, you died. When the owner of a diamond dies, the diamond is free. The first Unaltered to touch it becomes its owner. No relinquishment is required. I collected the shards of your diamond and healed your heart. I was extremely careful not to touch your shard. Once your heart began beating on its own, you became the owner of the piece within your heart. I owned the other pieces, because I was the first to touch them in their 'free' state, until I relinquished them in the protective glass casings to the different clan leaders. Now they own them individually."

"But the clan leaders aren't Unaltereds. Won't the diamond kill them?"

"As long as the diamond shard remains in its protective glass amulet, they can safely harness its powers.

I rub my temples. "This is a lot to take in."

"If some other Unaltered was present when you died, and touched the diamond first, they would have gained ownership. I knew Freedom was after a Sanguine Diamond. When I relinquished the diamond to you at Harold's office, I placed it in the pouch for protection from Freedom. I'd envisioned the capture of the stone and realized I needed to protect it from Freedom's awareness. He set the situation in motion two-hundred years ago when he taught the Death Clan how to feel inside the body and how to manipulate healthy tissue. Prior to that incident, he'd sided with a different group of Healers, teaching them how to pull the life essence from people."

"The Vampires?"

"They were referred to as such, but they looked as normal as you or me. Freedom knew a diamond would be used to annihilate the Vampires and he thought he'd be there to claim it. A diamond was harvested from a Diamond Bearer, and one of your relatives named Duncan was used to eliminate the Vampire Clan in the same way as you for the Death Clan."

"Freedom obviously didn't succeed with that," I

surmise.

"No. He moved on to the Death Clan and started his quest again.

"Maetha, Freedom asked who died for me. Was he talking about harvesting, or whatever you just said?"

Maetha appears genuinely shocked by my question. "A very good friend of mine removed his diamond for the purposes of annihilating the Death Clan."

"What was his name?"

"His name was Gustave."

"He died?"

"Calli, Diamond Bearers live until they're decapitated or their heart is separated from their body. Gustave ended his own life by removing his heart in an effort to help balance nature."

"Wow! The diamond I carried in the pouch came from the inside of a man named Gustave? The piece inside of me right now—"

"Gustave was a relative of yours, Calli, and he approved of you to carry his diamond."

What a humbling revelation! I want to ask so many questions, want to know more, but I remain focused on the most prevalent question that has been burning a hole in my brain. "Are the Diamond Bearers Immortals, Maetha?"

"We can be killed if we stop paying attention to our surroundings and futures. As long as we continue to heal ourselves and protect our lives, we continue to live. If that defines us as Immortals, then yes, we're Immortals. You now have the same ability to sense imminent danger. With time and training, you can also preserve your life."

"I could be an Immortal?"

"When you had the whole stone on your chest, didn't you feel the power of awareness flowing through you? Did you feel the individual presence of everyone in the clearing?"

"Yes, I did. I was able to single out Chris's mind and I spoke to him with my thoughts. I also had a vision of my own future. That's when I realized I wasn't going to die."

"The ability to feel our surroundings and the individuals nearby allows us to avoid dying. We can detect threats and read intentions. We are not indestructible, but as long as we avoid death from unnatural causes, and heal our own ailments to prevent experiencing a natural death, we can live on and on."

"Can you explain how were you able to make me run fast at the track meet?"

"As a Diamond Bearer, I can use the powers of the diamond on Unaltereds. However, the Sanguine Diamond doesn't contain the ability to force someone run fast. I used my spell-casting on an additive in your drinking water. I enchanted the herbal ingredients and caused them to increase your speed."

"Is this why I was able to get the running power from holding Chris's hand? He shouldn't have been able to pass his power to me, because I'm an Unaltered."

"Yes, that's right. Clara's special Muck Soup also helped. Most of the Runners in the clan wouldn't be as fast as they are without Clara's secret ingredients."

"So, I really was on steroids."

"The ingredients wouldn't be detected in urine or blood tests. By the time the additive wore off, you had accepted the diamond and began using the diamond's power for running."

I pause for a moment, trying to process everything. Then I say, "So, Freedom has been running amok for a while now."

"Yes."

"Why don't you just read his mind or look for his

future and put a stop to him?"

"Calli, that's not always possible, even with a whole diamond."

"I don't understand."

Maetha takes another sip of her lemonade. "You figured out how to maneuver through mind-block walls and shocked more than a few people in doing so. The Readers were amazed more by that power than anything else. What you did was enter the mind in an angled fashion, different from the method regular Mind Readers use. Of course, your method is different because your power source comes from the diamond."

"Can't you break through Freedom's walls like I did with the Readers?" As I ask this question, I recall how I wasn't even able to feel his mind, similar to my mother's mind.

"You didn't break through walls. You found the holes and gaps and entered through them."

"I still don't understand."

"Imagine a game of checkers. All the disks are placed on black squares and can only move on black squares. You know the rules for checkers, such as when you can jump or when you can't. One of those rules is that you always move at an angle on the black squares, never on the red. If you got down at eye level to the game board, your checkers would appear to be in a straight line, not a zig-zag pattern. This is how a mind block is seen by Mind Readers: a straight wall. Diamond Bearers have the bird's-eye view and can play on both the black and red squares, so to speak. We are able to reach the back row because everyone else has blocks set up only on the black squares. We move diagonally on the red squares and enter through the blocks. However, Diamond Bearers can set up blocks on their red squares too, but not to keep Readers out, since they can't read our minds anyway, but to keep other Diamond Bearers out.

"This is the reason I exercise extreme caution when selecting a Bearer. I need to be certain you'll be a good agent of nature before giving you the diamond. Once you have all the pieces of your stone and have learned how to block completely, Diamond Bearers won't be able to enter your mind. I, along with the other Bearers, will be able to sense where you are at all times, but won't be able to read your mind if you don't want it to be read. At least, that's how it's been up till recently."

I angle my head, wondering what she means.

She continues. "Freedom has found a way to prevent all communication from the other Diamond Bearers. He has figured out how to be 'invisible' in a sense. We cannot track his location all the time. We cannot see his future, either. The day he appeared to you, he resurfaced momentarily. I bi-located to his location, outside your mother's clinic, and watched him communicate with you and then turn and walk away."

"You were there? I didn't see you."

"I wasn't there to be seen. I had a fix on Freedom and I needed to follow him. My eyes held onto his physical form, but I could no longer track him using the diamond's power; he'd gone 'invisible' again. Being able to see him, yet not feel him, confused me greatly."

"What do you think he's doing to hide from you?"

"I don't worry so much about the logistics of his ability to block us as much as I worry about his reason. The 'why' is much more disconcerting. Freedom disagrees with my choices and feels life on this planet should play out chaotically with disasters and illnesses keeping the population under control. To an extent, that is nature's will. However, the Unaltered bloodline, which you are a part of, would have ended during the Black Plague in 1348.

"The Diamond Bearers chose not to eradicate the plague because it would have been in direct violation of nature. The world's population suffered a huge hit, but without it the planet would be overrun with humans right now. However, Freedom, his wife, and their two children were infected and were going to die. I stepped in and healed Freedom and his oldest child, a son, to keep the bloodline going. Freedom became the next Diamond Bearer, and his son continued the line. From what I could sense, nothing about Freedom indicated he would stray from the path of nature, but once he became a Diamond Bearer and learned what I had done, his true-self surfaced.

"His son lived a full life and had several children, the first of whom was Unaltered, thus passing down the trait to continue the line. In Freedom's mind, what I had done was not right, and as his son aged, it angered him more and more. The fire was fueled with the deaths of his grandchildren and his great-grandchildren. Freedom feels I took away his choice, that I forced him into this immortal state against his will. In essence, he's right.

"This is something you'll need to wrap your own mind around, Calli. Your present family will die before you will. Your future family will die before you, and some will die *because* of you. The first born from every generation will be protected and guarded, placed on the ready, should any be needed in the same way you were needed."

My mind cannot imagine my own children. *Yikes!* "So, is every Diamond Bearer a descendant of yours?"

"Many are."

"Am I?"

"Yes."

"So you're like my great, great, great, great . . . how many greats?"

"Over two-hundred generations. I stopped counting years ago."

"You're the greatest grandmother ever! How is it you've kept your existence a secret? I mean, you and all the other Diamond Bearers."

Maetha smiles a little. "You are comparing the lives of twenty-one individuals to entire empires and civilizations. A small handful of people, regardless of their powers and abilities, slip through the cracks of time. We have intervened and erased some documentation of our existence, while other information is preserved, like Clara Winter's books about Immortals."

"You know about those?"

"Yes. They are necessary to keep the belief of Immortals alive amongst the clans. They also propagate the misinformation about the Sanguine Diamond."

I say, "With as many people who witnessed what happened at the clearing, I don't imagine the belief will be dwindling anytime soon."

"You're right, Calli. This is the reason we hold off on using a diamond until there is no other choice. Consider the fact that the last time we used a diamond to wipe out a clan there were no cell phones, no satellites, or any other kind of recording devices. We have to be extremely careful when we expose ourselves. Now, do you have any other questions at this time, Calli?"

"Do I have to go back to school? I mean, honestly, what's the point? Shouldn't I be training with you?"

"As your greatest grandmother, I'm ordering you to finish school."

"Going to pull that card, are you?"

"I knew a man once, a Healer, who lived at a time when illness and injury were treated with spells and the healing power. As you know, sometimes the healing power has limits. This man became determined to learn how to help the human body without using magic. His thinking was what if the powers went away? How would anyone survive? His experiments and methods live on today and they inspired many great individuals throughout history. His name was Hippocrates. Now imagine where we'd be today if the only way to be healed was through a Healer or Spellcaster? What if you somehow lost your diamond abilities? Wouldn't you still like to be able to help others?"

"I would. Wait! You knew Hippocrates?"

She nods. "I think all Diamond Bearers need to explore other ways to accomplish tasks without using their powers, like Hippocrates."

Her story makes me want to go do some research on the man. It would only make sense that he was a Healer. "All right. I'll continue with school. What about my parents? Should they know what's going on with me?"

"Not yet. All in due time."

"Maetha, what do you know about the Shadow Demons?"

"They are the consequences of using a diamond to wipe out a group of Healers."

"So, they *are* the dead Healers?"

"Yes, their desire for power holds them to this world. That's also why they only go after people with powers."

"Can't we get rid of them?"

"Oh, there have been attempts to do so throughout the years, but so far nothing has been successful. All we've come up with is how to push them back with light. I am of the mind that they live in an alternate dimension, with our darkness being their windows. They are not present in all dark corners of the world, only those where they can smell the powers in existence."

"Yeah, I've figured that out already. Is there another

way to wipe out clans without using a diamond?"

"Our group of twenty-one 'Immortals' can kill any group of Healers, but when we openly use our powers, it only sparks the development of many more immortality-seeking Healers. Like I said, in the current technologically-advanced world we live in, it's downright dangerous for us to step out of the shadows. Governments would love to capture us and find out what keeps us alive. We have enough trouble with the government already. We certainly don't need them hunting Immortals."

"I'm going to find a way to eliminate the Demons, er, dead Healers, Maetha."

"Calli, I believe you will try, but I don't see that in your future."

"Well, things can change."

"Yes, they can. For now, I want you to try to enjoy your childhood, enjoy your youth."

I laugh. "What? Are you serious?"

"I'm completely serious. You need to go out with your friends and go on dates."

"I'm not interested in any of the boys around here."

"Calli, I'm not telling you to forget about the vision you saw concerning Chris. I'm simply telling you to broaden your horizons and experience life for what it is. You have several years before fate intervenes. Get out there and be a kid."

"I don't know. I'll try, but I've never really fit in."

"That's the purpose behind my encouragement. You need social interaction to learn how to blend in better, to learn the social conventions of the age, to keep up with the trends. Before you knew how old I really am, would you have been able to guess I wasn't from your time?"

I shake my head.

"Some of the other Diamond Bearers are not as

cultured or up to date with the world, and they are actually handicapped by their refusal to press forward with advancements. I don't want that to happen to you. Social interaction on the basic level is the first step to staying current."

"All right. I'll hang out a little more."

"Good. I'll visit you again down the road. If you run into the Diamond Bearer Freedom, keep your distance."

"You're leaving?"

"Yes. I have other pressing business to attend to. In the meantime, you need to practice meditation. Learn how to control your mind. Learn how to bring yourself to a place of neutrality."

"I thought you were going to teach me how to spot auras? What do I do in the meantime?"

"I will come to you when the time is right, and I'll bring Beth. Until then, try to find your place in nature. Keep current with the world's news and you may be able to spot our interventions."

"How do I get a hold of you?"

"You won't have the need. Besides, you're a smart girl. Use your intuition and gut instinct."

Maetha leaves me sitting in my chair under the giant umbrella pondering everything she's revealed. What would it be like to be Maetha and watch the world change and evolve over her lifetime? What will it be like in my own lifetime? Even if I only live five-hundred years, what kind of changes and advancements will I witness? The idea boggles my mind, and I put it out of my head. The issue of hanging out with other kids my own age has my stomach in knots. I simply don't relate to the kids from school. The other day at the mall with Suz was proof enough of that.

Chapter 4 - Brand New Power

I go out often at night, looking for the Shadow Demons, but I can't find them anywhere. How can I investigate them further if they are nowhere to be found?

School starts soon, thank God. I'm tired of Suz's constant whimpering about Brand and his lack of attention. I've tried on multiple occasions to read his mind only to be perplexed at the mess he has inside his head. Looking for his future is worse; I don't quite know how to describe what I see. For one thing, I can't actually see what he'll do next because there are too many possibilities of where he'll go. Never before have I actually seen several possible outcomes in someone's future. Brand has become my new project because I don't like things I don't understand. I feel compelled to learn what his ability is.

School has been in session for one week now, with everything just as I left it in the Spring. No one pays me any attention. Even the teachers look right past me to the point that I am beginning to wonder if Maetha had something to do with this. However, I'm torn. I don't care for attention, yet I miss it—somewhat.

In my English class, Brand sits on the other side of the room, surrounded by doe-eyed girls who stumble over themselves to win his affection. I don't understand it. He's not even that good looking. I hear he has a different girlfriend just about every day, yet everyone keeps vying for his attention. An even more confusing fact is the girls he dumped still like him.

Today, I'm even more confused. From where I sit in the cafeteria at lunchtime, I have a clear view of Brand as he charms his table of girls. I read his lips as he looks at each girl and tells her what her favorite color is. Then he points around the table and names off all their favorite movies. It's a sickening display. I feel into his body, checking to see if he's a Reader, but no.

"Hey Calli," Suz comes up and sits beside me. "Watching Brand again, I see. Do you like him?" Her voice holds surprise and suspicion.

"What? No. He intrigues me, that's all."

"He intrigues everyone. It's like he can read minds. He's like the David Copperfield magician guy that every girl wants, but Brand doesn't want every girl."

"That's because he's already *had* every girl, Suz."

"Not you."

"Nor will he. I'm not attracted to his type. He's a player, manipulating the system somehow. He's getting his information from somewhere and using it to charm the ditzy girls."

I realize I've probably just offended Suz with that comment, but at the moment I don't care. Suz is a cute girl and could have any number of handsome guys, yet she's fixated on Brand. Besides, I'm not quite over the fact that Suz feels obligated to be my friend—like I'm some kind of deformed throwback. Guilt can be a funny thing.

Suz says, "I heard Blake Simmons is going to beat him up after school because Brand stole his girlfriend, Tiffany."

"Blake Simmons?" I choke out my question. "You

mean Black-Belt Blake?"

"The one and only. It serves Brand right for moving in on Tiffany. She's someone else's girl." I can hear the jealousy in Suz's words, but also the longing. If she had her way, she'd be Brand's girl.

"Well, this I've got to see. Where's the fight going to be?"

"My guess is the parking lot."

Finding Brand after school isn't too difficult. I simply follow the worried girls. Blake Simmons stands out at the far edge of the parking lot by the chain-link fence. A large crowd of boys surrounds him. No doubt Brand has offended nearly every one of these boys with his over-zealous flirting. Brand is leaning up against the fence, popping his knuckles. The expression on his face makes him seem almost bored—definitely not worried. Apparently Blake is waiting for his other friends to arrive before tearing into Brand.

Blake is as tall as Brand and ripped with toned muscles. It's a well-known fact Blake has won many martial arts trophies, which doesn't look too good for Brand. Yes, Brand is the best quarterback the school has ever had, but that doesn't mean he's strong. It just means he can throw a ball straight.

Blake, on the other hand, is a trained fighter. His muscles look bigger than normal with his arms folded across his chest, and his broad shoulders make his whole upper body look massive. A glimpse of his mind shows he is eager to put Brand in his place.

The crowd has grown so large that Suz and I have to jump into the bed of a nearby truck in order to see Brand.

Tires screech in the distance as a car rounds the corner at a high rate of speed. The sports car comes to a halt nearby and five tough-looking guys climb out. I enter one of their minds and find the boys are fellow black-belts from the same dojo as Blake. Brand still doesn't appear worried. Strange.

He pushes off from the fence and approaches Blake. "Are we doing this or what?"

"Yeah!" Blake yells to the crowd. "This idiot thinks he can steal anyone's girl. It's time to put an end to it."

The crowd is a mix of shouting and cheering with basically the girls cheering for Brand and the guys rooting for Blake.

Blake rushes Brand with a series of swings, kicks, and jabs—all of which Brand avoids by moving ever so slightly. Brand's movements aren't skilled or masterful, but they aren't awkward or clumsy either. He appears to have faster reflexes than Blake. Could Brand be a Runner? No. I didn't sense anything special about his body back in the cafeteria. So how is he doing this?

The volume of the crowd increases as the girls cheer louder for Brand. Blake's groupies shout, "Kick his butt!"

I look into Blake's mind, out of curiosity. I mean, really, what must a guy like him be thinking at a moment like this? His mind opens up, revealing his astonishment at Brand's maneuvers and his ability to predict his next move. Blake is clearly aware Brand has some advantage over him, but realizes Brand has not tried to land any punches on him. Blake is not used to fighting air; none of his strikes are making contact. Normally his moves are countered by his opponent, but this is more like shadow boxing. Blake's mind reveals what he intends to do next: bring in his five dojo buddies.

I look into Brand's future to try to see the outcome,

only to be assaulted with possibilities—there are many moves Brand can make, and in all of them Brand gets his butt kicked. Looking into his future feels almost the same as looking at his mind, but instead of thoughts I see futures. Some of his injuries will be serious. At least I think so. It's so hard to tell what I'm looking at. This makes no sense to me.

I look for Blake's future and see he will concede and accept Brand's offer to call off the fight. He will shake Brand's hand and slap him on the back. Brand will be unhurt and one of Blake's five friends will be lying on the ground in pain, while the rest huddle over him.

What?

Before my very eyes, I watch the five other black-belts join Blake and attempt to pummel Brand. Although Brand is surrounded, he still dodges every attack. The most amazing part is how he avoids anything thrown by the dojo-buddies *behind* him, without ever looking at them. Not one of them can land a successful strike, whether they stand in front or behind him.

Brand steps aside as a snap kick, aimed at his groin, travels on to hit Blake square in the jaw. As Blake recoils and clutches his mouth, Brand weaves through a gap in the circle of fighters, grabs one by the arm and pulls him to the ground. Brand retreats several feet away as the fighter scrambles to his feet and charges. A well-placed knee to the charger's family jewels stops him abruptly and he falls back on the pavement again, groaning in agony.

Blake and his four confused dojo-buddies now face Brand, their fallen friend lying on the ground between them. One of Blake's cronies speaks up. "I thought you said this guy was an idiot. He's obviously a trained fighter."

Blake doesn't respond, but he doesn't need to. His dumbfounded expression says everything.

Breathing calmly, Brand says, "Blake, do you really think beating me up is going to change the fact your girlfriend chose me over you?"

"She said you made her do it!" Blake fires back.

"I didn't force her to do anything against her will. She made that choice all on her own, and she didn't choose you."

Tiffany's shrieking objection is heard by all. "You tricked me, Brand!"

"No I didn't. I gave you an opportunity and you acted on it."

"Blake, honey," Tiffany changes her approach. Blake looks back and forth between Brand and Tiffany. "Who are you going to believe? Me or this scammer?"

Before Blake can answer, Brand dips his chin and lowers his voice. "Look, it wasn't cool of me to do what I did. I'm sorry. How about we end this?" Brand extends his hand to Blake.

Blake stares at Brand for a long second, then takes his offered hand. The girls cheer and scream with delight, while the male onlookers are in a state of shock. Blake pats Brand on the back. They both turn their backs to Tiffany.

I watch the scene unfold exactly as I saw it few moments earlier, and the confusion in my mind ups another notch. I decide to stick close to Brand until I figure out his secret. I'll start by tailing him tonight.

Later that night, my mother sits in her favorite recliner with a glass of wine, watching the ten o'clock news. I mull over many different phrases in my head, trying to decide which one my mother will accept as a good enough reason to leave the house this late at night so I can follow Brand.

Telling the truth is out. Something tells me she won't agree to me going "Demon hunting."

Since I cannot use my powers on my mother, I look for my own future. I systematically go through each scenario and then view the future to see how my mother will react. Mothers can be so overly protective. She's not going to go for "we're out of milk," or "I need school supplies." I consider using Suz as an excuse. The future looks good on this one. *Here goes nothing.*

"Mom, is it all right if I drive to Suz's house to drop off a book?"

"It's late, Calli."

"I know, but I will only be a few minutes and she needs the book tonight to study for tomorrow's test."

"All right, hurry back."

I leave, feeling guilty about manipulating and lying to my mother.

I drive to Brand's house, pondering his different abilities. Does he have the Seer ability? Is it possible he used it to dodge those top-notch fighters today? No, I'm certain he doesn't possess any of the powers I'm familiar with. Perhaps he's an Empath, able to influence others by using their emotions. That would explain how he keeps landing new girlfriends and why his ex-girlfriends still like him. It would also explain why Blake so quickly shook his hand. However, it doesn't explain how Brand won the fight.

No, Brand has some kind of skill or perhaps multiple skills that are undetectable by me, a Diamond Bearer.

I round the corner and park several houses away from Brand's and decide to walk the remaining distance. As soon as I open the door and step out, my nose is filled with the all-too-familiar stench of the Shadow Demons.

Sure enough, the shadows around Brand's home are

filled with dead Healers. I'm not surprised to see them, because I figure Brand is wielding some sort of super-power, but I'm still unsure what the power or ability is. I wander into the shadows and watch as the hideous creatures float out of my way.

The neighbor's tiny dog runs toward me, stopping short at the property line fence, barking with a little yappy-yap voice. I don't think the dog senses the Demons. It seems more interested in me. The Demons don't pay much attention to the dog, but they also don't go near it. The dog stops barking momentarily and I notice the Demons spreading out a little, moving closer to the fence, that is until the dog starts barking again. The Demons slide away from the four-legged annoyance. Very curious. One thing is for certain, if I linger, the dog's owners will investigate to see what has the dog so riled up.

Now that I've figured out where the Demons are located, I can try to experiment with them, but the proximity of the nearby homes has me a little concerned. People might call the police if they see me wandering around in the shadows. I can always escape by running, but what if they have my description?

As I drive home, a thought comes to me: if I can lure Brand out after dark, the Demons will follow him. I could take him to a location where we wouldn't raise suspicions and experiment with him there. All I have to do is figure out how to get him outside after dark.

My answer comes in the form of a sport: football. The season has just begun.

Normally I don't care for football, but I am curious to find out how Brand handles himself out on the field. More than anything, I am dying to find out how he copes with the looming sunset. Further into the football season, the sun will be down before his game even starts. Yes, this will be interesting to watch.

Tomorrow night will be the season's first game, and I plan to be there.

I arrive back at my home and park my car. I realize I still have the book I was supposed to be taking to Suz. I stuff it deep in my purse and then open the back door. My mom is still watching the news. She nods my way, turns off the television, and says good night.

I head to my room and check my email. Beth has sent me a letter:

> *Hey Calli,*
>
> *How are you doing? Things around here are so-so. A couple new members arrived the other day: a boy and girl about age thirteen. They're twins. Imagine that, twins! What are the odds of that happening? I've never heard of twins holding a cosmic power.*
>
> *There's a bit of unrest between the clans these days. The amulets have eliminated the need to have representatives from the other clans remain with us, and with that change comes distance. We no longer have the same relationship we used to have with the other clans. Clara wears the amulet for our clan, which is just fine with me, but a division in our own clan is forming because of it. Some feel the fastest should wear the amulet, others feel Clara should, while the rest believe one of the other adults should wear it, not the leader of the clan or the fastest. Personally, I'm happy with Clara wearing the amulet.*
>
> *I have to imagine the other clans are having the same type of problems. This change wasn't necessarily a good one, and no one can find the Spellcaster, Maetha, to ask for help. Do you know where she is?*
>
> *I'll talk to you later.*
> *Beth.*

I typed a quick message in reply:

Beth, I'm not surprised to hear the diamond shards are causing unrest. I saw the leader of the Readers' Clan a while ago. He had one of the amulets around his neck.

Twins, huh? I read recently twins were on the increase across the nation, so I'm guessing this will happen more often.

As for Maetha, I don't know where she is or how to contact her. The next time I see her I'll let her know you're looking for her.

Later,
Calli

♡ ♡ ♡

My first football game is cold and wet. Rain pours down the entire time of the game. Ugh! I listen to the spectators around me as they critique Brand's quarterbacking skills. I hadn't realized I was watching anything spectacular because I've never cared to watch football before. Brand is completing every pass he throws, and the game is wrapping up quickly. The spectators all comment on how brilliant Brand is as an athlete to have such accuracy on a muddy, slippery field.

I guess they have a point.

When the game ends, the players all file through the door at the end of the stadium that leads to the locker room. I watch to see if Brand ventures outside the artificial light, but so far, there hasn't been any need to. I leave the stands and sit in my car, dripping wet from the rain. I am near Brand's car, which is by the locker room exit. The parking lot lighting is sufficient to keep the Shadow Demons at bay, so I know he won't have a problem staying safe.

Brand exits the door and walks quickly to his car. A couple of other teammates holler to him that they are going to a local diner to celebrate, but Brand tells them he has a headache and is going to go home.

A headache, yeah right. Probably from all those times he didn't get sacked.

I follow Brand home and watch from a distance as he enters his lighted garage. He still hasn't gotten out of his car as the door closes, and I lose sight of him. It's obvious to me he understands the dangers lurking in the dark.

I attend the next few football games, both at home and away, to study Brand's behavior. Rarely does he fail to complete a pass, and he's never sacked. He's caught the eye of several university athletic scouts, and the local reporters plaster him nightly all over the news. Brand already seems to thinks a little too highly of himself. This notoriety isn't going to help.

I sit in the cafeteria at my normal empty table and stare across the room at Brand and his endless fan club of girls, contemplating everything I know about him at this point. All I know is this: I don't know much.

Brand's gaze meets mine and locks in place. A warm smile creeps over his face.

I avert my eyes and look down at my lunch for a few seconds. When I look up, he's gone. Class is going to begin soon, so I clear my tray and walk to my locker.

I pull the books for the next two classes from my

locker, jam them in my backpack, and slam the door shut. Brand is hiding behind my locker door and startles me with his sudden presence.

"Hey Calli," he says, dragging out the vowels.

"Are you talking to me, Brand?"

"There's no one else in this school named Calli, so yes." He gives me his best seductive smile.

"What do you want?"

"You."

"Is *this* how you land all your girls? Wow, they must be more stupid than I thought."

Brand's whole demeanor changes. Through clenched teeth, he asks, "Why doesn't it work with you?"

Is this guy for real? I shake my head and walk to class. What a jerk! But what can you expect from a jock?

The next day in English class, Brand moves from his normal spot to the vacant desk next to me.

"Hi, Calli."

In a synchronized movement, all the female heads in the room turn to me and shoot nasty glances my way.

"Let's grab a cup of coffee sometime," he says, almost as if we're in the middle of a conversation.

I hear some gasps from the girls. Opening my folder and pretending to go over my notes, I say, "No thanks, Brand." I prepare myself for another emotional outburst.

"Oh, okay," he says, obviously deflated. I'm able to pick up on one clear thought from his mind. *Why doesn't this work with her?*

Part of me is curious about him, wanting to understand his power. The other part of me is defensive, wanting to protect myself. Of course, with the diamond's power, I can protect myself pretty well. I guess I just don't want to be made a fool.

A little later in class, when the teacher is turned away, writing on the board, I glance over at Brand. He's about to flick a folded up piece of paper in the direction of the teacher's desk. A nearby girl whispers encouragement, challenging him to hit the cup of coffee on the desk. Brand turns his head to me and whispers, "If I hit the cup, will you go with me to a movie?"

"No."

"What if I make it land inside the cup?"

"That would be impressive, but still a no."

"I'll settle for impressing you then." He pauses a couple seconds, working on his aiming, then flicks the piece of paper. It flies up through the air and lands inside the coffee cup.

My eyes widen at the sight of his incredible luck, which only adds more to my list of things to figure out about him. What kind of power would it take to be able to control objects like a piece of crumpled paper, or say a football? Telekinesis? That still doesn't explain how he does everything else.

The bell rings and he jumps to his feet. "See you later, Calli."

I'm surprised by his niceness. "Bye," I respond.

One of Suz's friends named Tawnya moves in front of me, blocking my way. "For your information, he's taken."

"By you? Does he know that?"

"He might if you'd get out of the picture." Her head bobs around almost comically as she speaks.

"I'm not trying to get Brand. The question is why did he just ask me out instead of you?"

She storms off in a huff and I resist the urge to laugh at her possessiveness.

When I get home from school, I ponder on the tidbits I was able to pull from Brand's mind. His actions don't reflect his thoughts, well, as much as I can tell. I also think about Tawnya and the other girls. What is it about Brand that has all these girls clamoring for him? It's almost as if he radiates charm and pheromones.

Today drags on as I wait for English class. I'm curious to find out if Brand will attempt to flirt with me again. At lunch he sat with his back to me. I don't think it was on purpose, though. He did make eye contact with me before he sat down, which surprised me.

I enter English class and sit at my usual spot. Brand isn't in the room yet. I note the empty desks nearby and the group of girls huddled in the far corner talking quietly. I thumb through my notebook, acting as if I can't hear them talk about me with my super-hearing.

Brand enters the room and sits next to me, not surprisingly.

"Hi Calli."

"Hi." I focus on my notebook.

What can I say? I've tried everything! His thoughts ram into my mind.

I wonder what he means by everything. Even though curiosity is killing me, I resist the urge to look at him. I can hear the girls' jabs and insults about me, but I doubt Brand can hear them.

Brand lets out a huff. "Calli, I don't get you."

He's caught my attention. I turn to face him. "What's not to get?"

"You! I can't get *you.*"

"What makes you think I want to be got? Besides, you

have plenty of options over there." I nod my head toward the girls in the corner.

He doesn't answer and his thoughts are so confusing I don't try to read them. My head hurts whenever I try. I'm relieved when class begins and I have to change my focus.

I've dealt with Brand's strange type of behavior for a couple of weeks. I'm glad I only have him in one class. If he'd taken my rejection and moved on I'd have respected him a bit more, but he didn't. He follows me like a lost puppy, trying with all his might to land a date with me.

Today, I've had enough. I've come up with a plan, a test of sorts, to get him to back off. When the bell rings, ending English class, I turn to him and say, "Okay, I'll go out with you, Brand."

"Really?" he says, obviously surprised by my sudden change of mind.

"Yeah. I'll meet you in the park Friday night at eleven.

He looks like he could pass out. "Eleven at *night?* Why?"

"I'll see you then." I stand to leave and he grabs my arm.

"Let's meet at my house, and . . . and then I'll drive us to the park, okay?"

Yeah, right. "No, I'll meet you at the park, or no date."

"Calli, why are you so persistent?" His voice squeaks a little.

"Why are you so sensitive?" I let him continue to hold onto my arm as it provides a stronger connection into his body. However, this doesn't help my powers at all. I still can't find anything to indicate what kind of power he has. "You know, I'm beginning to think you're afraid of the dark," I tease.

He drops his hand and says, "No, I'm not. It's just . . . well, the park is dangerous after dark."

"Since when? There hasn't been any crime in that park since I can remember."

"But why invite it?" He smiles, unleashing his dimples.

"You know what, forget it." I start to walk away.

"Wait!"

I turn and face him.

"Eleven is past my curfew."

"Then no date." I walk away before he can come up with another excuse. His mind revealed a tiny bit of information. He's well aware of the Demons and the dangers they present. I also got the impression he's giving up on me.

It's about time!

I follow Brand from a distance over the next several months, hoping to witness something that will help me better understand his power. He appears to be able to see the future; he acts as though he can read minds; and he's demonstrated his uncanny athletic ability through football, even though the team lost early-on in the State playoffs.

That only proves a team is made up of more than just one superstar.

The holidays come and go, and Brand attends the winter dance with a sophomore. Apparently he's exhausted all his senior and junior female options. He has moved on to jailbait.

Suz was crushed when she heard.

With spring comes track. I don't plan to run this year, and it's hard to get Coach Simms off my back, but I can't risk accidentally displaying my abilities. I am tempted to make up a lie of some kind. Instead I simply tell him no. It feels better anyway to be honest with myself.

College applications have been mailed, acceptance letters received, and scholarships awarded. They all mean nothing to me. Naturally, my parents have worried incessantly about my lack of excitement, even to the point they recommend I take an antidepressant. The only way I can get them off my back is to accept one of the university offers and begin planning for the fall.

Suz is accepted at the same university I'll be attending. We plan to room together. I know she needs to save money on rent, otherwise I would have arranged private accommodations.

I've come to accept that Suz changed my life with the firecracker incident. I don't hold it against her. She made a bad choice as most kids do once in a while. One thing's for sure, she's been beating herself up with guilt ever since. I'd let her off the hook if I could find a way to do it without her knowing I read her mind.

What I really want is for Maetha to come train me how to view auras and teach me more about the Diamond Bearers.

Chapter 5 - Do Over

The month of May is chock-full of activities and adventures for the senior class. One trip is to Cedar Point Amusement Park in Sandusky, Ohio.

We leave the school early in the morning, and almost everyone sleeps on the bus ride until about an hour out. As each individual awakes, the level of excited chatter picks up.

Suz, who sits next to me, awakens as the noise grows. She looks out the window and says, "Calli, will it be all right if I hang out with my other friends for some of the day?"

"Why wouldn't it be?"

"Well, you know, I don't want to leave you all alone."

"I can take care of myself, Suz. I don't care who you hang out with."

That's all it takes for her to cheer up—my permission for her to abandon me. I really don't like looking for Suz's future, but I take a peek to see if she'll be hanging out with me *at all* today.

Through her eyes, a scene opens up. I see myself from a distance, hugging Brand, and I feel her anger at my betrayal. She will most definitely not be hanging out with me today. In fact, this day will mark the end of our friendship.

This is why I don't like looking into her future.

Why on earth would I be hugging Brand? Is he going to deliver a top-notch pick-up line that finally melts my cold heart, causing me to fall into his arms? Not a chance. Is he going to have an emotional breakdown so I'll feel sorry for him and give a "there, there" hug? I try to look into Brand's future but cannot decipher what I see. I figure I'll just have to wait to find out how all this will happen.

♡ ♡ ♡

Cedar Point, located on an island in Lake Erie, is breathtaking to behold. Roller coaster heaven! This is going to be fun. We dash off the bus with the instructions to be back at six o'clock sharp for the return trip home. Buses from other high schools are already parked with their seniors in line to enter the park. The girls behind me squeal with delight at the sight of fresh meat. I shake my head.

Inside the park and already abandoned by Suz, I search out the location of the nearest restroom. It's quite a long walk away. I've been struggling to hold my bladder for the last two hours. I shouldn't have consumed so much soda on the way here. Now I'll be doing the scissor-walk all the way to the bathroom. A thought occurs to me: perhaps I can use my healing ability to ease my discomfort a bit. Sometimes I forget exactly what I can do.

As I leave the restroom, I see a large board with a map of the amusement park and the "You are here" red star. Wow, this place is huge!

"What are you going to ride first?" I hear a voice behind me, and I turn to find Maetha.

"Maetha, what are you doing here? You scared me. You should get a cell phone or something and let me know when you're going to pop into my life."

"When you've been alive as long as I have, you're not

quick to jump on the latest gadget bandwagon."

"Cell phones aren't things that are going to go away, Maetha."

"Are you so sure? At some point, people will want to return to their quiet lives, tossing away the conveniences that both bind them to society and allow the world to keep tabs on them. Cell phones are still rather new, and the novelty is fresh, but it will get old when the wrong people overstep their bounds, causing the general population to scramble to go off grid."

"You sound like one of those talk radio alarmists. Did you look into the future for that one?"

"No. It's the nature of the beast. Anyway, I was passing through the area today and realized you were nearby so I thought I'd stop in and give you an update."

I chuckle. "If you had a cell phone you could have just called."

She ignores my comment. "I apologize for my delay in getting back with you. A new power has emerged, one not contained within the Sanguine Diamond. Three of us have been investigating two individuals, trying to figure out what the power is. I need to put my focus on this matter for now. I'll come after the school year is finished to teach you how to see auras."

"That will be fun. So, what's this new power like, Maetha."

"Let's get some refreshment first. I would love one of your homemade lemonades, but an artificial one will have to suffice."

We walk to the nearest food vendor. Maetha steps up and orders two lemon slushies, then directs me to a shaded area where we can sit.

Maetha doesn't seem impressed at all with the frozen lemonade. "I remember the first time I had a lemon drink.

It was in Egypt, 1037 AD. The sugar back then tasted much better, but so did the lemons. I'd been out of the country for a while and I guess they'd been making this drink for some time before I sampled it." She takes another sip of her slush and squeezes her eyes shut. "The new ability I spoke of is a confusing one. It seems to have roots in the Seer's and Reader's powers, almost like a mixture of the two."

"Let me guess. When you look into their mind, all you see is a jumbled mess?"

She reaches out and grabs my arm. Eyes opened wide, she says, "Yes! You know someone with this power?"

"I think so. He has Shadow Demons around his house, so it's some kind of cosmic power." I chug a large amount of the awful drink. It tastes like all-purpose lemon cleaner. "His name is Brand Safferson, and he's a pervert."

"A what?"

"Well, he's always trying to hook up with new girls. He's a player, a scammer, a pervert."

"I hardly think a young man wishing to mate qualifies him as a degenerate."

"Mate?" I laugh. "If he were looking for a relationship that'd be one thing. He's just after a quick fling."

"The all-consuming drive for a male to 'hook up' is what keeps the population growing, Calli. It's nature at its most basic level."

"Yeah, but the last time we spoke, you were talking about all the deaths brought about by the Black Plague and about how if they hadn't died, our population would be overrun in today's day and age. Now, you're implying nature's most basic level is a good thing. So which is it?"

"They are both nature's will."

I shake my head and take a deep breath.

She continues. Look, when populations grow exponentially, a virus has more individuals to infect, and natural disasters will affect more people. It's all a natural cycle. However, if the desire to procreate ceased, the human race would die off within a few decades. So, one of the most basic natural instincts is to further the human species." She pauses, then adds, "When I come back, perhaps you can arrange a time when I can meet this over-zealous, mystery-power-wielding young man."

"He's here. Do you have time to meet him today?"

She stands immediately and throws her mostly full drink into the nearby garbage can. That is answer enough. I join her and we start walking.

"Maetha, I don't know how long it will take to find him. This park is huge."

"Imagine his face in your mind for me."

I do as she orders and feel her access my thoughts. She pulls out of my mind and stares straight ahead. I follow her line of vision, but can't tell what or who she's looking at.

"Calli, I'm looking into the minds of others for his face. Once I locate him I can delve deeper for a location."

"Wow, move over Homeland Security."

"There, that boy with his britches hanging down to his testicles has seen him recently at the Corkscrew ride. Let's go."

As we near the ride, another teen's mind reveals to Maetha that Brand has left with a girl and is headed to a grassy area nearby.

I find it amusing how everyone approaching us scratches their head as they walk by. The sensation of having their minds read must be the same for regular people.

We walk around a large hedge and find a group of boys who have circled around Brand. He's clearly stepped over bounds with his choice of girls, once again, and now a gang is about to beat him up, or so they think.

"Maetha, have you ever seen one of these new people with powers in a fight?"

"No, I haven't."

"Let's get a better viewing spot, because you're going to like this."

We reposition ourselves behind a nearby vendor's shack and watch the scene unfold. Brand has apparently ticked off a guy who has several juvenile delinquent friends, and they are all about to violate their probations.

If I was an opportunist, I'd go around and take bets on Brand, but I'm guessing Maetha wouldn't approve.

The situation escalates, and the offended boy rushes at Brand, ready to punch him in the face. Brand shifts to the side at the last second, and the boy's hand makes contact with a post directly behind Brand, making an audible crunching, cracking sound. The attacker's wailing is deafening, and the crowd lets out a sympathetic "Ooooh." His buddies all jump forward at the same time, and a glimmer of silver catches my eye.

Maetha's eyes dart over to mine. "Calli, I can't see his future well enough to know if he'll be all right. I don't want him killed."

"He won't be hurt."

"How do you know this?"

"You have to look into the future of the knife bearer to see if he'll win the fight."

"What? Oh, wait . . . I see. Everything will be all right."

Sure enough, the fight plays out like the one in the high school parking lot and is over in a matter of thirty seconds, with each of the hoodlums curled up in agony on the grass, holding their private parts. A six-inch blade pokes up out of the grass with the handle still waving back and forth.

Maetha turns to me and says, "Calli, I'll be out of sight, observing, but I want you to take him somewhere more private and reveal to him you have the healing power. He will then reveal his power to you."

"You've seen that happen? Then why don't you just tell me what his power is?"

"Future sight will not reveal a paradox. If I could see what he will reveal, there would be no need to have him reveal it."

"Huh?"

"Your future reveals you will learn his power and help him understand it better. It does not show me his power."

"Ugh, too confusing. All right, what should I say to him to get him to talk?"

"Whatever you feel you should."

I watch as Brand picks up the knife and closes it. He wags it in front of the owner and says, "Thanks." He pushes the knife into his pockets and walks away. The girl the fight began over rushes to one of the downed boys. I use that opportunity to approach Brand.

"I see you're busy keeping the peace, Brand." I fall in step with him and note his tired expression.

"Oh, you saw?"

"Yeah, I did. You've got quite a skill there. You should go into Ultimate Fighting or something."

"I've been hit enough times, thank you very much." He doesn't look at me. He simply keeps walking at a brisk pace.

"What? You never get hit."

"That's what *you* think. Why are you even talking to me, Calli?" He glances over at me with a puzzled expression on his face.

"I think you and I have a lot in common."

He stops and says, "So are you going to change your mind about me, about us?" His emotion and voice inflection change on a dime.

I can tell he's weighing his options with me. *What is it with male hormones?* "No, Brand."

"I don't know why you won't change your mind. I don't know why I can't change *your* mind."

"What makes you think you could change my mind?"

"It's a gift."

"Do you really think it's appropriate to use your gift on people in that way?"

"Who cares? It's what I do. My time here lasts so much longer than anyone else's. At least I can score with the girls while I'm at it."

What is he saying? I don't want to interrupt his willingness to open up, so I add to his statement. "Yeah, you've succeeded with all the girls except Suz."

"And you," he reminds me and starts walking again.

"Why have you passed her up?"

"I don't want to talk about it." His tone is laced with finality and anger. He walks up to a beverage vending machine and feeds a couple of bills into the slot and makes his selection for water. He struggles to get the bottle out of the machine and then twists the cap off. As he lifts it to his lips, he looks at me and pauses. "Do you want a drink?" He extends the bottle toward me.

"No, thank you. Why do you say your time here lasts longer than anyone else's?"

Brand guzzles the water as if he's been traveling over miles and miles of hot desert. He wipes his mouth and lets out a slight belch. "It's true, literally. My day lasts longer than anyone else's. Of course it's my own fault, but I can't help myself. I like things to go my way. I like to win the fights, and I like to get the girl if I can." He pauses and stares at me for a couple of seconds and then answers the question I was about to ask. "Because I've had a lot of practice."

"How did you . . . ?" My amazement is hard to hold back. Had he read my mind? No, it isn't possible, because I'm an Unaltered. Only other Diamond Bearers can read my mind.

"Calli, I can tell you all about yourself. For instance, you like the color red, your favorite food is anything Chinese, and you used to have a cat named Fluffle-up-a-gus. You don't want to go to college, but you figure you have to please your parents and great grandmother."

I laugh out of pure shock. I'm not even sure Suz could spout that much information about me. How does *he* know this stuff? "Can you read minds or something?"

"Or something."

I step closer to him. "Brand, can we go somewhere more private? I have something to tell you."

"Wow, are you finally ready to jump my bones?"

"Dream on."

We walk through the crowds until we find a maintenance shack with a small area behind protected by a fence. Once we are safely behind the building, and I'm sure no one's following us, I say, "Brand, I know why you wouldn't meet me in the park after dark that time."

He exhales and glances around nervously. "No, I don't think you do."

"I've seen them, Brand. They're called Shadow Demons, and they only attack people with special abilities. You have a special ability and so do I."

He lifts a single eyebrow. "You can actually see the . . . whatever they are? Why can't I see them? How many times have you been attacked by them?"

"Never. They're not interested in my ability."

Now I really have his attention. He asks, "So, what's your ability?"

"I'm a Healer. I can heal most any ailment or injury with my mind."

"Really?" He laughs. "With your mind?" He pulls the recently-acquired knife out of his pocket and opens the blade. "So you're saying if I stabbed myself, you could heal my injury? How fast?"

"Fairly fast."

"Faster than two minutes?"

"Yes, I think so."

Before I can even brace myself, he thrusts the blade deep into his thigh.

With blood gushing, he looks at me and says through gritted teeth, "The clock's ticking, Calli. Show me what you can do."

I focus on his injury and feel the cold steel inside his flesh. I begin repairing the sliced muscle from the inside out, pushing the blade out in the process. The knife drops to the ground; the skin on his thigh closes. All that's left is a tear in his blood-covered jeans, but his leg is in perfect condition. He stares slack-jawed at the knife on the ground, then pushes his fingers inside the slit to feel his leg.

"Calli, what did you do?" His voice cracks with his amazed discovery.

I feel exhilarating and can't help but smile. This is the first time in a long while that I've used my healing power on someone who is actually aware of what I've done.

Brand pulls his finger out of the knife slit in his pants. His hand is covered in blood. "I'm impressed, but can you fix my jeans? This is my favorite pair."

"You're the one who jabbed a knife into them, moron. Get a needle and thread and sew them up. I only fix humans."

"Well, what good is your power if you can't fix my jeans too?"

I can't believe he isn't shocked out of his mind with my healing ability and that he's throwing such a fit over a pair of worn-out jeans.

"You showed me yours, now I'll show you mine." He takes my hand and looks me directly in the eyes. "You want to see something cool?"

Excitedly, I nod.

"Come with me and watch." He squeezes my hand, and everything around me begins spinning around in a nauseating blur. When the spinning stops, Brand asks, "Faster than two minutes?"

I instinctively answer "yes." I let go of his hand, look at the knife in his other hand, and then down at his unharmed pants. No blood. No rip. He hasn't stabbed his leg yet, and I keep waiting for him to do so.

He looks at me and says, "See, I fixed my pants."

"Did we just travel back in time, Brand?"

"Nope."

I rub my forehead and squeeze my eyes shut, trying to pull my thoughts together. Had I only imagined him stabbing his leg? The memory is etched in my brain, and yet he hasn't done that yet. Am I going crazy, or is this some sort of déjà vu? Maybe Brand has the power to make me think an event has happened when in fact it never did.

Brand hasn't taken his eyes off me. "Are you all right, Calli?"

"What did you do, Brand?" An echo of a memory fixed in my brain is of Brand asking me that same question after I healed his self-inflicted stab wound.

But he hadn't stabbed, and I hadn't healed.

Brand speaks slowly. "We rewound the same stretch

of time, but I didn't stab myself this time."

"So, you remember stabbing yourself?"

"Yes, and you remember also?"

"Yes."

"See, now you know how I was able to fight the gang."

"I'm not sure I understand."

"I keep repeating segments of time until I figure out how to avoid getting hit. The gang fight took around two hours to complete. I was hit many times, and those guys broke my nose repeatedly, but once I finally made it through the fight and successfully landed my groin kicks, I didn't need to go back and repeat any further. That's the version you saw. I spouted all that stuff about you, but only because you gave me every one of those answers just moments before. You didn't remember giving me the answers because I repeated the time back to where you hadn't said anything yet, but the memory remained in my head. There were plenty of questions you wouldn't answer such as: if you're a virgin, or who's your dream guy?"

I blush and my mouth falls open involuntarily.

"I stabbed myself, knowing if you were full of crap I could simply repeat the time sequence and my leg would be fine. In fact, if you'd been fooling me, I'd have gone back even further, and you'd never know exactly what it is I do."

"Well, why don't you repeat back to the moment right before the gang tried to beat you up? You could avoid all that mess and wasted time."

"Because I can only repeat the last two minutes, no further."

I hear footsteps and reach out and grasp Brand's arm, thinking it might be the gang of guys.

Brand looks at me as is he's been betrayed. "Your friend is coming. You set me up, didn't you?"

Maetha rounds the corner and joins us behind the shed.

I ask Brand, "How did you know . . . why would I set you up?"

He points an accusatory finger at Maetha. "She's been spying on us."

"It's okay, Brand. This is Maetha. She helped me understand my power and the dangers associated with it. She can help you too."

"I don't need anyone's help." Brand shuffles his feet uneasily.

Maetha launches right in with questions. "Are you aware of other powers and abilities out there?"

"What, like besides Calli's healing? No. Unless the monsters in the dark count."

"When did you first see the Demons?" Maetha doesn't mince words.

"I can't see them. I only know that if I walk into a dark area, I get attacked."

"Then you repeat time and remove yourself from the situation, right?" Maetha concludes.

Brand exhales, relaxing his tense shoulders.

"So to speak. As long as I don't stay in any situation longer than two minutes I can always have a do-over. After all this time, two minutes is constantly counting down in my head."

"Have the shadows held danger for you all of your life?" Maetha asks.

"No, only since I discovered I had this ability to fix the problems in my life. So, a couple of years. It seems much, much longer than that, though. Hey, if you two know so much, then tell me how to deal with the Demons."

I look at Maetha, who stares at him. I think she's

waiting for me to break the news.

I answer him. "We don't know, Brand. Light pushes them back, but you probably already know that. I've seen them shrink away from a barking dog, too. Actually, I have some experiments I'd like to do, and you can help me."

Maetha speaks to my mind. *His ability is more powerful than I thought.*

I know, I respond. *He used his power on me, Maetha. How is that possible? I'm an Unaltered.*

Brand doesn't know we are able to have a private conversation, and he responds to my request about experimenting. "Oh sure, I get it, you just want me around so I can be your Guinea Pig."

"Yeah, pretty much. You have a problem with that?"

"No, why would I have a problem with flesh being ripped from my bones?"

Maetha's eyebrows draw together. She looks over her shoulder briefly, then says with urgency, "The angry boys are coming this way. We should move to a different place."

"There," Brand says, pointing to a large bush not far away, "they won't see us if we move over there."

"How do you know?" I ask Brand as the three of us hurry over to the bush.

Brand cocks his head to the side. "Remember that one time when I showed you my power? In about two minutes, they will come by and not see us. Gee whiz, Calli. Pay attention."

We reposition ourselves behind a bush across the pathway from the maintenance shack and wait. Brand asks Maetha, "How do you know they are coming? Can you repeat time too?"

"No, I can see the future."

"You can't see the future," he says while he chuckles.

"I find it fascinating, Brand, that you are so quick to

reject the existence of other people's superpowers when you yourself possess one," says Maetha.

"Yeah, I see your point. I keep thinking my ability will go away someday, like it's because of something I ate, or the result of radiation or gamma rays like the cartoons portray with some superheroes. Every day when I wake up, I test my ability to make sure it's still there, and every night I avoid the shadows. But this—you two—she's a Healer, and you see the future. This is freakin' me out."

Maetha puts her hand up, motioning us to be quiet. "Here they come."

Twenty or so scary-looking boys, including the ones Brand had rendered incapacitated only minutes before, round the corner and stop by the shack. One boy gives orders and divides the group into a few smaller groups to cover more ground. Then he checks behind the maintenance shed before moving on.

Maetha speaks to my mind. *Calli, I am needed by the others and I must go. For now, only display the healing ability. Teach him about the will of nature and help him understand that repeating time for his own gain could be dangerous. Help him stay out of trouble.*

Maetha steps away from the safety of the bush. "I'm sorry, Brand. I must leave you. Calli will help you learn more about your gift and how to use it properly." Before Brand can respond, she walks away into the crowd.

"Humph," Brand grumbles. "I don't need anyone to teach me how to repeat, no offense, Calli."

"I think what she meant was I have a lot to teach you about the world of powers. For now, we'd better get ourselves to a safer location."

We walk through the park, keeping our eyes peeled for the group of thugs who want Brand's head. At one point we see them coming from the other direction and divert off into an arcade with multiple exits. I try to look into Brand's future to see if this move will be successful, but I can't get anywhere. His power provides a virtual roadblock.

"Do we need to repeat?"

"I already did, Calli. We ran into them up ahead by the Wack-a-Mole game. There were too many of them, and I didn't really want to fight, so I repeated back here."

"Wow, this is messed up, Brand."

"Tell me about it. Maybe I should just face them and let them beat me up. Then they'd leave us alone. Plus, you could heal me. It's a win-win situation."

I try to look for his future to see if that would work, but naturally I can't determine one way or the other how things would work out. "Yeah, well, I don't think we should risk it. I can't bring you back from the dead, so we better keep dodging them."

We dash out the side door and wander through the park. Over the next couple of hours, I inform him about the cosmic energy rays and how he wasn't that far off in thinking he'd been exposed to radiation. I give him a brief explanation about the different known abilities—the Healers, Readers, Seers, Hunters, and Runners—and how his power is a new development. Maetha is investigating some others like him, I tell him, but hadn't figured out what their power is until today.

We talk about the clans and how people with powers have been around forever. I leave out the part about the diamonds, and the events that took place with the destruction of the Death Clan. I don't tell him Maetha's age, or say anything about unaltered humans.

When I began to tell him about the will of nature, he takes my hand and pulls me toward a game booth. "Come on, Calli. I'll win you a stuffed animal."

"No you won't. You'll cheat. You'll repeat until you

win, all on the same amount of money."

"So what? I still have to beat the game. I'll bring you along so you can see how many times it takes me to win."

Well, how can I resist that temptation? "All right. Win me the large puppy."

Brand goes up to the vendor and gives him the money for three baseballs. He will need to break a plate, and not just any plate, but one with a prize sticker behind it to win the smallest prize. He will then have to break three winning plates to win the big puppy. He raises his arm and hurls the ball, hitting one plate directly in the center, busting it into three pieces. I'd forgotten he is the star quarterback. His plate isn't a winner, so he throws the next ball and then the last one. Each breaks a plate. One plate has a winning sticker, and the vendor reaches up to a hanging cord and waggles it wildly. The cord is attached to a cow bell up in the top of the booth and is obviously meant to attract attention.

"And what does the lady want?" The vendor smiles, revealing a few missing teeth. I choose a small purple lizard with huge bulging eyes.

Brand takes my hand and says, "Second row down, third plate from the left is a winner." The air around us whooshes and everything goes blurry for a microsecond. I blink and it's over. We are back to standing at the game booth with Brand being handed the three balls and the purple lizard back on the shelf.

He immediately aims at the known winning plate and smashes it to pieces. The cow bell clanks its aggravating sound, the toothless vendor asks for my selection, and I am handed the lizard. Then Brand throws the two remaining balls and breaks two non-winning plates.

I look at him curiously. "It seems to me you should break other plates first and save the winner for last."

"Yeah, yeah, everyone's a critic. Come on," he mutters as he takes my hand and repeats back to the same spot as before. My head takes a moment to stop spinning.

This time, with the first ball, he's able to locate a winning plate on the bottom row, directly in the center. The vendor rings the blasted bell.

"And what does the lady want?" The decayed condition of his remaining teeth is a good reminder to always brush after meals. I choose the lizard, and Brand throws the second ball at the second row down, third plate from the left and smashes it with perfect accuracy. Again with the cow bell, and the vendor allows me to trade up to a medium prize. I choose a monkey with the long curly tail. Finally, Brand picks up the last ball and holds it out near my mouth and tells me to blow on it. I roll my eyes, not wanting to encourage his behavior. However, I really want to see how he uses his power, so I puff on the ball, and then watch as he throws it to the center bottom row plate . . . and misses.

I am surprised Brand hasn't repeated time yet, and even more surprised when he pulls out more money and buys three more balls.

"My lady wants the big dog, so I'll have to break another winning plate." The vendor hands him the balls after taking his money. Brand aims at a plate he hasn't hit before. No win. He winds up and throws the second ball at another new plate. No win. The third ball flies from his fingertips, but not in the direction of the winning plate on the bottom row. Instead it crashes into another new plate, sending pieces flying. A winning plate!

The vendor clanks his bell ridiculously and then, using a hook on a long pole, reaches for the big puppy. He gives it to Brand so Brand can give it to me. By this time, we've drawn a lot of attention from other park attendees.

I lean close and ask, "Why didn't you repeat? Why did you purchase more tries, and why didn't you go after the plate on the bottom row?"

He doesn't answer. Instead, he places his hand on the small of my back and guides me through the gathered crowd. The huge stuffed puppy in my arms makes it difficult to see where I'm going so I'm all right with him helping me. Although I think he could have done so without touching my body.

Once we're away from the crowd, he says, "I don't always repeat. Sometimes I like to spice things up. Like the last football game of the season. I stopped repeating my throws so we could lose and be done with it. This little amusement park game was a metaphor for my life: sometimes I stick with one thing until I succeed, and other times I let chance determine if I'll succeed. You probably noticed the same things happened each time we repeated, such as the crowd was always the same, the same people looked our way when the toothless wonder would ring the bell, and the man always stood in the same place to hand me the set of balls. This is how I won the fight you saw earlier. I knew when I was going to be punched, and I repeated until I could avoid the punch. Every hit and punch hurt, especially the knife to my gut. Repeating takes my body back, not my memories, the same as you just witnessed."

From out of nowhere, two large guys rush toward us. "There he is. Grab him!"

I feel Brand take my hand. The world spins around me, faster than being on the Octopus ride. When the spinning stops, we arrive at the moment when he's about to hand me the stuffed puppy.

I look at him admittedly confused.

"Let's go a different direction." He guides me away

from the crowd, walking briskly without looking back. Once we've put enough distance between us and the gang, he stops me beside a bench and takes the puppy out of my arms and sets it down. "You know, Calli, you and I would make a great team. We have a lot more in common than anyone else, wouldn't you say? We should hang out more often."

"We will be together plenty. We'll be working on the experiments I mentioned earlier."

He shuts his eyes and shakes his head. "That's not what I mean."

"Brand, I'm not going to date you."

His eyes meet mine. "Don't you like me?"

I take a deep breath to gather my words, carefully thinking about his power and what it means to me. I also consider that Maetha asked me to teach him about nature's will. If I upset him with my answer he might not hang out with me. "Look, Brand, I like you and all, but I just want to be your friend."

"Just a friend?" He sounds let down.

"Yeah."

"Can friends hug?" He smiles big, and executes the dimples, his only true weapon in softening a girl's heart.

"Yeah, as long as you don't try anything."

He opens his arms in invitation for my hug. Somewhere in the back of my mind I realize Suz is watching this from a distance, and yet it doesn't stop me. I step into his embrace and hug him like I would hug my father. I can't speak for him, but I don't believe for a second he's hugging me like he would his mother. Brand is an opportunist, and I've just fallen into his opportunistic arms.

I push him back and scan the area and find the backside of Suz's head as she walks away. Strangely, I don't feel sad. I realize she's never really been a good friend to me, that I am more of a burden to her. I guess this is one way of letting her off the hook without divulging my secrets.

I think about her infatuation with Brand and how it must really hurt her to see me hugging him, but instead of empathizing with her, I decide to get to the bottom of why Brand shunned her in the first place.

"Brand, what happened with Suz? Why did you break off your friendship?"

"Where's that question coming from?"

"She said you two had something going for a little while."

"I'll only tell you this if you swear you won't tell Suz."

"Suz and I aren't friends anymore. Besides, I'm a vault, Brand." *More than you know.*

"Okay. I was making out with Suz one day when my mother busted in on us and freaked out, saying I was kissing my *half-sister*. My father and Suz's mother had had an affair, and Suz is the result. I knew about my parents' rocky beginnings, but I never knew who my dad cheated with. I was able to repeat back to before my mother came in the room. I hurried Suz out the back of the house in order to keep her from being embarrassed. I've had to give her the cold shoulder to suppress her attractions to me ever since. I suppose I could just tell her why and develop a brother/sister relationship, but that would devastate her. Honestly, Calli, I believe I did the right thing by getting her out of the house before my mother ruined her life."

"Yeah, I agree. I think you did the right thing. I won't tell her."

"Can I have another hug?"

"Nope."

"Does he have a name?"

I look at him for a long moment. "I'll tell you in two and a half minutes."

"Damn, you figured me out."

"How many times did you ask me for a hug, Brand?"

"Many."

"So, what did you change to soften me?"

"It was winning the stuffed puppy for you and doing it honestly. Your eyes softened and I knew you'd be more likely to give me a hug."

"But that was more than two minutes ago."

"It's all a long process. I've learned to recognize signals and body language that will have a better chance of being directed the way I want."

"You mean manipulate, don't you?"

He shrugs his shoulders.

"Let me guess. You thought by answering my question about Suz you'd be able to win me over some more, right?"

He nods.

"So, now you figure I have a guy?"

"No, you told me you did when I tried to kiss you."

I slug his arm—hard! "You tried to take advantage of me? You're a pig, Brand."

"Well, you may be right, but I have to say, you are the strongest-willed girl I know, and I can't seem to win you over, so, you have my complete respect."

"His name is Chris Harding, and he's going to kick your ass someday."

"You know, you could have just told me you already have a guy and that's why you don't want to date me."

"Would that have mattered? It didn't stop you from going after Tiffany."

"The difference is Tiffany responded to my flirting. When I tried to kiss her, she let me, and she kissed me back."

On the bus ride home, Brand sits by me. Suz sits with her other friends, throwing me dirty looks. I close my eyes so I won't be tempted to read lips or minds. I think about the day and how enlightening it ended up being. Maetha was able to get more answers about the unknown cosmic power, I got to know Brand better than I thought I would, and now my mind is swimming with possible experiments I can perform with Brand and the dead Healers.

As I rest with my eyes closed, my head continues to spin from all the repeating we did today. Brand and I repeated so many times. I eventually had to ask him to stop dragging me along. Even though Brand and I didn't go on any of the rides—we were too busy staying one step ahead of the slew of angry boys—I'm probably just as wiped out and dizzy as everyone else on the bus. The difference is I can heal my motion sickness.

Chapter 6 - Deadly Shadows

Brand shakes my shoulder, waking me from my deep sleep.

"Calli, what am I going to do?"

I note his panic immediately. I look out the bus window and realize right away what he's concerned about. Apparently our sleepy little town had been hit by a lightning storm because the power is out. We drive down the eerily darkened street toward the school.

"We'll figure it out, Brand. Don't panic."

"Don't panic? Are you kidding me?" His voice rises into a high-pitched squeal I feel sure everyone can hear. "Calli, repeating will only put me back on this bus, headed for the same end! And you say don't panic? Oh, I'm panicking! There's much panicking going on here!"

He's in big trouble. I wish I'd had time to develop some tools or gadgets Brand could use at this very moment to ward off the Demons. Once he's safely in his car, he'll be fine. He'll drive home and pull into his lighted garage . . . *crap*, I realize, *his garage will be dark as well.* He'll have to stay inside his car till the lights come back on.

The whole situation makes me wonder what the clans did before electricity. Did they carry lit torches with them all the time? Did they keep dogs around to deter the Demons?

We pull into the darkened high school parking lot, and everyone's murmurs and whispers increase. "Brand, let's let everyone else get off the bus first," I say.

That will give me time to think of a solution.

One by one, the students exit the bus, and soon we are the only ones left.

I walk up to the bus driver and say the first thing that comes to my mind. "My friend here is deathly afraid of the dark, and this power outage is freaking him out. Would you mind holding up a second longer while I drive my car around here to the door?"

"Hurry it up, then." He yawns, and waves his hand in the direction of the door.

I look back at Brand and jump off the bus. The Demons are thick outside the door and continue to gather. I hurry to my car, unlocking the door with the remote as I run, then climb in. I drive quickly around the lot and up onto the sidewalk with the passenger door right next to the bus door. I reach over and open the door toward Brand, who stands on the bottom step of the bus. The light spills out from the interior of my car and I see the Demons slink away.

"Get in!" I shout.

Brand jumps in my car with a fluid motion, slamming the door shut. I can see the bus driver shaking his head. Ignoring him, I put the car in gear and drive away. "See? That wasn't so bad."

He sputters and coughs. "I need to repeat again, Calli." He pulls his blood-covered hand away from his stomach.

I yank the steering wheel to the right and pull over. "Again?"

"They get me every time." He continues to mutter curse words.

"Wait. Maybe I can heal you," I say, then quickly scan his body and find his injury is pretty serious, but not irreparable. "Brand, I can fix you."

"But the blood, your car, if I repeat—"

"No. Lean toward me." He leans, or more like falls against me, and I quickly pull his shirt up from his waist and rest my hands on his torn skin. I sense the major damage first. A Demon's claw punctured completely through his body, narrowly missing his spine, damaging his liver, and exiting out the front of his body. I feel the mending within him as sliced muscles and organs right themselves. The exit wound on his stomach is the last to heal together, but he's lost a lot of blood. I search my own body for excess energy to transfer to him, extra plasma, so to speak, to sustain him until his own body can replace the lost blood. Instinctively, I take my hands and run them over his upper body mere millimeters above his skin and clothes, transferring my energy to him.

Brand takes several deep breaths and starts to gain strength. "Calli, you're amazing. What does this Chris guy have over me?"

I can tell he's trying to downplay the seriousness of the situation. "Knock it off, Brand."

"Sorry about your car. Sweet ride, by the way."

"It will clean, don't worry about it. The bigger question is how we're going to get you inside your home." I pull back onto the dark street and continue to Brand's house. My body shakes and I can tell I'm weakened from using the healing power. I don't want to alarm Brand, so I take slow, deep breaths and focus on the road.

The power is restored before we arrive at his house and the porch light effectively lights his front yard. Problem solved.

"You left your big puppy on the bus, Calli," he says as I slow to a stop in his driveway under the bright floodlight.

"Oh no. I guess I had more important things on my mind." I smile and look beyond him toward his front door.

"No danger, Brand. You're good to go."

Brand looks at his bloody hands. "What should I tell my Mom about this blood?"

"Tell her it's not real and it was a prank pulled by some other boys."

Brand begins to lean toward me as if he's going to kiss my cheek, but I put my hand up and stop him. "Good night, Brand."

"Sheez, you're strong willed." He gets out of the car and jogs up to the door.

I drive away once he's safely inside. What a day! I decide to hit the twenty-four-hour car wash and shampoo the interior of my car before I head home. First, I call my mother and tell her I am back in town, but will be delayed getting home so she won't call out the cavalry. I tell her someone threw up in the passenger seat and I am going to go clean up the mess at the car wash. She buys it.

Graduation comes and goes without much fuss—well, if you don't count Suz and all her exaggerated antics of jealousy and self-inflicted depression, then there wasn't much fuss. My parents are curious about why my friendship with Suz ended, but the new development of me hanging out with the all-star quarterback has them a bit preoccupied.

I try to tell them Brand is just a friend, but they don't believe me. Even more frustrating is the fact that Brand has apparently attached himself to me and is no longer playing the field. All the girls who used to swoon over him now throw dirty looks my way. *So much for anonymity and blending into the shadows.*

Now that school's out, I no longer have to ignore

snide remarks or pretend not to hear the animal sounds directed at me. However, one of the last days of school was particularly fun when one of Suz's snotty friends made a pig snorting sound and actually snorted a bunch of phlegm into her throat. She hacked and coughed and dry heaved. I guess she really was a snotty friend.

One week after school ends, Maetha and Beth come to visit me late in the afternoon when my parents are gone.

Beth jumps forward and hugs me tightly. "It's so good to see you again, Calli. You look really good. You're all grown up."

"Beth, it's only been a year since I saw you. I can't have changed that much. Look at you. You've changed more than me." I am amazed to see creeping color redden her cheeks. She has confidence and composure even though she still wears a bit too much black eyeliner, but that's just my opinion. I guess it doesn't really matter how a confident woman dresses.

Maetha says, "Calli, Beth and I will be in town for a few days and will be staying at the Riverside Inn. I think it's best if we do our training there. I want you to bring Brand with you. Here's our room number." She hands me a card. "A phone number is on the back."

Beth interjects, "It's my number."

"What? You get to have a phone at the compound?"

"Yes. Although most of the time it's in Clara's office. You know, rules. The number is easy to remember, what with all the sevens."

I glance again at the card and see her point. I say, "I'll find out when Brand's available and get back with you."

"Good, We'll see you then." Maetha turns to Beth.

"I'll be in the car."

As Maetha walks away, I say to Beth, "So, you and Maetha?"

"Yeah. Thanks for letting her know I was looking for her."

"I didn't."

"She said you did." Beth's eyes narrow.

"She must have read my mind or something."

"Or something. I think there's more to her than she lets on." Beth throws a quick glance over her shoulder.

I draw the conclusion Maetha hasn't told Beth about the Diamond Bearers, so I follow her lead. "Probably so."

Beth's expression brightens and she says, "I'm so happy to see you again! I knew you were different the first time I saw you. It was your incredible aura." She steps back and looks above my head. Then, she dips her chin to her chest. "I'm sorry for the way I treated you."

"Hey, don't worry about it. We're good."

Her eyes meet mine with a mile-wide grin. "Thanks. See you soon." She waves and hurries to the car.

They leave and I immediately call Brand.

"Hey, what's up?" he asks.

"Remember the woman from the amusement park? She's in town and wants to meet with us again."

"Why?"

"Why?" My first thought is: is he serious? Then I consider he doesn't know Maetha the way I do. I say, "She wants to share some of her knowledge with you."

"Don't you mean she wants to learn more about me?"

"Probably."

"All right. Pick me up in the morning. After ten o'clock."

"Lazy. Okay."

"Great. It's a date!"

"It's not a date—" I try to add but he's already ended the call.

I call Beth to let her know when to expect us.

♡ ♡ ♡

I pick up Brand the next morning and we drive to the hotel.

"So, what are we doing today?" Brand asks.

"I think Maetha's going to teach me how to see auras." I pull the car into a parking spot and see Beth heading toward us.

"Ah, come on. Don't tell me you believe in that crap," he grumbles his reply. I'm about to respond when his voice changes, indicating his extreme interest in something. He says seductively, "Oooh, hellooo! Who do we have here?" Brand's eyes follow Beth's every movement as she approaches. I have to remind myself he's probably never seen a Runner before.

"Stop drooling, Brand, it's unbecoming." We get out of the car and Brand walks right up to Beth.

"Hi there. I'm Brand." He extends his hand to Beth. She takes it in a firm handshake. "Calli didn't tell me I'd be meeting her beautiful friend."

I can't say I'm surprised by his actions. This is, after all, fairly standard behavior for him. I step near them and say, "Brand Safferson, this is Beth Hammond."

Beth smiles. "Nice to meet you, Brand."

"Your eyes are mesmerizing, Beth." He sounds like he's gazing into the windows of heaven.

"Thank you," she stammers.

His eyes travel over her body. "I bet you're an Olympic athlete. You have a perfect body, I mean, body structure. You must be amazing."

Beth's mouth hangs open and her eyes twinkle.

It's so obvious to me what Brand is doing. I jump in and ask, "What room are you and Maetha in?"

Brand answers before she can. "She'll take us there, won't you?" Then he puts his arm around her shoulders, and *she lets him do it!*

"Sure," she says, her voice soft and airy.

I smack his shoulder and say, "Stop that, Brand."

"Stop what?" he replies. "No one ever flirts with her or tells her how beautiful she is. She needs this. Besides, after the way her low-life ex-boyfriend treated her, she needs some positive affirmations."

Beth stops dead in her tracks and glares at Brand. "I never told you anything about Justin. Are you a Reader?"

Brand doesn't answer. He steps back, closer to me, takes my hand, and squeezes it. Then the ground and surroundings begin to spin crazily as he rewinds time. Once the spinning stops, I find Brand standing next to Beth with his arm around her shoulders.

Beth says, "Sure." My mind replays the moment she responded to Brand's assumption she'd take us to Maetha.

Brand smiles at me.

Oh, boy. This is going to be a long day.

The day is tedious, and it doesn't matter how many times Beth explains the process of viewing auras, I still can't see anything. Maetha spends a long time talking privately with Brand, probably asking him questions about his ability. Every now and then I notice something peculiar about Maetha's behavior, that's not at all like her regular business-like manner.

Brand must be repeating.

Later on I speak with Maetha and tell her what I witnessed.

Her breath catches in her throat when she hears my words. She lowers her voice and asks, "Are you saying he was able to manipulate *me* to get me to answer him the way he wanted?"

"Not exactly. Your own free-will cannot be controlled, but everyone has their breaking point or 'button,' and when pushed, tend to behave the way he wants them to."

"To what end? What does he have to gain from manipulating me?"

"Perhaps it's just an experiment on his part. To him, you're a Seer. Maybe he wanted information about his future."

"I wouldn't be able to tell him anything. His future is incredibly difficult to see."

"Then don't worry about him. He doesn't have control over your free-will."

"My bigger concern, Calli, is that he can use his powers on *me and you*. I don't know what I've told him. How do I know what he knows or doesn't? We're in all new territory as Bearers, and having people like him running around is frightening."

"I'm going to have to talk with Beth and warn her about what he's doing." I approach the two of them and clear my throat to get their attention. Beth turns and faces me. I look past her and address Brand. "Have you ever tried real communication? You know, the kind where no powers are used."

Beth's eyebrows furrow. "What are you saying, Calli."

Pointing to Brand, I say, "He's using his powers on you."

"What?" Beth's head whips around to Brand. "How dare you try your power on me!" she yells. Her teeth are clenched together and her words sound more like a hiss. It's nice to see the Beth I knew from a year ago.

"I'm sorry, Beth. I was caught off guard by your beauty." Brand's smooth voice flows like a melody.

"My what?"

"I sensed you were feeling down this morning and I only wanted to cheer you up. I haven't lied about anything I've said to you. I only used my power to get to know you better, but I acted poorly. Can you forgive me?"

"Well, just don't do it again."

I turn to Maetha and put my thoughts out for her to read. *Do you see what he's doing? Beth isn't the sort of girl to back down so quickly, and it can only mean one thing—he's still repeating. He's rewinding and trying different phrases until he finds the one that gives him the desired result. By making one attempt after another, he eventually gets his way. Keep watching. I'll bet she ends up hugging him soon. He always ends with a hug.*

We watch as Brand leans forward and whispers something to Beth. She giggles and then hugs him. I catch Brand's eye and shake my head. He shrugs his shoulders as if to say, "Sorry, I can't help myself."

I leave them and walk back over to Maetha.

Maetha speaks to my mind. *Calli, Brand's power is dangerous. He needs to learn how to use it properly and in a manner that supports the will of nature. You need to take him under your wing and teach him about the greater good. Remember, I'd asked you to teach him.*

I reply with my thoughts. *As far as I can tell, he only uses his power to get girlfriends, win fights, and not get sacked on the football field.*

Well, Beth won't become one of his conquests on this trip, Maetha says. *I can assure you of that. However, I do see a certain level of attraction to him on her part, so keeping them apart long term isn't going to be up to us. His future is a crazy plethora of pos-*

sibilities, and only some of them reveal Beth as the one he ends up with. His mind is all about percentages, I'm finding. I'd say he has about a 15% chance of ending up with Beth. Maetha puts her hands to her head as if she's experiencing discomfort. She says out loud, "Wow, his head is a mess. How do you navigate through it, Calli?"

"I've found it's better to steer clear all together. I don't like the headache that navigating brings on."

"I understand what you mean. This pain is horrible."

"I call them Brand-aches."

Maetha closes her eyes and holds still a moment. I figure she's using her healing ability. "I've experienced these headaches with the other Repeaters also," she says.

"Repeaters?"

"Yes. One of the other individuals with this power refers to herself as a Repeater. I think the name suits well enough. Soon after Brand's power was identified, my associate in Columbus, Ohio used the information to befriend the female Repeater named Nicole and gain her trust. I met with Nicole and experienced the same explosion of pandemonium and pain within my head. However, she doesn't use her power the same way Brand does. Nicole is a juvenile delinquent."

"There are others like me?" Brand joins in on the conversation as he walks over to us.

"Yes. So far we've identified a small handful of Repeaters—five, possibly six, all close to the same age."

His bounces up on his tiptoes with a big grin stretched across his face. "I want to meet them."

"Someday you will, Brand." Maetha smiles at him. "For now, let's get back to training."

We spend the rest of the afternoon learning about the energy fields around humans and the colors associated with them. It might as well be a foreign language because it goes right over my head. I don't know that I'll ever be able to detect auras, at least not as long as I view the whole idea as ridiculous. However, when I recall the memory in Chris's mind of what he saw when he looked at me, I'm reminded that auras are not hogwash, because through his eyes I saw my own iridescent glow. If only I could see it with my own eyes.

Before we part, Maetha takes me aside and says, "This has been a productive day, Calli."

"How so? I can't seem to see any auras."

"That wasn't the major focus of this meeting." She nods in Brand's direction. "He was. I've learned much more about his ability and his possible intentions."

"Intentions? What do you mean?"

"It seems the way Brand uses his power has to do with his basic personality and his life experiences before the power emerged. His power of persuasion and charisma, coupled with his ability to manipulate endlessly and tirelessly, says to me nothing would stop or deter him from succeeding at whatever he sets his mind to. I want you to study and learn his intentions and what he desires. Try hard to sway his mind in a good direction. Keep his allegiance and don't lie to him, or you'll lose him. I would take him under my own wing, but I can tell he doesn't trust me the way he trusts you."

Maetha and Beth leave us and I make plans with Brand to meet at his house a few days later in the evening when his mother will be gone. We will be able to run a few experiments with the Shadow Demons and hopefully gain a better understanding of them.

The sun sets out my bedroom window in a brilliant

scene of orange and red, with a few streaks of clouds reflecting the warm colors of the summer sky. Sunsets must be so ominous for people with powers. I figure there's only about an hour left until the shadows become dangerous again.

If not for Brand's insufferable personality, I would feel terrible for using him as my test subject. However, knowing he can repeat out of bad situations opens up the opportunity to learn more about the Demons, something that hasn't been possible before.

I select an old, worn-out shirt from my drawer and stuff it in my bag. Ms. Winter's "shirt into the shadows" demonstration was incredibly effective for visually dramatizing the fierceness of the Demons. I still remember how petrified I felt after seeing my shirt ripped to shreds. I know Brand fully understands the ferocity of the Demons, but we still need something with his scent for experiments. He will have to give me one of his shirts.

Before I leave the house, I dig through the coat closet and retrieve my father's camera case. He has a light meter that I think will come in handy. After finding the meter, I put it in my bag with my shirt.

When I arrive at Brand's house I find him reclining on his well-lit front steps. As I walk up to the house, he declares, "My date has arrived."

"This isn't a date, Brand." I reach in my bag, pull out my shirt, and toss it to him.

"Sure it is." He catches the shirt. "You even brought a change of clothes. You must have big plans."

"Are you kidding me?" I struggle to contain my irritation. "I'm here to perform research on the creatures that want to kill you, and you can't take that seriously. I guess I'm just wasting my time." I turn around, as though I'm going to leave. I'm not, but he doesn't need to know that.

"Wait! I'm sorry."

I turn back. "This isn't a date."

"Okay, okay. You're one stubborn girl, you know that?"

I pretend to ignore his comment. In reality, I've probably made him want me more, which disturbs me because that isn't my intention. Pulling a list out of my pocket, I say. "All right, I've made a list of the experiments I'd like us to try."

He takes the paper, looks it over, then says, "I have a few requests of my own, if you don't mind, Calli."

"Like what?"

"Well, I want you to show me exactly where the Demons are. Show me where the light is not bright enough to hold them back. I need to know how far away from the house I can safely go without being attacked."

His smart request happens to be number two on the list of experiments I want to carry out. I have different reasons for wanting to map out the Demons' territory than he does, though. Brand wants to know where they are in the thinning light—where his safety zone ends—whereas I want to find out how much injury he will sustain in the not-quite-dark, not-quite-light border area. I hope he's up for this.

I point to the two nearby lights: one across the street, the other next to his driveway. "The streetlights will interfere with our experiment."

"Not a problem," he says as he opens his front door, reaches inside, and pulls out a rifle.

"What are you going to do with that?"

"Turn off the lights," he says with a devious smile. "Don't worry, it's just a BB gun—a high-powered BB gun." He steps off the porch and walks to the safety of the light at the end of his driveway. He aims at the light across the street and pulls the trigger. I hear a pop from the gun and a clinking sound as the BBs bounce off the metal pole. He cocks the gun and tries again. This time he successfully cracks the protective glass at the top of the pole, allowing the next shot to shatter the bulb. Then he walks back to the porch before aiming at the light at the end of the driveway. The crashing sound of glass hitting the cement below startles the neighbor's yappy dog, causing him to do what he does best . . . bark.

I turn to Brand and say, "You missed the first shot and didn't repeat. How come?"

"I don't always repeat, Calli."

"Huh," is all I can say. This is interesting. Is Brand becoming more honest with me? Less fixated on determining the outcome of every situation?

I decide to change the subject. It's time to get to work. "Okay," I say. "I'll walk out there and stand at the line of Demons. I can see right where they are. I brought a light meter with me so we can measure how their presence relates to specific light levels. I suspect there's a particular level that will mark the point at which the Demons can be present, kind of like the way ice forms at the freezing point." I show my meter to Brand and step off the porch into the gathering darkness. I walk all the way to the sidewalk and stand toe-to-toe, nose-to-nose with the dead creatures, who swarm menacingly in front of me. They grope with their talons and hiss through their dagger-sharp teeth. Their glowing red eye-sockets are like hellish fireflies dancing in the dark. I can smell their putrid, rotten breath and see the congealed slime oozing from their jaws, but I know I am safe: they are not interested in me. They want Brand.

A couple of white snakes with red eyes and enormous

fangs slither on the ground toward my feet, disappearing as they cross the line of light and darkness. Maetha mentioned she suspects the Demons actually live in a parallel dimension and that perhaps our darkness is a window or entryway into their world. The thought makes me wonder if it's possible to enter their dimension or to read their minds. I try reaching out to them with my mind, but I feel nothing to read. My Healer senses don't feel anything either, and the Demons don't have a future to see. The only power that notices their presence are my Hunter's senses, making me wonder if regular Hunters can smell or see the demons.

I look at my light meter. My night vision has improved dramatically since getting the diamond shard in my heart, but it's still too dark to see the numbers. I deduce that getting a proper reading will depend on where the light meter is positioned. Obviously this particular meter isn't going to give me the results I need. I'll have to shop around for a different one, one that will be easier to read or one that can transmit the readings to a computer.

"What can you see?" Brand asks. "Where are they?"

"I'm standing in front of them now." Then I step directly into the line of Demons, who shrink away from me so they won't make contact. "Now I'm standing with them."

Brand walks forward and slows to a stop before reaching me. Three jackal-bodied demons lunge toward him but fade to nothing before they reach him. The rest float beside me calm and tense, waiting for their prey to make a mistake. Brand asks, "What does your meter say?"

"It's too dark to read it. I'll have to go get a different one and try later."

"All right, so without the streetlights, the light from the front porch reaches as far as the sidewalk. I already know the Demons are thick anywhere just beyond a defined line between light and darkness, like around the corner of the house.

"Come closer, Brand."

"I don't really want to. Even though I can repeat back to the safety of the porch, it still hurts to be attacked."

"Have you ever been killed by the Demons?"

"Well, uh, I'm alive, so no."

"So the Demons don't kill you? Or you just repeat before you die?"

"I don't exactly know, Calli. My power just kind of kicks in automatically, so I haven't died yet. The pain, however, is what scares me most."

"Brand, you are the only one who can give us a better understanding of the Shadow Demons. This is for the betterment of everyone. Now, put on your big-boy pants and help me out here."

"If I take three steps forward, they'll attack me."

"How do you know until you try?"

"Calli, I just did. Honestly, did you already forget who you're dealing with here?"

"No, but how am I supposed to observe their behavior if I don't get to see it?" I can't believe he'd repeated without me and prevented me from seeing what happened.

"Fine!" he declares.

I move forward to take his hand, but he pulls back. "I don't need to be touching you to pull you back with me." He touches his pointer finger to his temple and says, "It's all done in here."

I am actually shocked to hear this. "Then why did you hold my hand at the amusement park?"

"Because I could." He smiles, exposing those blasted dimples, probably in the hopes I won't be mad.

"Seriously?" Red-hot anger fills my blood. "I traipsed

around holding your hand for no reason?"

His smile falls and he looks to the ground. "I don't know what would happen if I have physical contact with you when they attack. I won't risk you being injured."

I let my frustration out with an exaggerated exhale. "You can just repeat me back, Brand."

"Yes, I could, but I don't want you to feel the pain." He takes a deep breath, steps forward three paces, and I watch in horror as the Demons viciously attack him. His body is actually lifted from the ground, picked up by two jackal-bodied Demons, while other Demons tear into him. Blood oozes, clothing pieces fly through the air. He screams out in agony for a split second, then the world whizzes around, back to the point just before he stepped into the darkness.

The scene I just witnessed is now racing through my mind, and I feel sick. My stomach muscles contract and I run to the fence to throw up on the lawn. The neighbor's dog, being oblivious to the horror that just happened, starts barking at me again.

Brand looks at me briefly, then turns away and bends forward, placing his hands on his knees in exhaustion. His head hangs down while he takes deep breaths. *He must be feeling pretty sick too.*

I recover and walk over to him, the nausea still lingering in my stomach. Whatever desire I had before to see him shredded by the demons is now replaced by extreme guilt. "I'm so sorry for pressuring you, Brand."

"Yeah, whatever," he brushes off my concern.

"I've never seen them kill anyone before, it's more horrible than I imagined."

He stands upright and turns to me. "Where do the Demons go in the daytime?"

He's obviously pushing the conversation away from

himself, so I follow his lead. "No one really knows. That's why we're conducting these experiments."

"Okay, can you tell me if the Demons can enter my house if the lights are off?"

"Haven't you tried to find out for yourself?"

"You're smart, Calli. I like that." He smiles and I let out a huff. He sure makes a quick recovery. "Let me rephrase my question," he says. "Why don't they enter my house when the lights are off?"

This has been a question of mine ever since Clara Winter demonstrated the Demons' ferocity at the Runners' compound. I suspected it was because there were always lights on inside and outside the building, but what if the power was out like the night we came home from Cedar Point? Would the Demons be able to get inside? There's only one way to find out.

"Brand, I want to try something. Where's the outside power box for your house?"

"On the side of the garage. Why?"

"I'm going to flip the switch while you're standing inside your front room with the front door opened. If the Demons get you, you can repeat back to safety. If they don't come, don't repeat and I'll walk through the house with you." I go to the side of the garage and find the power box. A massive Demon lurking beside the house scares the stuffing out of me. This Demon is a bear-bodied, black-scaled beast with curled horns and eagle talons. After seeing what they're capable of, I'm hesitant to get too close. The demon floats out around me, giving me access to the power box handle that cuts all power to Brand's home. I pull it and wait. Brand doesn't repeat, so I head back to the front door.

The Demons are crawling all over each other just outside the open doorway. I see a wolf-bodied Demon stand on its hind-legs and plant its front paws on the open entrance, as though leaning against a wall. The Demon doesn't seem to be able to move through it.

Brand's quivering voice is heard inside the house. "Calli, is that you?"

"Yeah. This is very interesting, Brand. I can see their shapes outside your door, but they aren't entering. There's some kind of invisible wall preventing them from entering. Let's go look through your house." I enter and take his hand and note right away he's trembling. This experiment is testing his resolve and bravery. I imagine he hasn't been this afraid since his power first emerged and he accidentally walked into the shadows.

We do a quick walk-through of his home in the dark, bumping into a few corners and chairs. We open all the doors and find no Demons whatsoever. We even open a couple of windows to see if they'll come in, but they don't. Again, I see a Demon lean against the open space, but it seems unable to enter. I deduce this must be the reason the people with powers of centuries past weren't killed in their homes. My mind completes the thought that perhaps Maetha, who can also see Demons, told the villagers they were safe inside their homes after dark. It still doesn't explain *why* they were safe, though.

I remember the Hunters were safe inside a flimsy tent, so the strength of the walls doesn't matter. How big does an opening have to be before the demons can enter? Would Brand be safe under a structure with only a roof and no walls, like a pagoda?

"All right, Calli. Turn the lights back on please."

I jog to the side of the house, push the handle upward on the power box, and restore power to the home. We move on to the next experiment.

"Brand, go get me one of your old shirts, one you

don't care about."

He does so, and I retrieve the shirt I'd brought with me. We walk to the side of the house, where the porch light etches a clear line of darkness on the ground.

"Have you ever tried throwing some of your clothing into the shadows?"

"No."

"My introduction to the Shadow Demons was done this way: by throwing shirts into the shadows." I bundle the two shirts together and toss them up and beyond the corner of the house. I've seen this done before, yet it still amazes me how the two shirts are torn differently. A far cry from the horror of watching Brand get attacked, though. Brand's shirt is completely shredded and lies in little pieces on the sidewalk, while mine is only ripped a little. However, it *is* ripped. I hadn't even thought about the fact that when Ms. Winter threw my shirt at the Demons, it was torn into long strips, and now, looking at my ripped shirt confirms the suspicion that if I'd held Brand's hand when he walked into the shadows, I'd have been attacked also.

"Holy crappola!" Brand shouts. "That was cool! I've never seen anything actually shredded, well, except for parts of my own body." He grimaces momentarily, but then he's all excited again. "This is amazing, Calli. Even more so, because I didn't have to get hurt. Let's do it again."

"All right, but this time, I don't want you standing nearby."

"But I want to watch."

"I want to see if it makes any difference if you're nearby."

"Fine, I guess I can watch my shirts get shredded any night of the week."

He repeats with me back to before I tossed the shirts into the shadows.

"Brand, I want you to go inside the house to the opposite end while I do this experiment, and I want to repeat *with you* so we can try a few different variations. Give me thirty seconds, then repeat back to now, all right?"

He grunts some kind of complaint and walks away. Once I hear the front door close, I look into the shadows and find the creatures floating around the sides of the house, following him. I toss the shirts into the dark, and as I expect nothing happens; none of them move from their chosen spots in the backyard. They seem to be attracted to his presence and perhaps his smell.

The dark and the light then swirl together in a dizzying array, and I find myself holding both shirts with Brand beside me. "Well? What's the verdict?"

"Nothing happened. The Demons were gone. I tossed your shirt, and it landed on the ground, untouched. Let's do it again, but this time you stay by my side." He smiles a seductive smile, and I remember—as if I could forget— he's just a typical teen boy who finds double meaning in everything.

I throw the shirts into the midst of the freshly assembled Demons, and once again Brand's shirt is shredded in mid-air. I turn to him and say, "Repeat."

The swirling effect nauseates me. We are back to the starting point once again. This time I have a new idea. "Brand, go get your cologne. I want to spray my shirt to see if it will attract the Demons."

He does as instructed, and soon we repeat back because the Demons haven't attacked my shirt.

Brand rubs the back of his neck. "Maybe it's only my natural scent they're attracted to? I guess that rules out you taking one of my shirts to experiment with."

"Yeah, I think you're right. I think we've done enough for tonight. Let's pick this back up tomorrow night."

"All right," he says, stretching his arms as he yawns.

Chapter 7 - A Kiss for Good Luck

I head home and look up light meters on the Internet as soon as I get there. I learn that I don't know much about the subject. Some research needs to be done before I'll be ready to test light levels. My dad's friend, Chuck Stowley, owns a photography studio, and I figure I can glean some information from him.

Another thing I need to do is figure out some way to test the Shadow Demons against the sound of a heartbeat, preferably my own. After Ms. Winter brought it to my attention that my heartbeat is much louder than a normal person of powers, I wonder if sound could be a factor in pushing the Demons back or at least create a deterrent. I decide I will record my heartbeat tomorrow morning at my father's office, but for now I need to sleep.

The next day I head to my father's office and enter through the staff entrance.

My father's secretary, Mabel Lilenquist, greets me. "Hey, Calli. I haven't seen you in a while. You're all grown up." She gives me half a hug with her one free arm as she tries not to drop the files in the other. Her short height and round midsection make it difficult for her to do much of anything except sit at the computer and take calls.

"It's good to see you, Mabel. Is my dad busy today?"

"Always, but I know he'll make time for you. Have a seat in his office. There's a cheese and olive tray in the fridge, dear."

I go into the lounge area and peek inside the fridge. There's a big label "Courtesy of Rodgers Pharmaceuticals" and I figure the representative came by during lunch and brought food and snacks so my dad could eat while the rep talked up his company's latest drug. I grab a plate and put a few olives and cheese slices on it along with a small meat and cheese sandwich. I also take a bottled water and head into my dad's office to wait for him.

One hour and an old edition of the *New England Journal of Medicine* later, my dad shows up. "Calli, what brings you by?"

"It's nothing urgent. If you need to finish up with anything, go ahead."

"I should make a couple quick calls."

I nod and pick up a medical instruments magazine and thumb through it. However, I'm not really paying attention to the pictures and words, instead, I eavesdrop on my father's calls. I find that with my heightened hearing I can hear the voice on the other end of the line quite clearly.

Apparently someone has just been diagnosed with a brain tumor and the prognosis is dismal. Another patient is suffering chronic migraines, but the medications aren't helping, so she's being referred to a pain-management specialist.

I consider for a moment that with my powers I could help these individuals. I have to shake my head in an effort to toss aside the notion of saving everyone.

"All right, Calli, all finished. What did you need?"

"I was wondering if I could record the sound of my heart beating on your ultrasound machine."

My father chuckles and sits forward in his high-back leather chair. "Why?"

"I'm conducting an experiment, that's all. You've always encouraged me with my scientific experiments."

"Yes, I have, but you don't know how to operate the machine, and the tech doesn't come in till Friday."

"You know how to operate it, Dad. Just flip a few switches for me and I'll do the rest. I don't need an ultrasound. I only want to hear and record the sound of my heartbeat. I can wait till you have more time if necessary."

"Now is as good a time as any. Your mother and I have a charity banquet tonight, so I won't have time after work to help you. Come on. Do you have a recording device?"

"My Mp3 player can upload the recording from your machine."

He leads me down the hall to the room where the equipment is and has me climb up on the bed. "You'll need bare skin above your heart so the wand will be able to do its job."

I unbutton my blouse a few notches, and he applies a small bit of ultrasound gel. Then he turns on the machine and positions the wand. "Let's take a look while we have you all hooked up, shall we?"

I bolt upright instantly. "What? Why?"

"It doesn't hurt Calli," he chuckles. "Come on. I know what I'm doing. Lay back down."

I can't have him looking into my heart. What if he sees the diamond shard? "Never mind. I changed my mind, Dad."

He must sense my frustration, because he changes his approach. "Calli, I'm sorry. Here, I've turned it on. There's no picture, only sound. When you're done, plug your USB cord here and move your file over." He smiles hesitantly and turns to leave the room. Then, placing his hand on the doorknob, he says over his shoulder, "Again, I'm sorry. I didn't realize you were still so traumatized from your accident."

Accident?

I enter his mind and see the day Maetha explained to my parents that I'd been in a vehicle accident while in Montana, and that some windshield glass had lodged inside my chest. It's a plausible lie to explain the small scar on my skin. She told them I'd panicked in the hospital and they had to give me a heavy sedative to calm me down. My father figures I must have had a moment of PTSD, and he's upsets he brought it on.

"Dad, it's all right. Don't worry about it." I lie back on the bed with the ultrasound wand in my hand and listen as my father gently closes the door. Then I press the wand into the goo and locate my heart. The gentle pumping, swooshing, and silent stretches sound through the speakers, and I experiment with different locations to see which will yield a better sound. When I finish, I clean the wand and upload the file to my player.

After I arrive back home, I go into the garage, looking for something to hold the Mp3 player. Perhaps we could use Duct tape and strap it to Brand's body. I decide against that. Wearing a fanny pack probably isn't going to fly with Brand, either. I look up on the wall and find the solution: my father's fishing vest. It's perfect, with lots of pockets on the front to hold various things. I pick off the ornamental fishing flies and empty the pockets.

Now I'm ready for tonight.

♡ ♡ ♡

The sun has already set, and my parents are still not

home from their banquet. I send a text message to explain where I am and then leave the house and drive over to Brand's.

When I arrive, I pull out my father's fishing jacket. "Brand, I have something for you to wear."

He looks at the jacket and then at me. "What's that for?"

I unfasten one of the pockets and remove my Mp3 player for him to see.

He reaches forward and touches the device. "You still use one of these? Most normal people just use their phones for music these days." He throws me a sarcastic glance.

"Duh. But I don't want my phone permanently attached to this vest." I show him the two small external speakers strapped at each shoulder. I press play and watch his face to see what his response will be. He raises an eyebrow, but doesn't react much beyond that.

I say, "My heartbeat's significantly louder than other people with powers, and I have a hunch it's an important factor in what we're doing." I help him into the jacket, and at one point our faces are very close together. A warm smile spreads across his face, and I step back from him cautiously.

"Man, you're stubborn," he says, nearly whispering. "You react the same way every time."

"You should know me by now, Brand. You'll have earned my respect when I see you using your power for good and not for gratification. Even then, you won't be successful in your attempts with me, but I'll see you with better eyes."

"Huh . . . let's do this experiment already." He walks away and over to the corner of the house. "Turn me on, Calli."

Frustration mounting, I mentally order myself to

remain calm as I walk over to him and press the play button. "Ok, you're all set."

"Can I have a kiss for good luck? You know, I'm about to suffer more pain, all in the name of science."

"No."

"Can I kiss *you* then, as a thank you?" He looks as though he's trying to contain a grin that wants to explode.

"A thank you for what?"

His smile erupts uncontrollably. "It works, Calli. The heartbeat works. Watch."

Brand steps forward beyond the line of light and into the darkness. His feet are still on the ground and his body is not injured. Brand approaches the Demons. Every thump-thump of the heartbeat pushes them back five feet like an invisible shockwave. As he spins around joyfully in the darkness, a white snake demon stands like a cobra, but can't move any closer to him. The Demons circle and prowl around him, looking for a weakness or an opportunity to strike. They seem confused, ears perking up while sniffing the air, as though they know instinctively both to attack and not to attack.

I step into the shadows as well and walk a circle around Brand, watching the Demons glide to and fro out of my way. A sense of pride fills my chest. *I did it! I figured out how to repel the Demons.* "This is amazing, Brand!"

Before I realize what he's doing, he grabs me by the waist and pulls me to him, kissing me on the lips. Not a long kiss, but long enough to mean something. I freeze in place, completely shocked by his actions.

He lets me go and steps back, of which I'm relieved. I hope he can't see me trying to catch my breath and analyzing what just happened. He dips his chin to his chest, making me think he's about to apologize. Instead, he says, "Thank you, Calli. I haven't been able to be in the dark for so long, but now, because of you I can be." He brings his gaze up to mine. He tilts his head to one side. "Oh, and don't read too much into the kiss. It was strictly platonic."

Having caught my breath and regained my rational thinking, I fire back. "Platonic? That was platonic? In what universe?"

He shuffles his feet and wobbles his head back and forth. "I *did* ask if I could kiss you."

"But I didn't say yes."

"Do you want me to repeat back so you don't remember?"

"Haven't you already done that?"

"No. I really am thankful to you. You know the phrase: 'I'm so happy I could kiss you?' That's how I feel. Do you want me to repeat?"

"No. Just don't do it again. Use your words next time."

"Sometimes words aren't enough. You didn't exactly push me away, you know."

"You caught me off guard. Next time I'll punch you."

"You already have," he mutters.

"What?"

"Never mind."

"No, what do you mean?"

"What's the difference how I do things if you can't remember?"

"Uh, dude, that's called date rape and it's not okay. You have an amazing power, but you must make better choices. Yes, you asked permission, but you didn't respect my wishes. That would be like me asking you if it's okay if I kick you in the nuts, then not respecting your wishes."

The nearby floating Demons begin zooming around the two of us wickedly fast. Then I realize we are repeating. The spinning stops as I've just finished saying, "This is amazing, Brand!"

This time he just stares at me instead of grabbing my body, a huge smile is plastered on his face. "I really am happy, Calli, so happy I could kiss you. But I won't."

I nod my head. "I'm really happy, too, Brand. We figured out how to be safe in the dark. This is going to help so many people."

"Will you ever let me kiss you?"

"Not romantically. Brand, let's get something straight. I'm not attracted to you in that way. So can we just admit we make a good team and are good friends and leave it at that?"

"Okay."

"Come on, let's try some different settings." We step back into the light, and I press the volume button down a notch. "There, try that."

He just stands there, looking at me for a moment, then he presses the volume button, reducing the sound to a barely audible level. "This is the lowest level I can use without being attacked."

"You've already tried?"

"Yes."

"Oh. Well. I guess we're done for the night then."

"It's been a good night, Calli. May I keep this heart-attack jacket? I'll buy you another one." He smiles at me and runs his hands over the front pockets.

"Don't worry about it, I'll replace it. Keep in mind the batteries will only last just so long, so you won't want to be caught off guard. I'll work on another version of the device and try to find something with external speakers included in the unit."

"How about attaching a light, too? I can't see very well in the dark."

"Good idea. Well, goodnight, Brand. I'll talk to you

later." I wave as I walk to my car.

On the drive home I think about the wide range of emotions I experienced tonight. Brand's kiss was my first kiss from another boy besides Chris. However, Brand forced himself on me, so I don't consider that to be a real kiss. Technically, Chris hasn't actually kissed me. Mouth-to-mouth or a kiss on the forehead when I'm unconscious doesn't count in my book.

The success Brand and I had with the Shadow Demons tonight is cause for celebration. I still feel light as air, proud of my accomplishment.

When I arrive home, I stumble upon my parents whispering about me inside their room. My father mentions my ultrasound.

"Charlotte, it was all wrong. She doesn't have normal sinus rhythm, and I think we should have her checked out. She must have sustained damage in the accident."

"Relax," my mother replies. "I don't think it's anything serious, otherwise it would have shown up in her file from the hospital."

I walk away from their door and go back down the hallway, then I turn and announce my presence loudly, "Mom, Dad, I'm home."

My mother immediately opens their bedroom door and greets me. She doesn't mention anything about my father's concerns, nor does she ask about my evening with Brand. We say goodnight and I go to my room and close the door.

Over the course of the next seven days, I meet with Chuck Stowley, who teaches me about the history and physics of lighting. For twenty bucks an hour, one hour a day, I think I've made a good investment. Chuck seems happy about the exchange as well.

I learn the amount of light put off by one candle flame is equal to one lumen. Now I know why light bulbs all indicate lumens as well as watts. Watts indicate how much power is needed to run the light bulb. LED and fluorescent lights require much less power to run, and the amount of light they produce can be equivalent to that of incandescent lighting. I learn about reflected light, visible light, luminous flux, lux, light amplification, and photo multipliers, plus a lot more than I can remember or even understand.

I also had my first physics lesson about the nature of light and electromagnetic radiation. I learned a light wave is shorter than a radio wave, an x-ray is shorter than a light wave, and a gamma ray is shorter than an x-ray. Shorter waves tend to carry more energy with them, and can cause cancer without proper protection. Any kind of electromagnetic wave can be dangerous if it has enough energy. Apparently, that's why we're not supposed to point lasers in our eyes.

According to Chuck, Earth is bombarded by cosmic radiation all the time, but most of it is filtered out by our atmosphere. I remember when I first arrived at the Runners' Clan and Ms. Winter told me powers come from cosmic radiation, but Chuck told me the same radiation causes cancer when it's strong enough. Science proves Chuck is correct and the comic books are all wrong, so that makes me wonder if there's a different kind of radiation that causes the superpowers, one that doesn't cause cancerous mutations.

If there is, then who would know?

Mr. Stowley is reluctant to let me borrow a digital light meter that measures lux readings, so I have to purchase one. The meter I choose has a separate unit which displays the light reading, and can store the measurements I take. Mr. Stowley is more than happy to make the sale.

As we complete the transaction, I read his mind and am shocked to find he doesn't really like being around my father. He only likes the free fishing trips on our boat where my father provides a day of relaxation complete with food and drinks. My purchase is only helping Chuck profit further off my father and mother because, let's face it, my money isn't really my own.

I guess the world revolves around fake friendships, disingenuous relationships, and the ability to get others to part with their money. Oddly, I don't allow myself to become offended by this revelation because it comes with the understanding that my father needs his friendship with Chuck, no matter how dysfunctional it may be. They both serve each other's needs, and where a friendship can't exist between two people, the exchange of money can still bring them together.

The world is a strange place, and people are even stranger.

I begin measuring lux readings all around Brand's house and yard, charting my findings in a tablet. The most important number, the level at which Demons are prevented from crossing the line and coming into the light, is not as cut and dried as I thought it would be. The further away they are from a light source, like Brand's front porch light, the more they can exist in random locations. Light doesn't travel through the body, therefore, when the body blocks the light source and creates a shadow, the Demons can attack—as in the incident when we returned from Cedar Point. The light from the inside of my car was sufficient, but Brand's body created a shadow behind him and the dim interior lighting from the bus wasn't strong enough to properly illuminate his backside.

I decide a minimum safe reading is twenty lux. Brand's shadow at this level isn't so low it will invite an attack. I am inspired by the nightlight in the hallway outside my door, which has a sensor to indicate low levels of lighting, at which point it will turn on automatically. My devices will operate on the same principle, plus that will save battery power.

I explain all the technical information to Brand and find he isn't interested in how or why the device will work. He only wants to know if it *will* work. Apparently he's been thoroughly enjoying his new-found night-time freedom and hasn't really missed me at all over the last week.

Chapter 8 - Matchmaker Calli

It's that time of the year again: my birthday. As in years past, my birthday signifies the end of summer, the nearing of another school year, and one additional candle on the cake. This year I officially become an adult, according to the state of Ohio. I certainly don't feel any different being eighteen and I have no desire to purchase tobacco in any of its forms or a firearm, so becoming another year older really only means I'll soon be off to college.

My parents give me supplies for my dorm room, nothing too expensive. Brand gives me a new Mp3 player and a set of small external speakers. My mom eyes him curiously, and I resist the urge to read what she's thinking. I decide it's better not to know. The last thing I want to discover is whether my mom is disappointed that Brand didn't give me jewelry or perfume.

I receive another bouquet of roses and a card from Maetha, wherein she reemphasizes the importance of meditation and learning how to calm my mind. Between my struggle to visualize auras and feeling like an idiot whenever I sit in the lotus position to meditate, I haven't made any progress toward mastering either. I have been too afraid my mom will walk in and make fun of me for succumbing to some sort of Eastern hooey. She's an advocate of stress-relieving methods and often prescribes relaxation techniques to her patients, but if she sees me meditating, she'd probably question me about what's bothering me.

Maetha reminds me in her letter that I need to socialize at college, and she also applauds my decision to pursue a medical degree. One particular paragraph stands out in my mind.

It reads:

> *Brain scans are being used to study the brain's activity during the thought process. Similarities and differences between people are emerging, and the data is being catalogued. Someday, a brain scan will be able to determine whether someone's lying, or whether a crime was committed out of premeditation or self-defense. The future of this science is unforeseeable, as the ones who will perfect it haven't been born yet. Placing yourself on the frontier of medical advancements will give you insights into the possible directions these types of inventions might go. No one is immune from something like a brain scan. We are, after all, just humans. -Maetha*

The next four weeks fly by rapidly. I've located a possible manufacturer to produce my Demon devices, and I've sent my written requirements via email with my shipping address listed as my college dorm. The developer estimates the prototype will take three months to kick out and the $900 price is much lower than what the other manufacturers wanted. Unfortunately, I exhausted all my savings for this prototype. At least Brand is covered adequately with the fishing jacket.

My parents follow me to my dorm and help me move in. My room is in the same co-ed building that Brand will live in, not that I want to be located so close to him, but he's kind of handy to keep around for all those moments when a do-over is needed.

Suz was originally going to be my roommate, but opted out after graduation or more like after she felt like I betrayed her with Brand. *Huh, go figure.* We had a really nice off-campus apartment with a hot tub picked out. I guess that's the way the cookie crumbles. She'll really flip a brick when she realizes I'm in the same building as Brand.

It's a tough day for my parents. I catch my mom wiping her eyes a couple times, and it makes me feel sad. It isn't like I am moving away for good or anything: I'll be back at Thanksgiving. She really would be amazed and upset if she knew what I'd been through in Montana. Handling dorm life and college can't possibly compare.

I say my goodbyes and try to settle into my new life.

Brand never ceases to amaze me. He was offered a full-ride scholarship in football, but he denied it and went into Performing Arts instead. What the heck? I am not the only confused person to find out Mr. All-Star Jock wants to be a singing actor. I haven't questioned him about it yet, but I fully intend to do so.

College life is a real rush, to say the least. I think what amazes me the most is observing the minds of everyone on campus and just how different people are in their thoughts and behaviors.

Take, for instance, the girls from my high school who are attending college with me. I saw their behavior in high school when they were stuck-up, holier-than-thou gossips. They never missed an opportunity to criticize all the other girls who were "too easy." However, now they are in a reverse role where they have become the "too easy" girls, chasing after the jocks without a relationship in mind. It seems when girls like these move out of mommy's and daddy's house, they go wild. Hmm, the girls who were once mild are now wild. Someone could write a song about that. Someone probably has.

On the other hand, many guys who were horn dogs in high school, and too dense to actually score, are still horn dogs, but now they actually score in college. What's the reason for this? Have the guys become smarter or have the girls relaxed? Based on what I'm seeing, I'm leaning toward the latter of the two.

In my dorm I discover that some girls seem to wear much less clothing than at the beach, and guys like to walk around without their shirts all the time. I'm not complaining. As a pre-med major, I fully appreciate the many muscles that make up the human abdomen and chest, but as an inexperienced female who doesn't leave my room without being properly covered, I still blush a bit when I run into that much skin.

My class schedule is quite manageable, leaving a lot of extra time for studying and practicing my abilities. Acting on Maetha's advice to socialize and mingle, I begin an experiment of sorts in the cafeteria which involves unsuspecting students and faculty. I read minds, looking for girls who have the dreamy gaze in their eyes for a particular guy, and then I read the guy's mind to see if he likes the girl, or if he even knows the girl exists.

One day while reading minds, I find a girl staring longingly across the room. In her mind I see the image of the boy she's attracted to. I scan the room, locate the boy, and read his mind. I find that he likes her too, but is too shy to act on it. It's more than this, though. These two are in a couple of classes together and take turns looking at each other.

As a female who appreciates love, I have to help out. I walk across the room to the girl and say, "Excuse me, I couldn't help but notice you were checking out that guy over by the soda machines. I hope I'm not butting in too much, but when you look away from him, do you know he looks back at you?"

"What? Are you sure?"

"I'm Calli, by the way, and yes, I'm sure. I'm fascinated with body language and have a pretty good sense for it. His body language is screaming for you, but I get the idea he's really shy and afraid to talk to you."

"I thought he was looking at me in class. I'm Pamela Gilespy. Nice to meet you, Calli."

That's all it takes. Suddenly I have a new friend. Over the next few weeks, Pamela and the guy, Spencer Wainsfeld, become acquainted and really hit it off. They seem to be a perfect match with similar interests and backgrounds, and it makes me very happy to know I helped them out.

Pamela hangs out with me more often whenever she isn't with Spencer, and today her friend Stacy Nelson comes along too.

Pamela introduces us by saying, "Hey, Calli, do you think you could work your magic on Stacy too? There's a guy she likes, but it's unclear if he likes her or not."

"Sure. Where do we find him?"

"He'll be at the mixer tonight. Are you going?"

"I wasn't planning on it, but I guess I am now."

"Spencer has to work tonight, so it will be a girls' night out," Pamela adds.

The two girls become all giddy and giggly, female aspects I really don't like. They help me pick out an outfit to wear and play with my shoulder-length hair, experimenting with different "do's" —another detestable activity.

Later that evening, after layer upon layer of makeup has been applied and I've tried on several pairs of high heels, eventually settling on a pair that will match the skimpy emerald green dress one of them finds for me, the three of us leave for the party. Pamela and Stacy are quite comfortable in their barely-there dresses and heels, and it amazes me how different I am compared to them. Still, like Maetha had suggested, I am determined to learn how to blend in.

As we approach the large house, the pounding music is heard though the closed door. I'm happy I'm not trying to use my Hunter's enhanced hearing power or else I'd have a massive headache. We enter the building and at once a nauseating wave of sweat, booze, and pheromones hits my nose. We zigzag our way through the crowd and find a good vantage point on the staircase where the entire room is visible.

Pamela points in a less than stealthy manner and yells over the blaring music, "Over there, by the large fern in the corner. He has blond hair and is wearing a dark blue polo shirt." Despite her yelling, I still have to use my mind-reading power to understand what she's saying.

I find him and connect with his mind. *Yuck!* His name is Jake Jones. This guy doesn't have a good cell in his body. His mind is not just in the gutter, it's already down the drain and in the sewer. I look for any recognition of Stacy and don't find anything right away. I detect within him a strong athletic ability. His mother must have been close to a cosmic energy event, but not quite close enough for him to become a Runner.

"So . . . what do you think?" Stacy is excited to hear my opinion of the guy.

"Why don't you walk over that way and mingle with people around him. I'll watch his body language from here."

Stacy and Pamela push through the crowd until they are in his line of sight. Jake spots Stacy and gives her body a once over. Then he turns to his friend and dismisses Stacy without a second thought. I am pleased with our little covert mission and am happy to find the disgustingly-minded Mr. Jones isn't interested in Stacy, but I know Stacy will be let down when I tell her Jake is a "no go," so I watch different guys as the two girls make their way back to me. A couple of guys are attracted to Stacy, but more are drawn to Pamela.

"So, what do you think?" Stacy asks me when they return.

"He wasn't interested, sorry. But there were other guys who were. Do you want me to point them out to you?"

"Really? Are you sure about Jake? Because I thought I picked up on a vibe."

"You're welcome to go after him, but beware, he's nothing but a Conquistador if you ask me."

"A what?"

"A Conquistador, a con-man who will knock you on your keester, then kick you out the door when he's done with you. Look," I nod beyond Stacey's shoulder, "an interested guy is coming over for you, gray jacket, black hair."

She turns, checks him out, then turns back to me. "He's cute. What do you think about him?"

I've learned that individuals with good hearts have a certain feel to them when I look into their minds; recognizing the feeling makes it easier to figure someone out, and this guy is a decent guy. I look Stacy in the eye and nod my approval because he's now standing right behind her.

Pamela and I watch as he introduces himself as Allan

Kingston and then leads her out to dance. They are a cute couple, and upon closer inspection, I see in Stacy's future she will be married to Allan. He will be a successful lawyer, due to his extraordinary memory and speaking ability, and Stacy will teach music lessons from her high-end suburban home. I pull out of their future and realize Stacy is a gifted musician. Why hadn't I paid attention to that aspect of her before? I read her thoughts and learn she dreams of being a musical performer. Yet, in her future, she will give up her dream. I look at Allan. He's a good guy, and the vision of their future appears to be positive, so maybe everything will work out.

The pulsing bass of a new song brings my attention back to the party. I glance over at Pamela, standing nearby, talking to a group of girls. What cosmic ability does she possess? I feel into her body, but sense nothing unusual. I connect with her mind and find she has a reliable gut-instinct that helps her make better decisions as well as staying out of trouble. Her memories show she sometimes has vivid dreams, and she is always shocked when they come true. She must be a weakened version of a Seer, with powers not strong enough to attract Shadow Demons.

I look around the room, trying to detect and cat-egorize the many different minor abilities. I find that everyone excels in one area or another, but not everyone has chosen majors reflecting their gift. Some people don't know what their ability is, and are floating through college classes hoping they will figure it out. There are also people whose talent does not have an associated college degree, like natural comedians. I discover that many of these minor gifts and abilities are not related to the five cosmic powers of the clans. Also, each grouping of individuals, such as the athletic, have varying ranges of intelligence, which I find fascinating. Not all jocks are idiots! *Oh dear, that kind of thinking will get me beat up.*

A boy by the punch bowl catches my eye. He holds up two glasses of red-colored liquid and nods to me. Even an ordinary girl would be able to read his body language. He's asking me if I want a drink. I shake my head in refusal and smile. He doesn't persist and sets the extra glass down. I am a bit shocked that he gives up so easily, but when I feel inside his body for his cosmic ability, I realize he doesn't have one. I can't sense anything. It feels like he isn't there. I try to connect with his mind and am shocked to find nothing, just like my mom's. He must be an Unaltered. Through the chaos of noise, stench, and dirty intentions piercing the air all around me, I can't tell if he has a scent. One thing's for sure, this one boy stands out like a clean spot on a filthy pig.

I put two fingers in my mouth and whistle loudly to catch his attention. It works, and I nod and point at the drink. I follow him with my eyes as he weaves through the crowd, climbs the stairs, and hands me a glass of punch.

"Hi, I'm Travis." He has to shout over the music. He has a pleasant smile, too-tanned skin, short light-brown hair, a trim body, and manicured nails. I don't know why I notice his nails, but they are beautiful—well, for a guy. He wears a basic rock band T-shirt and faded blue jeans.

"Calli." I reach forward out of habit to shake his hand. I wonder if this is normal. Do I come across as being too formal? I'm not sure, but he shakes my hand.

"Are you here with someone?"

"My friends. Girl-friends, that is." I am nervous for some reason. Travis is a good-looking guy, no doubt about it, but my interest in him is strictly due to the fact he is unchanged by cosmic energy. I take a sip of punch and my whole mouth feels like it's on fire. My Hunter's taste figures there is more alcohol than punch, and even a tiny drop is overwhelmingly disgusting. I raise the glass to my lips as though to take another drink, but discretely spit the punch back out instead. A quick yuck-shiver wracks my body and I imagine the expression on my face looks like a pug chewing on a lemon. I pull myself together and ask, "Where are you from?"

"Central Ohio. You?"

"Northwest area. What's your major, Travis?"

"I haven't decided. I'm doing my generals. You want to step outside so we don't have to yell at each other?" he asks.

I nod, set my glass down on the nearest surface, and follow him as he pushes his way through the crowd.

Once outside in the warm night air, we continue our conversation. I become enthralled with his expanded vocabulary and deep insights into normally boring topics, and how he's able to paint a visual picture in my mind with his words. More than anything, I'm fascinated to have met another Unaltered besides my mother.

I try to read his mind again. Nothing. I look for his future again, but no visions arrive. I smell the breeze as it flows past him, but all I smell is his cologne and deodorant—no personal scent. Maetha said Diamond Bearers can use their powers on Unaltereds, but I can't. I have to assume I can't because I only have a piece of the diamond.

We talk for a little while until Stacy and Allan interrupt our conversation. Stacy says, "Thanks, Calli. See you later." The two of them hold hands and walk away with a bounce in their steps. Pamela arrives soon after.

"Calli, are you ready to go . . . or are you—"

"I'm ready to go," I say. "Nice to meet you, Travis," I say, shaking his hand once again before walking away.

As we walk away I hear Travis mumble under his

breath, "Nice to meet you too, Calli Courtnae."

I stop and whip around, but he is already gone. I never told him my last name.

♡ ♡ ♡

A couple of months go by without any sign of Travis. I've kept my senses on alert, scanning crowds for Unaltereds, but haven't found any.

College life, classes, and homework consume most of my day. I'm still waiting for my Demon devices to arrive, which should be pretty soon. Brand is hard to find, what with his nighttime freedom. Any extra time I have is spent matchmaking. It seems I've become quite popular in some circles for my matchmaking abilities. After the successes of Pamela and Stacy, I've been searched out by many other girls who want a better shot at finding love. Not every girl takes my advice. Some end up with guys who only want quickies or to be "friends with benefits." I find it hard to understand why a girl who's looking for a relationship settles for a guy who's not.

I've found that matching individuals who are physically drawn to each other results in success, at least for the short term. Individual personalities are far too complex to determine how small habits and pet peeves will be received by the other. I resist the urge to look far into the future on anyone. After learning that Stacey will give up her musical dreams to be Allan's wife, I've felt responsible for her future loss. But maybe that's just my perspective. I'm certainly learning more about socializing and interacting with people. I travel home for Thanksgiving and am surprised to be visited by Maetha and Beth when I stop at a gas station.

"Maetha, Beth, what are you doing here?" I exclaim,

locking the gas nozzle to full flow. Stepping over the hose, I give Beth a hug.

Maetha says, "We've been tracking some potential threats to the clans. Not much to report. We're on our way back to Beth's home so she can be with her family for Thanksgiving."

A grimace spreads across Beth's face. "I just want to be there for my little brother, that's all."

Maetha addresses me, speaking in a more cheerful tone. "So, Calli, how is everything with you?"

"Well, I've made some headway with the Shadow Demons. The sound of my heartbeat confuses them. I made a device for Brand to wear that emits my recorded heartbeat. He's able to go out in the dark."

Beth's eyes widen and her mouth falls open. "What do you mean? Like *in* the shadows?"

"Yes. I've sent my plans to a manufacturer. I should hear back from them soon."

"Wonderful," says Maetha. Her head turns and her eyes scan the area. I wonder what she's looking for. She faces me again and says, "If you run into problems with your manufacturer, I may know someone who could help."

Beth says, "I don't know where you find the time to work on that, but I'm really glad you're trying. If you figure out a way to mass produce them, I definitely want one."

Maetha says, "If Calli figures this out, it will be a first with the Demons. Right now the only person with cosmic abilities who would dare wonder into the dark would be someone who can repeat back to safety."

Beth changes the subject. "Hey, guess what? Chris came back to the Runners' compound to be an instructor."

"Really?" I ask, my voice flying a little higher than I want it to.

"He's not pleasant to be around, though. He always

has a somber look on his face and never smiles, but that doesn't stop the girls from crushing on him. His doldrums seem to be bringing out the 'fixers' in the girl's hall."

"The what?"

"You know, all the girls who choose a troubled guy or a 'sick puppy' to fix. I don't understand it either. But what do I know? I chose the verbally abusive guy."

Right, she chose Justin. She also dumped him, so that's saying something. "What's Justin up to these days?"

"Don't know, don't care."

"Oh." My mind draws a blank, so I say nothing.

Maetha clears her throat. "Beth and I need to get going."

We say our goodbyes and they walk away. I finish filling my car with gas and return the nozzle to the pump. As I drive the last few miles to my parents' home, I think about what Beth told me about Chris. I wish he could be happy, and it saddens me to think he walks around in a state of detachment without hope. The worst part is, I know I can't do anything about it. I can't let him know everything will work out in the end, because if I did, it could alter the future in a way that nullifies the vision I had. I rationalize that perhaps Chris has to go through this dark dreary stage in order for the future to pan out.

♡ ♡ ♡

Thanksgiving was delicious as always. I enjoyed every moment of the three days I was home.

I return to my dorm on Sunday morning. I find that Brand has been busy while I've been gone and has success-fully ticked off a couple of fraternity guys by stealing their sorority girls. The guys plan to fight him this afternoon by the river dunes. I hear all the details several times over before I even reach my room due to the fact that everyone knows me now as Matchmaker Calli and because Brand is my friend.

As I climb the stairs I pass a cluster of girls and notice Suz is among them. A quick mind read reveals she's catching a ride with her friends to the big fight. Brand knocks on my door frame after I put my bag down. "Mind if I come in?"

"Brand, I leave you to your own devices for five days, and this is what I have to come back to? Can't you keep it in your pants for two seconds?" I lay on the sarcasm extra thick.

"It's not a big deal, Calli. Can I help it if these girls want a little more attention than what they're getting from their boyfriends?" Brand walks casually to the chair at my desk and sits down.

"Just because you *can* repeat doesn't mean you *should*." I continue to unpack my bag.

"That's easy for you to say. I'm in heaven here on campus. It would be a sin *not* to repeat."

"Don't make me take your Demon device away, Brand." I wag my finger at him.

"When will the new devices get here?"

"They're still about four weeks out."

"Your parents would be so proud of you if they had any idea what kind of work you've been doing, but they never will. Still, it must make you happy to know they'd approve."

"Don't you get much approval from your parents, Brand?"

"I've always been a failure in my dad's eyes."

"I can't believe that. What about all those football games you won? Wasn't he there to watch?"

"He was only there to see me fail."

This is a side of Brand I'm not used to seeing. "Why do you feel that way?"

"My parents divorced when I was young, a few years after my dad's affair. After they tried to make it work, he moved out and me and my older brother would go see him on some weekends. He always had a different girl at his place whenever we arrived, and his attentions were on her the entire time. It was as if we didn't exist. Some weekends he'd cancel our stay because of his new girlfriend. Why couldn't he see there were more important things in life, like his kids?"

"I'm sorry, Brand."

"I thought playing football would make him proud, especially since he played when he was young. Isn't that what fathers want—for their sons to follow in their footsteps? Well, not my dad. The last game in the State championships—the one we lost—my dad was there with a new girlfriend. After one particular play, I looked over at him and saw what looked like a glimmer of pride in his eyes, so I made sure the next play was over-the-top spectacular. When I looked at him, I finally saw what I'd been yearning for over the last eighteen years of my life: my father's approval. As soon as it was there, it was gone, replaced with the all too familiar look of disgust. You know what the sad thing is? I repeated the play over fifty times to get him to look at me that way. It was my proudest achievement, and my biggest disappointment. I decided right then I was going to live my life for me, not him. I continued the game, not repeating again, and we lost. The look on his face wasn't any worse with my loss than it was after my fantastic play. Now, do you understand why I went into Performing Arts instead of football? I've moved on, Calli."

"I had no idea, Brand. I'm sorry. So, you want to be an

actor?"

"Yeah, movie stars get lucky all the time!"

I shake my head. "I don't believe you've moved on, Brand. You're still seeking your father's approval."

"What?"

"You continue to seduce girls, getting what you want. You want your father to be proud of your triumphs. You want him to say, 'Like father, like son,' or 'That's my boy,' so you continually chase after girls, just like your father."

Brand throws his arms in the air. "What, are you a shrink now? What am I supposed to do? Stop chasing girls? It's what comes natural to me, and it would be a shame to stop."

"Don't you find it strange you chose your major based on the amount of 'action' you'll get?"

"Hey, I'm a guy!"

"No one's arguing you aren't. I just find it interesting that one of your biggest issues with your dad is being played out in your day-to-day life. Aren't there more important things in your life, Brand?"

"I'm not like my dad! He abandoned my mom when she needed him most. I would never do that. What kind of a man would cheat on his pregnant wife? The day I was making out with Suz and my mom came in and interrupted us, I took Suz home and then came back and talked with my mother. She of course didn't know I knew about the affair because she had no idea she'd told me. Imagine her surprise when I sprung it on her."

Suz appears in the still-opened doorway to my room, where she has clearly been eavesdropping, and confronts Brand. "You liar! Your mother never came into the room!"

Brand looks at me. "What do you think, Calli? Should I continue to protect her or should I let this play out?"

"Protect me from what?" She puts her hands on her

hips.

Brand looks at Suz and says, "Suz, I'm your half brother. Your mother and my father had an affair."

Suz's face turns red with rage. "You're nothing but a son-of-a-bitch liar! I don't know what I ever saw in you."

Brand turns to me. "Should I repeat?"

"Nope," I say, "she needs to hear this." I'm not entirely sure if I am making that decision based on what the future will hold for her or if it's my own mind wanting Suz to know the truth so she'll lay off her all-consuming attention to Brand.

"What are you talking about?" Suz says.

Brand explains. "You and I are half brother and sister, Suz. I found out and put a halt to our relationship rather than tell you."

"My mother never cheated on my father. You're lying."

I try to help Brand. "Come on, Suz. He's telling the truth."

"You're both trying to screw with my head. That's a really low thing to do. You both hate me and want me to hurt."

I can't let that comment slide by without a rebuttal. "Are you saying *you* never screwed with anyone, Suz?"

"What?"

I continue, "You've never purposefully hurt anyone? You've lived a lie for years. There's an old saying about liars: 'it takes one to know one.' You only suspect Brand is lying because you're so good at it yourself."

"I don't—"

It's time for me to tell Suz the truth. "I know you set off the firework in middle school, Suz. I know you only became my friend because you felt guilty about what happened to me, and it's been one huge lie for you to continue pretending to be my friend. You were relieved when you saw me hugging Brand at Cedar Point, and used that moment to justify finally breaking off our friendship."

Suz's face drains of color, and her voice drops to a whisper. "How . . . when . . . I never told anyone about that firework."

Uh-oh. My face must show my thoughts because Brand says, "It's not too late, Calli."

Suz points a shaking finger at me. "Wait! I told my therapist. Your mom must have spoken to her. It's the only way you could have figured that out. That's a breach of patient-doctor confidentiality. I could sue your mom!"

"You could sue your own therapist, but not my mom."

Suz posture stiffens and she lets out a grunt. "I've always hated you, Calli. You get everything you ask for. You never have to struggle for money or clothes, and everything always works out for you. *You* ended up with Brand instead of *me*."

Brand jumps up from the chair and gets in her face. "Haven't you been listening, Suz? You are my sister. Can you say *incest*?"

"I don't believe you. My mother would never cheat on my father."

I throw in, "Brand and I are not a couple, Suz. We're just friends."

Suz mutters, "That's still more than what I ended up with. All right . . . well, what about the fact that Brand said his mom came in while we were making out? That never happened. We kissed and then he stopped and took me home. He's lying."

I realize things have gone too far. "All right, Brand, fix this," I say.

Brand shakes his head. "Can't undo it now. It's been longer than two minutes." Then he turns to Suz. "Suz, there's something I need to tell you."

Nervously, I jump in. "Brand?"

"Suz, I have an ability that I use on people, mainly girls,"

"Brand!" I warn.

He smiles at me with his head turned in my direction so Suz can't see. "Suz, I'm a hypnotist."

Suz wrinkles her brow and stares at Brand. "No you're not."

"Yes, I am. I'm able to get people to do and say what I want them to, and I'm able to mess with their memories to cover up what we've done. In fact, the day my mom came in and caught us making out, you told me about the firework in the bathroom and about being Calli's fake friend. As soon as you told me, you immediately regretted it, so I made you forget you'd ever said it."

I know he's lying, but I appreciate his effort to come up with a plausible explanation for how I could have learned Suz's secret. That will take the heat off her therapist and my mom.

Suz isn't convinced, though. "I'm not buying this, Brand. No one has that kind of control over someone else's thoughts."

"What about the hypnotist at the school assembly last year? Are you saying those kids were faking it? I don't know about you, but Arnold Hoffman seemed to be telling the truth when he said he didn't remember picking his nose in front of everyone, yet we all saw him do it. Why couldn't I be able to help you forget certain aspects of your memory? What you need to ask yourself is, was it so wrong of me to want to protect you from the pain of your own bad choices? I was trying to help."

"It can't be true, Brand."

I can tell she's wearing down.

Brand moves closer to Suz. "Believe what you will, but I was looking out for your best interests. And I didn't tell you we're half brother and sister because I didn't want you to hate your mom for having an affair. Our kinship is the only reason I turned my back on you, and believe me, no one wishes it weren't true more than me."

Suz's expression relaxes a little more. "Really?"

"Yeah. If it weren't true, I'd be with you right now. Why don't you ask your parents about it? Tell them you think you might be pregnant and I'm the father. That'll get them to fess up real quick."

Suz frowns. "What if my parents' story doesn't match your mom's story?"

"Then come and find me. For now, give me a hug and try to believe I only want your happiness, and it's why I did what I did." Brand and Suz hug, with Brand holding the hug a little longer than Suz, and then she leaves.

After he sits back down, he runs his fingers through his hair and exhales loudly.

I look at him and ask, "Brand, do you really feel that way about Suz?"

"What do you think?"

"I'm not sure what to think."

"I think you nailed it on the head when you said I'm like my dad. I guess learning of his affair affected me more than I thought, and I went on a binge of a 'what does it matter?' kind of thinking."

"Perhaps you were trying to fill the empty space inside with much-needed love and praise. I've noticed you need everyone to like you and can't stand it when someone doesn't. I'd say that goes back to your need for your father's approval too."

"Yeah, well I haven't accomplished much. My world is still rocked every time Suz comes near me."

"I'm sorry, Brand. I didn't know, or I wouldn't have lit into her just now. But thanks for covering for me. I appreciate that."

"I did it more for your mom. I don't want her getting in trouble for telling you."

My eyes shoot to the floor. "She's didn't tell me."

"Then how did you find out?" he asks.

"I can't say."

"That's cool. You don't have to tell me. You know, Suz went on and on accusing me of lying, and yet she's been lied to her whole life, as have I. It's not very fun to find out everything you thought to be real really isn't."

If Brand had any idea how completely I understand him, he'd be shocked. "I stand corrected, Brand, on when you should or shouldn't use your powers. You have a reliable gut instinct and a quick wit. I'll have to trust you when you decide to repeat."

He throws his head back and laughs. "You have no idea how many lines I tried in order to come up with that hypnotist line. In fact, Suz threw it at me on one of my tries."

We are interrupted as I look up and see three bleached-blonde, excessively endowed girls bounce into the doorway.

The one in the middle says, "Hey Brand, do you want to come hide out in our room?" Obviously they know about the upcoming fight.

Brand looks at me and smiles, exposing his dimples. His looks have definitely matured in the last year. He is much more handsome than he was in high school and I can see what the girls are excited about. Plus, he owns his confidence, at least on the outside. I've just seen his inner self-loathing side, and I must say it really changes my image of him—for the better.

"Thanks ladies, but no, I have to face my mistakes."

The three let out a collective sigh and put their hands on their chests—as if they need to draw any further attention to that region. Then they bounce out of the room and down the hall.

"Calli, are you going to come and watch?"

"Wouldn't miss it."

Chapter 9 - Freedom to Choose

A few hours later we leave the dorm and climb into my car. The river dunes are located out of town and are a popular place for Indie-band concerts because of the natural stadium seating and acoustics. It's also a perfect location for parties or the occasional fight because of its secluded location. However, most events take place in the summer months, not at the end of November. Luckily, we haven't been hit yet with a substantial amount of snow, and what did fall melted with the rain that followed.

When we pull up to the parking area, we are both surprised by the number of vehicles.

I cast a glance over at Brand. "How many guys did you tick off?"

He doesn't answer.

We get out of my car and walk toward the edge of the dune overlooking the river below and find roughly two hundred people have gathered to view the carnage. We begin our descent through the damp sand, and as we near the bottom I notice the large group of guys waiting for Brand.

"How many different fraternities did you offend, Brand?"

"Oh damn," Brand mutters under his breath.

I follow his line of sight and find Suz and a group of her friends huddled together in matching fur-trimmed parkas. I quickly read Suz's mind to find out if she is here to see him go down or to watch him kick butt. She is here to watch him win, and she's apparently told all her friends about his fighting skills . . . and they've told all their friends, and so on and so on. I touch on a few other minds and find they are here because of what they've heard about Brand.

"I can't believe you're more upset about Suz's presence than the thirty guys waiting for you down there."

He grunts something inaudible in return.

"I'm going to stay up here. I know I don't need to wish you luck, Brand, but good luck."

"Piece of cake."

He continues down to the bottom of the dune, and I sit down on the damp sand at the top of the hill in a spot that gives me a good view of Brand and most of the onlookers. Suz shoots some nasty daggers my way, causing me to turn my head, and that's when I see him.

Freedom stands by the edge of the river with his arms folded across his chest. He's wearing his sunglasses and long leather trench coat. I'm not sure if I should communicate with him or not. Of course, if I wait long enough, he'll probably talk to me, like last time. However, I'm not sure if he's seen me yet.

My attention is brought back to Brand, who's being circled by a crowd of buff college guys. *Sheez, Brand, you never do anything half-way do you?* The boys yell insults and curse words at Brand, who looks positively bored. I recognize one of the boys as Travis from the mixer a few months back. I remember he's an Unaltered. My mind fills with an alarming realization that at least two-thirds of these angry guys have unaltered DNA.

Why is there such a concentration of people *without* powers about to fight Brand unless . . . my eyes shoot over to Freedom. I try to read his mind, but only find a strange blackness. His blocking ability is really good. A few of the boys glance over at Freedom, who nods back, and then they attack Brand.

I am afraid for Brand initially, but within five seconds Brand proves he can hold his own and has already taken down three boys. I wonder how many repeats Brand had to do. A couple more boys drop to their knees, vomiting up their lunches due to Brand's signature moves. As more boys go down, it's easier to see exactly what he's doing. He really is a flawless fighter, landing perfect hits and punches, disabling his foes with one or two hits. The whole crowd gasps when Brand successfully eagle-claws one unfortunate soul, who falls to his knees in agony.

My eyes find Freedom again. He has a smirk on his face that I can't figure out. I hate the fact he's wearing sunglass because I can't see where his eyes are. I can't tell if he's looking at me or not. Only Freedom can understand the possibilities and advantages of having a group of Unaltered guys attack a person with powers.

Brand is down to five final contenders, who are nervously dancing around him, not wanting to engage. Finally, the cheering crowd urges the battle on to the finish. To everyone's surprise, except mine, Brand is the last one standing. I am very proud of him, and my beaming smile is evidence of this.

Brand steps over a couple guys and approaches Freedom. I want to yell, "Wait!" or "Don't!" but it's too late. All I can do is read lips at this point because I can't read either of their minds.

Freedom says, "You don't need to be in college, son. I can offer you employment right now."

Brand's head bobs as he replies something back. I can't tell what, since he's facing the other direction, and there are too many other people talking to focus my hearing on Brand's voice.

Freedom laughs and says, "Well, I'm sure you are, but this job would not be lacking in women. However, I need to know, would you have a problem with fighting at night?"

Yep, there it is. Freedom is trying to figure out if Brand is a person with powers.

Brand answers.

Freedom asks for clarification, "You don't have a problem with fighting in the dark?"

Brand's head shakes back and forth.

"Where did you learn to fight? Have you had any formal training?"

I see Freedom reach into his pocket and pull out a business card and hand it to Brand, then he turns and walks into the crowd and disappears from my view.

Brand turns his head and searches the crowd until he finds me, but before he can move toward me, he's surrounded by a swarm of girls. He doesn't look too happy, and he pushes his way through them, ignoring their advances.

I look over and see Suz leaving with her friends. That's a relief, at least. We won't have to worry about her confronting Brand again. The new concern floating through my mind is whether or not she will spread the rumor that Brand is a hypnotist. If she does, I wonder if it will fly as quickly as her rumor of Brand being able to beat any number of fighters.

Brand finally finds me. "Did you see the creepy-looking dude I talked to?" he asks.

"Yeah, what was that all about?" I ask naively.

Brand hands me the business card. "He wants to hire me as his bodyguard. There's more, but I'll tell you in the car."

I look over at him, admittedly shocked, knowing he must have sensed Freedom is more than what he appears to be. We ascend the hill, shrugging off congratulations along the way, and climb inside my car.

He launches into his pent-up concerns. "Calli, that guy knows about the Shadow Demons, I know it! He was very concerned about the dark and nighttime, as if he knew the dangers associated with it. Only another person with powers would know that."

I look at the business card closely. It says "Top Jobs Consulting" and lists a phone number. I figure I'll try to call the number at a later time just to see who answers. For now, I need to calm Brand down.

I say, "I used my Healing ability to feel inside his body, and yes, he has powers. You were wise to turn down his offer."

"I know. I repeated several times once he began asking about the dark. One time he asked me about my relationship with you. He didn't use your name. He only referred to you as the girl I arrived with."

So, he had noticed me. "Brand, the Shadow Demons are the common denominator in the world of powers. They bring everyone down to equal footing. I think he was trying to determine whether you are just a good fighter or if you have an ability strong enough to attract Demons. His last questions about your skills and if you'd had any formal training were—"

"How did you know he asked me that?"

I look over at him, feeling more than a little sheepish for slipping up, and make an impromptu decision. "Brand, when Suz blew up the firework in middle school, it blasted my eardrums. I was deaf for many months, and during that time I was taught how to read lips. I'm a lip reader. I saw

Freedom's side of the conversation."

"Holy cow!"

"No one knows, not even Suz. I need you to help me keep my secret, Brand."

Brand nods. "You know, Calli, you've slipped up more than a few times. I couldn't quite put my finger on it, but I could tell you knew more about me than anyone else."

"I used to read your lips from across the room in the cafeteria last year."

"Hey, is that how you found out about Suz and the firework?"

"Not exactly. There's more to me than just reading lips, but now's not the time to go into it. I'm going to call this number later from a secure phone line and check it out."

"Let me know what you find."

We drive back to town. Brand chats the whole way about all the many repeats he did to win the fight, how many times he was hit, and other testosterone-infused bragging. My mind is troubled by the fact that Freedom is involved with this whole deal. I need to tell Maetha somehow, but how? She really needs a phone.

A couple of nights later I find my opportunity to call the number on Freedom's card. I am in the Biology lab completing my studies. I ask the professor if I can use his phone. I go into his office and dial the number.

A cheerful female voice answers. "Top Jobs Consulting. How may I direct your call?"

"I was given this number by a man. I didn't get his name."

"Hold, please."

I wait for a moment, not sure if I should hang up or not. Then Freedom's voice comes on the line. "I was beginning to wonder if you'd call at all, Calli."

"How did you know it was me?"

"Because the card was meant for you, not your happy-go-lucky friend."

"Why are you interested in Brand?"

"I was, but I'm not any longer. I'm worried for you, Calli, concerned that you are being manipulated into a life you wouldn't choose for yourself."

His comment confirms what Maetha told me about him. He felt she'd forced a life on him he didn't want. "Where did you find all those Unaltered guys to fight Brand?" I ask.

"Unaltereds are a dime a dozen where I come from. The question you should be asking is why I did what I did."

"I already know why."

"No, I don't think you do."

"You're free to think what you want, Freedom."

"So, Calli, you understand what I have to offer you? You won't get the same offer from Maetha, only an eternity of servitude."

"Tell me how your offer would differ."

"I can remove the shard from your heart and return you to your natural state, so you can live your life the way nature intended, not the way Maetha intends. You'll be spared from having to watch all your loved ones die, knowing you could save them, but not being allowed to do so. You'll be free to grieve properly, not be forced to become as cold-hearted as Maetha would prefer. You can be freed from this terrible future and regain your identity as a human being, living life to its fullest."

"What do you get out of it?" I ask.

"Simply the satisfaction of knowing I've saved a young girl, with her whole life ahead of her, from the pain, anguish, and horror I've been forced to live because Maetha decided otherwise."

"That's not why you're making this offer, and you know it. You only want my shard. You couldn't care less about me. If you felt the life Maetha forced you to take on was so horrible, then you'd surrender your diamond and be done with it. I think you like your power too much and you want more."

"Calli, I'm impressed with your level of understanding. I have a better offer for you then, because I sense you also like your power too much to part with your shard. Join me, Calli, and I can help you live life as a fully independent Diamond Bearer answering to no one."

"Would you teach me how to block out everyone the way you do?"

"Of course, but only when I believe you are committed to me."

"Committed to you? What happened to 'fully independent Diamond Bearer answering to no one?' "

"I can't very well teach you my methods just to have you take them straight to Maetha. So what do you say?"

"Let me think about it." I hang up the phone and turn to leave the office. My professor stares curiously from the doorway.

"What's a Diamond Bearer?" he asks.

"Just a club." I smile and walk past him out the door.

When I arrive back at my dorm, I crash on my bed with so many thoughts running through my head. The mixer I attended at the beginning of the semester exposed me to Travis, and Travis turned out to be one of Freedom's thugs. Freedom has been following me this whole time. He's been placing individuals in my path to try to sway me to his side or at least get me to willingly give my shard to him. If he wants my shard that bad, why doesn't he just kill me and take it? I deduce that he really *does* want me to join his side. He must feel I'm still impressionable enough to change allegiances.

Well, he's wrong.

How can I be certain Maetha isn't the bad guy, as Freedom implies? The more I think about it, the more I realize that if Freedom is more on track than Maetha, then the other Diamond Bearers would join forces with Freedom, and since they haven't, I come to the conclusion Freedom is the one off balance.

I stare at the ceiling, feeling at peace with my conclusion, when a vision fills my mind. I see a young boy's running ability surfacing in a town on the New York border. He will be in P.E. class, competing on an indoor track, when his super-speed will reveal him as a DNA-altered individual in need of protection from both Demons and evil clan members who will try to kidnap him to use his powers. A representative from the Runner's Clan will come for the boy, and that representative will be Chris. He will be punctual, and the boy won't be taken by those who would do him harm.

The vision ends.

I roll over in my bed and hug my pillow. My mind revisits the day on the bank of the river while I was on the journey to deliver the diamond to the Death Clan. Chris would have died in any other normal situation, but he begged me to save him, and I did. Freedom had made a point when he said I wouldn't have to watch the ones I love die when I knew I could save them. I try to imagine what that would be like; however, I don't have to imagine too long. I've already experienced that feeling with Chris.

On that day by the river, I felt his deep love for me, and I've often wondered how he could have felt that way about someone he'd only met a few days earlier. However, since handling the whole Sanguine Diamond and experiencing the feelings within other people when I read their mind or view their future, I have a much deeper sense of understanding. When I looked into Chris's mind in the Healer's cabin before I left for home, I felt his emotions when, in the future, he sees me enter his hospital room.

Maetha said that without the love between Chris and me, and my desire to alter the outcome to ensure he lived, the delivery wouldn't have resulted in success, meaning I wouldn't have become a Diamond Bearer. The fact that I possess the proper traits of self-sacrifice and generosity, according to her, makes me qualified to be a Diamond Bearer.

Suddenly it hits me like a 300-mile-an-hour train: Freedom is after *Brand*, not me. Freedom already knows I have the proper traits to be a Diamond Bearer and my allegiance cannot be shaken. He knows someday the other diamond shards will reunite within my heart, making me his equal, and when that happens, I'll have as much power as he does . . . but I'll also have Brand by my side, making me more powerful than Freedom. Freedom has these thugs who are immune to Readers, Healers, Seers, and so on, because they are unaltered humans, but I have a guy who can render Freedom's Unaltered thugs incapacitated within seconds *and* is immune to Readers and Seers.

I reach over for my phone and call Brand.

"Hey Calli. What's up?" Brand answers.

"I called the number on the card, Brand."

"Did you talk to the guy?"

"Yes, he's a psychopath. He arranged the fight just to watch you in action. I'd go the other way if you see him again."

"I planned on it anyway. He made my skin crawl."

♡ ♡ ♡

The holidays come and go, and the arrival of the New Year is celebrated with my parents and their friends. My first semester grades are all A's, and my parents couldn't be more proud. I have to admit I am quite pleased with myself as well. However, I had looked forward to Maetha and Beth surprising me again like they did at Thanksgiving, but that doesn't happen.

A big bombshell is dropped the day before my return to school. My mother comes into my room and sits on my bed and says, "Did you know Suz's parents are getting a divorce?"

"What? No." I sit down next to her.

"Apparently Suz purchased one of those over-the-counter paternity tests when she arrived for Christmas break, and she tricked her father into giving her a swab of his own saliva. She sent it off priority mail and got her results within a few days, showing that he isn't her biological father. He left that night, and Suz's mother drove her back to her dorm and packed up her stuff. Apparently, Suz has been dating her own half brother."

"Who?"

"Brand Safferson. Did you and Brand break up?"

"No. I mean, we weren't even together like that. We're just friends. I overheard their fight back at Thanksgiving time."

I go on to tell my mom most of the details of what happened. Of course, I leave out the Repeater parts and the "Oh, and by the way I have a diamond in my heart,

Mom," particulars. It makes me wonder when I'll be able to tell my parents about my secret.

I hug them both before I leave for college and tell them I'll see them on Spring Break in late March.

When I arrive back at my dorm, a small package is waiting for me. My new Demon devices are completed, and they look great. I need to find Brand so we can test them. I take a quick look inside his room, but he isn't back yet from the holidays. I wonder if his vacation was as bumpy as Suz's due to the fact that some delicate secrets were revealed.

Later there's a knock on my door, but it isn't Brand. It's Beth. I give her a hug and invite her in.

"What a surprise! How's everything going?" I say as we settle down to talk.

"Not well. The amulet has divided the clan even further, and I'm worried that anger and jealousy will tear us apart. I hear it isn't any different in the other clans."

"That's terrible."

"I wouldn't have thought it would turn out like this when the amulets were first handed out. I doubt Maetha knew it either. Some people say she knew all too well what would happen, and that was why she gave them out."

"How's everything *else* going?" I try to sound innocent.

"Chris is doing much better. He's cheered up a little, and every now and then I see him smile."

We are interrupted by Brand knocking on my door. He looks absolutely horrible. I guess life at his home was as rocky as Suz's.

"Oh, sorry," he says, "you're busy. I'll come back later."

"Hi, Brand." Beth jumps to her feet with a mile-wide grin.

I wave him in. "Come join us, Brand."

He shrugs his shoulders and enters the room.

I know what would cheer him up, but I don't know if

I should show him the Demon devices in front of Beth. I look into Beth's future and see the same vision as before: she will lead a task force to eradicate evil clan members. I look to see if I should give her a Demon device, and what I see flabbergasts me: someday she'll be leading the task force and will be searching for *me*! What? Well, I definitely won't give her a weapon she can potentially use against me in the future.

Instead, we carry out pleasant conversation with the down-in-the-dumps-Brand, and before the evening arrives, Brand is feeling better. Beth leaves before darkness settles in.

Once we're alone, I say, "My Demon devices arrived. Let's test them out tonight."

"I'm not really in the mood, but you know." He walks to the door. "Come get me when it's dark."

Brand and I head outside and find a good location that will allow him to return to a safe place should the Demon device be faulty in any way.

He holds up one of the devices. "I like how small they are, Calli." He seems to have cheered up a bit.

"They're a little different than what I imagined them to be. Don't you think they look like a top?"

"A what?"

"You know, a top, a spinner. You flick it between your fingers, and it spins for a while."

"Oh, yeah, I suppose." Brand turns on his device and attaches it to his jacket. "It doesn't make any noise, Calli."

"Hmmm, I hope for your sake it works."

"I'm used to being ripped to shreds." He attempts to sound as if he's joking, but I can tell there's a double meaning.

"All right, here I go." He looks around to make sure no one is watching and steps beyond the line of light. Within seconds his body rises off the ground and his head flies backward as his throat rips open, causing blood to gush all over.

The world begins to spin wildly as Brand repeats the scene, and I find myself back at the point where he's about to walk into the dark.

He bends forward and puts his hands on his knees, hanging his head. "Well, that's the perfect way to end my perfect day."

"I'm sorry Brand, I don't know what—" I have to make a huge effort to choke back the urge to vomit.

"It doesn't matter." He stands and arches his back, tipping his chin to the sky. "You'll get it right the next time. By the way, my other device is missing. Did you take it?"

"No."

Brand turns around and walks back inside the building, leaving me standing out in the cold, wondering exactly what went wrong with the new device, what happened at Brand's house over the holiday break, and . . . who took his other device?

The new semester kicks off with basically the same class schedule I had in the fall, and that is nice. It means I won't have to adjust my routine too much. The failed devices have been on my mind since the day Brand tried one out. I conclude it's a manufacturer's defect, and decide to search for a different manufacturer with a better reputation.

Suz's friends have taken over the job of shooting

daggers at me whenever I see them, and I guess that's all right. The news spread rapidly that Suz was pulled out of college by her mother, but it's fueled mainly by the juicy information that she and Brand are half brother and sister. Of course, the misinformation about Suz being pregnant found its way into the rumor mill as well.

As I'd suspected, Brand's lie about being a hypnotist spread like wildfire following the Thanksgiving fight by the river, and when added to the recent story about him impregnating his half sister, it makes for top-notch talk-show fodder. For the last few days, I've tried to calm the rumors, but I soon found I couldn't explain anything without revealing information that shouldn't be revealed.

Brand hasn't even tried to clear his name.

I suspect he's sunken into depression, and I debate every day whether or not I should heal his brain chemicals. One good sign, however, is I can't read his thoughts. This tells me he hasn't given up entirely and is still repeating. He's not, however, dating or seducing girls any more. The whole Suz thing has really affected him, along with discovering more about his own mind and his need for approval from his father.

The latter part of January is spent in matchmaker mode helping several unfortunate souls find each other, for better or worse. Valentine's Day is just around the corner, and being a single girl is something that weighs heavily on many minds. I don't know why so many girls feel they are less of a person if they don't have a significant other on Valentine's Day. I wish I could use my healing power to repair their self-esteem.

Maetha says I'm mature for my age because I'm an

Unaltered. It's not that I don't feel low once in a while, it's just that I've been taught by my independent mother that I don't have to accept anyone in my life who doesn't value me. If that's a super power of an Unaltered, then I wish every female had that power.

After Valentine's Day, I find a different manufacturer for my Demon devices and email the specifics to the designer. I use the credit card my parents gave me to pay for the prototypes, figuring once they see the charge, I'll be hearing from them. Maybe by then I will have figured out a good excuse for dropping $1,200 to a design shop in Texas. This new manufacturer requires me to file for a patent, which in turn requires me to give a name to my invention. I think long and hard and come up with "Pulse-Emitter" because the Demons are pushed away by the sound of my pulse and the device emits a heartbeat sound. Brand will probably think it's a corny name, but then again, he'd probably name it "The Demonator."

Three days before Spring Break begins, Brand catches up with me as I walk to class. "What are your plans for the break, Calli?"

"I'm going back home to help my mother sort through boxes in the basement."

"Oh, well, have fun with that."

He quickens his pace and positions himself in front of me and turns around and walks backward while he says, "I was wondering if we could make another device. I've been going nuts these last few weeks without my other one."

"You never found it?" I stop walking and stare at him.

"No," he says as he halts his awkward backward walk.

The hair on the back of my neck stands on end. Someone must have stolen the clunky device, but who? It would have to be someone who could appreciate the value of it, someone who knows about and fears the Demons.

I say, "All we need is another Mp3 and some speakers because I have the sound file on my laptop."

"I have everything already. Can we do this tonight?"

I nod my head, and he takes off in the other direction, right after flashing his dimples at me. I continue on to my math class, worrying about his missing device. I sit in my usual spot in the back corner where I can view everyone in the classroom. I've been positioning myself in the back corners of every classroom so I can locate other Unaltered students. So far, no one has surfaced, and today isn't any different.

That evening after I've eaten dinner, I return to my dorm and wait for Brand. I check my email and see Beth sent me a message:

> *Calli, I can't say I'm surprised this has happened, but the Seers' amulet wearer, Curtis Shultz, has disappeared with no sign of foul play. Personally, I think he had enough of the conflict and quarreling and separated himself from his clan. However, Clara doesn't believe that: she suspects kidnapping. I don't know who would do that though. I've recommended the Runners' amulet have constant security. I hope all is well with you and I'll talk to you later. -Beth*

Brand knocks on my door and pulls my attention away from my computer screen. I look up and smile. "Come in, Brand."

"Hey, Calli," he says as he dumps the contents of the paper bag he's holding onto the bed.

"Does your mom have a bunch of chores lined up for you too?"

"I won't be staying at my mother's house for Spring Break. I met a girl online and I'm going to crash at her place for the week." His eyes twinkle with excitement.

"Oh, I see. So you want a new device so you can party all night long." I connect his USB cord to my laptop and transfer the sound file. "You know, you could keep your own backup file of my heartbeat. That way if anything happens to this one, you can make your own."

"Wow, you read my mind!"

"What?" *Did I really read his mind? No, he isn't aware I can even do that.*

"It's a figure of speech, Calli. That's what I was thinking, and you verbalized it at the same time. Chill out, Calli," he scoffs, "as *if* you can read minds. You're only a Healer."

I change the subject immediately. "Why did you wait so long before asking me to make you another device?"

"I wanted to try to make it myself, but no other heartbeat works like yours. I know . . . I've tried."

"Really?"

"Yeah, I even got Professor Guthry to let me record another student's heartbeat on the classroom ultrasound machine, but it didn't work when I tested it."

Very interesting. "Well, I have a different company working on another version of devices. I've named them Pulse-Emitters, even have a patent pending. They should be done fairly soon."

"That's cool. I'm so excited to test them out and die again," Brand chuckles.

After Brand leaves my room with his new device, I begin packing for my trip home. I still have a day and a half of school, but I don't want to wait till the last minute to gather my stuff. I think about the email from Beth about Curtis Schultz. I try to look for the future concerning Curtis, but I only see the same strange blackness I saw when I tried to look into Freedom's mind.

I'm still curious about Brand's missing Demon device

and who would possibly haven taken it. I have a couple of possible suspects in mind—Freedom, naturally, and/or his army of Unaltered guys . . . none of whom needs one to survive.

The next day flies by quickly, and in the evening I receive another email from Beth:

Hi Calli. Two amulet wearers are missing now. Charles Rhondell has disappeared, too. There was no note or indication of a struggle, and I've voiced Clara's suspicion of kidnapping to the Healers and Hunters. I am personally overseeing the safety and security of our amulet and am confident no unauthorized visitors will get by my guards. Do you know how to contact Maetha? Please respond ASAP. -Beth

I type a response back:

Beth, I agree with Clara. This sounds like a kidnapping to me, too. I don't know how to contact Maetha. She doesn't carry a cell phone. Excellent idea to up security around Clara. Whoever is behind this won't stop until they have all the pieces. Perhaps Clara should be relocated somewhere else, or maybe the amulet should be hidden. I'm about to head home for Spring Break. Keep in touch. -Calli

The next morning as I prepare for my first class, someone knocks on my door.

"Come in," I shout, but no one enters. I walk to the door and open it to find Maetha standing in the hallway looking rather nervous.

"Calli, go grab your ID. We're going on a trip, and that's all I can tell you."

Chapter 10 - Project T19

"What about my classes?" I ask

"You'll miss them today. Hurry."

I grab my purse, and Maetha's voice fills my head. *Leave it, Calli. Bring only your driver's license. No phones, no devices, and nothing that can be stolen or traced.* I pull my driver's license out of my purse and follow her outside to her four-door sedan. We climb in and shut the doors, and before I can secure my seat belt she begins backing up and driving away.

I sit silently with many questions running through my mind as she drives through the city. I deduce she's heading to the airport because this is the route my parents take whenever they go on a trip. It would explain why Maetha had me bring only my driver's license. I can't board a plane without identification.

Maetha speaks to my mind again. *I'm sorry I cannot answer all of your questions. Someone needs our help, but were being followed at the moment. Just follow my lead in everything I do, and don't say a word.*

Okay, now I'm a little freaked out! I instinctually turn my head to see if I can spot who's following us, but all I see is cars, trucks, and buses. I don't know what I was expecting to see. Black cars with tinted windows? I look over at Maetha who appears calm and focused, like she's been through this a thousand times before. If she's right about us being followed, then she may be the safest person for me to be with right now. I suppose a several-thousand-year-old Immortal must have some tricks up her sleeve I haven't seen yet, so I let out a deep exhale to calm my nerves and clear my head.

She parks her car in the airport long-term parking and we ride the shuttle to the terminal. Once inside the building, we walk to the ticket counter, where Maetha purchases two one-way tickets to New York City. I show ID for my ticket and notice out of the corner of my eye Maetha's ID says her name is Janice Johnson. The photo doesn't look like her at all. She's pictured with dark skin and hair and I wonder why the clerk isn't contesting the difference between her appearance and her ID. We take our tickets and walk to the security gate. I keep my mouth shut, like I've been ordered, and wonder why we are going to fly when we could run to New York City.

We pass through security without any delays and head to the designated concourse.

We sit in the terminal for only a few minutes before the boarding process begins. I notice a few security guards standing in the distance, talking on their radios. One keeps looking in our direction. I try to read his lips but find it impossible due to the radio being positioned in front of his mouth. His mind and future appear the same as Travis's—empty and non-existent. I look at Maetha and place some thoughts at the front of my mind.

That guard is an Unaltered human.

I know, she says without looking at him.

Should we be worried?

Do as I say and follow what I do. That's all you need to worry about. Stop looking at him.

We stand and take our place in line to board the plane. Our ID's are checked once again before boarding, and we make our way out the door into the cool, spring air to the waiting commuter plane. As everyone ahead of us climbs the stairs one by one, Maetha's voice sounds in my head. *Calli, look to your right, next to the plane. Do you see the luggage cart? I nod. When everyone has boarded we will exit using our running power and hide behind it. Wait for my signal, and try your best to keep your head clear.*

What is that supposed to mean?

We climb the stairs and find our assigned seats, which are conveniently located by the door. I feel an ominous presence enter my mind, and a tingling sensation tickles the inside of my head. This feels different from when Maetha puts thoughts into my head, so I decide to take her advice and focus on clearing my mind. However, no matter how hard I try to calm my thoughts, they keep coming back. My memories of the past few days are surfacing without my permission, as though someone is pulling them out and analyzing them one by one. I realize now why Maetha encouraged me to practice meditation. What I don't understand is how anyone can read my mind if I'm an Unaltered.

There must be a Diamond Bearer nearby.

No more people are entering the plane and the flight attendant appears as if she is about to close the door. I look to my right and see Maetha's eyes are closed. Her face is focused and I feel her mind penetrate deep into mine. The two foreign minds collide within my head bringing about a claustrophobic sensation to my whole body.

A high-pitched screeching noise blasts through my mind. It sounds like a combination of a jet engine and an eagle dragging its talons on a chalkboard. Instinct forces me to cover my ears and bend over in my seat. The sound vibrates through my entire body, sending waves of agony through my muscles, and making me cringe with pain.

Maetha grabs my wrist, pulls me on my feet with a heavy jerk, and leads me toward the door. The noise in my head subsides and I notice everyone in the plane is looking down at their laps. The flight attendants busy themselves with take-off procedures, not noticing we are about to flee the plane.

Out we go, down the stairs and over to the luggage cart where we crouch to hide.

"Catch your breath, Calli."

"What just happened in there?"

"Freedom bi-located to us and was trying to extract your memories. I intervened. We need to go now. We'll talk about this later."

She takes my hand and begins running top speed across the large airplane parking lot, and once we are across the multiple runways she releases the hold on my hand. I follow her lead, leaping over the security fence and continuing to head west.

We run for at least an hour, covering many miles of ground before we stop at a park in Angola, Indiana.

"Very good," she says out loud and gives me a one-armed hug. "Thank you for your patience, Calli. We were pursued from the moment I picked you up till we boarded the plane. I suspect the government officials waiting for us at the gate in New York City will be frustrated when they're informed we aren't on the plane.

"So," I say, "we weren't going to fly in the plane, you only wanted it to look like we were. Am I right?"

"Correct."

"Where are we actually going?"

"I cannot tell you where we're going just yet. You understand, don't you?"

"I guess."

She does a quick scan of our surroundings, then says,

"Your mind can still be accessed, as you realize. Therefore, I won't be putting anything in it that can be read by our foes, our destination being one of them."

"Maetha, how long have I been followed?"

"A couple days."

"Was I in danger?"

"I wouldn't have let anything happen to you. I've been nearby, waiting for everything to line up properly before bringing you on this task. Being followed is nothing I haven't dealt with in the past, but it's getting more and more difficult to shake a tail once I have one." She smiles and motions for me to follow her.

We start running again, turning to the south and eventually stopping in Fort Wayne, Indiana, at a large, multi-story office building. We walk around, approach a side door with a keypad lock, and Maetha enters in a code that unlocks the door. We enter the building and quickly walk the long hallway to a door labeled "Food Additives."

Maetha puts her finger to her lips to remind me to be quiet before she opens the door.

A man of medium build stands in the far corner by a filing cabinet. He has gray hair and thick glasses and appears to be about sixty. He looks up as we approach and says, "You brought an accessory with you this time."

Maetha replies, "Calli, this is Hans Lindlbauer. He's our chief researcher in DNA studies, and is also a Reader." Maetha walks to the window and peers out. I meet Hans halfway to shake his hand.

"Did you transfer your research exactly as I instructed?" Maetha asks him.

"Yes. I'm ready."

"Let's go. Calli, you will hold his hand and transfer your speed?"

I grab his hand and follow Maetha out the door. When

we exit the building we turn on the speed and head in a southwest direction. I note the time on a large community clock: 1:00 PM. I also note the dark storm clouds up ahead. We are about to be drenched.

We run a short distance to a post office, where Maetha opens a mailbox and pulls out a package. From the package, she pulls out three running suits similar to the one I wore when I delivered the Sanguine Diamond to the Death Clan. The fact Maetha thinks we need the specialized running clothes means we are going to be running for a while, and normal clothing won't stand up to the friction. Mr. Lindlbauer seems to understand, and I get the feeling this isn't his first time to run cross-country.

We change quickly in the small bathroom and stuff our clothes in the mailbox after removing our valuables.

Maetha looks at the two of us and says, "I can't tell you where we're going. Just know it's a long run." She addresses Hans directly. "I had to find a secure location for you, Hans. The other was compromised."

"How can you be certain this next location won't be exposed as well?" He nods his head in my direction.

I can't believe it! He thinks I might be a snitch or a spy.

"Hans, Calli and I are of the same blood. You have nothing to worry about concerning her. Let's go."

We run for four hours, and the initial drenching our clothes took from the thunderstorm is no longer a bother. I believe we're still in Indiana, but I can't quite tell where we are until we stop at a building with a sign identifying it as the Patoka Lake resort. Maetha has a keycard for a room, and she opens the door.

Right away I notice this isn't any ordinary hotel room. This is someone's living quarters. I scan the room. The books on the shelving unit are old—very old—and above them I see several painted portraits of men, women, and children framed in intricately carved wooden frames. Antiques litter the room: oriental vases, snuff boxes, salt dishes, Fabergé eggs, nesting dolls, crystal bells, lamps, and shadow boxes filled with silver and gold coins.

I look at Maetha, realizing this is her room and these antiques aren't simply collected in the same manner an antiques' dealer would build a collection. No, these items have been gathered throughout Maetha's multi-millennial life, and each probably has special significance. Along one wall I see a long, glass case with an assortment of ancient helmets, swords, and spear tips inside, most of which are in pristine condition. In fact, most of the items in this room are beautifully preserved, and have been well taken care of. Any one of these antiques could be worth a fortune to a museum.

"Hans, your studies will arrive tomorrow. I've set up a mini-lab in the other room. Would you take a look to see if I forgot anything?" Maetha points in the direction of a door across the room, and Hans walks to the door and enters the room. She turns to me and answers the questions in the front of my mind.

"Yes, this is one of my residences. Yes, not many individuals know of its existence, and yes, bringing Hans here indicates the level of severity concerning our situation."

Hans comes back in the room. "You were very thorough in your preparations, Maetha. Now, tell me about the subjects I tested."

"Why don't you tell me what you found first?"

"All right, the new blood samples show inconsistent

alterations compared to other high-powered individuals. The alteration appears to have been forced upon the subject."

I look at Maetha, and her voice sounds in my head. *The blood samples were taken from Repeaters.*

I turn to Mr. Lindlbauer and ask, "Are you saying this ability is manmade?"

He doesn't answer, only stares at me for a few seconds, then asks Maetha, "How much does she know?"

"More than you, Hans. She's in direct contact with one of them."

He rubs his jaw and seats himself in one of the ornate high-boy chairs in the corner. "Until further research validates my studies, I cannot be certain, but the possible implications are monumental." He looks at Maetha and says, "Just before you arrived today, I learned the government has been working on two top-secret projects dealing with DNA modification. Twenty-five years ago, Project T19 was launched and focused on pregnant women, yet failed miserably when the exposed fetuses developed severe defects and deformities. T19 was in operation for six years before the plug was pulled. It was assumed to be a complete failure. However, the subjects' blood samples you submitted for testing fit the time frame and don't fit the bill when it comes to natural alteration. Oh, and all the samples have the same paternal DNA."

I look at Maetha for answers. I'm shocked to learn Brand's dad fathered other Repeaters. Maetha ignores me and asks him more questions. "What was the other project, Hans?"

He continues, "It was instituted in the early 1980's and is still in operation, although I don't know if it's anything to worry about. It involves sequestering men and women in government-run underground facilities in some sort of baby-making operation. According to my information, the women are kept in the facilities for the first five months of their pregnancies and are then released back into society. Each participant has always been a willing party. I don't know why they classified it as 'DNA modification' though.

"There's also a third project, Maetha. It's in the weapons' sector, but I don't know much about that one, other than it was headed up by General Harding and a male civilian whose mind is similar to yours."

Somehow I know this General Harding has to be Chris's dad, and I feel even more uneasy. Then I recall Freedom saying, "Where I come from Unaltereds are a dime a dozen." Apparently the government is creating Unaltereds, and Freedom is deeply involved with the program. That explains why he had such a large group of guys available to fight Brand.

Maetha's voice comes into my mind, acknowledging my supposition as she walks to the small refrigerator and pulls out three bottles of juice and passes them to us. I haven't seen this variety before, and when I taste it, I realize it's most likely something Clara Winter made. The flavor reminds me of the food and beverages served at the Runners' compound, which in turn reminds me of Chris. Hearing his father's name and tasting familiar flavors makes it easy to recall Chris's face and dredge up all the emotions and feelings buried deep in my soul.

Maetha asks Hans, "May I look into your mind to see the face of the civilian you're referring to?"

"Certainly."

I find it extremely interesting she asks permission to do something she could have done without him even knowing. Could it be this Reader has no idea who he's dealing with?

"Ah, yes. I know that man," she says to Hans. At the

same time, she speaks to my mind: *It's Freedom, and no, Hans doesn't know much about my abilities.*

Hans finishes his juice drink and glances around. "Maetha, how secure is this room?"

"I've lived here undetected for thirty years. The owner of the resort is my friend, and the staff never enters the room. It will remain safe so long as you don't venture outside."

"I don't see a telephone."

"Hans, your excessive telephone use is what gave your location away. If you're right about the blood samples and the individuals are government experiments, then you're the only scientist who knows T19 was actually successful and the results are potentially catastrophic for mankind. Your telephone communications were being listened to, and your Internet searches were being followed. I'm sure the government is aware that you know about these top-secret projects. However, I don't think they know you've identified the blood samples of living, breathing, government-modified DNA recipients. Calli and I removed you not two minutes before your office was going to be raided, Hans. You're safe here in my room, but I'm afraid Calli and I need to leave now. There's some clothing in the box by the computer and plenty of reading material to keep you busy until your research arrives."

He asks, "How exactly will my research arrive? I sent it to New York."

Maetha smiles. "Yes, I know. Your package will be intercepted and redirected here, and one of my associates will deliver it to you. I'll get back as soon as I can." Maetha shakes his hand and turns to me. "Let's go."

We leave the building the way we entered and walk out to the trees by the lake. Maetha stops and sits on the ground with her legs crossed, patting the ground for me to join her.

"Calli, do you understand why I brought you with me?"

"I'm not sure now. At first I thought it might be time for me to get the rest of the diamond pieces put in my heart. I wondered if you were the one rounding up the amulet wearers. I figured you were behind the disappearances."

"Calli, as I told you, once a splintering takes place, no one can alter the destiny of the diamond. I am not responsible for the missing amulet wearers. I am also not concerned with them because this is all part of the reuniting. This cycle repeats itself every time a diamond is extracted, splintered, and reborn, and I am not worried about it . . . and neither should you be. Everything must play out as nature intends."

"Did you bring me along so I could learn about Brand?"

"Yes. I wanted you to learn with me. I didn't know what Hans had discovered, just that he'd stumbled into a pit of vipers. I also brought you along with me in case I need help."

I can't believe my ears. Maetha thinks she might need help, and she thinks I'll be able to give it to her?

"Calli, I'm not all-powerful. I'm a human being with increased abilities, and that's all. So much of what I do and decide is done by following my gut instinct, and often it's decided on the fly. My wisdom and experience from living as long as I have guides my decisions as well. However, times are changing. Freedom is changing the times around us, and because you've had personal interaction with him, I figure you can shed some light on the situation. Your mind holds many clues to this big puzzle, and I needed you nearby when Hans divulged his findings."

I ask "What do you think about Brand's dad fathering all the Repeaters?"

"I'm not concerned. Brand's emotional rollercoaster is inconsequential in the big picture. I'm challenged with figuring out why unaltered humans are being bred and what type of weapon is being made. Calli, I must tell the others what I've learned and I need you to be my protector while I do so. Alert me if there's danger."

She closes her eyes and her body relaxes. She appears so serene and beautiful, and I marvel at how peaceful she is, even with the disturbing news we've just received, like the fact that Chris's father is working with Freedom on some kind of weaponry. My thoughts shift to Brand. He's not an authentic person of powers. He was created, and yet the Shadow Demons are drawn to him. Interesting. Maetha said the people following us at the airport were CIA, and just the thought sets me on edge.

Is it possible there are more people with created powers like Brand? How was he made? What kind of technology would it require to do such a thing? These questions swirl in my mind as I take in my surroundings. Two swans out on the lake gracefully glide through the water. The sound of chirping crickets brings my attention to the position of the sun and the realization that nightfall is only a couple of hours away. We won't be able to get back to Brand for several hours, and his safety worries me.

Maetha pulls out of her trance and says, "Calli, someday your mind won't be hampered by such details." Then she adds, "Brand is being moved to a secure location in Fort Wayne." She stands and says, "Let's go."

We arrive at a hotel in Fort Wayne and approach the

designated room, but even before we reach it I can hear Brand yelling at someone.

"Where is she? You said she'd be here!"

Maetha knocks on the door. Footsteps are heard. The door opens, revealing a tall man dressed in a police uniform, but I can tell right away he's a Hunter. My experience with Hunters in the past isn't one I like to remember, and this guy doesn't make me any more comfortable. He immediately strikes me as a shady character.

Maetha speaks to my mind. *He is a mercenary—a hired thug.*

We enter the room, and Brand rushes to my side.

"Are you all right? Are you hurt?"

"I'm fine, Brand." I glance over at Maetha and the Hunter, who are speaking quietly in the corner. The Hunter hands Brand's broken Demon device to Maetha.

Brand abruptly yells and points his finger at the Hunter. "That bastard lied to me and brought me here! He took my Mp3 away. He knew how to get around my power by stalling long enough so I couldn't repeat." Then Brand turns his anger on Maetha. "You told him how to do it didn't you? Why would you do that?"

Maetha calmly walks to Brand and says, "Your life was in danger, Brand. I did what I had to do to ensure your safety. Government agents were present the day when you fought by the river, and they were about to seize you today. This officer did as he was ordered, but he has no idea you have powers, and if you want it to remain that way you better repeat back and shut your mouth. Take Calli with you so she can remember this too.

He pulls me with him as he repeats back to the moment when we entered the room and he asked me if I was all right. As soon as the room stops swirling and tilting, I present my thoughts to Maetha and tell her Brand just repeated and this time he won't go on a rant, exposing his powers.

The Hunter hands Maetha the broken Demon device as I'd watch him do before, but this time Brand is silent. Maetha pulls a small amount of cash from her zipped pocket and hands it to him, and the man leaves.

After the door closes and the three of us are alone, Maetha sits on the bed and turns to face us. "Brand, you will be coming with me for the next while until it's safe for you to return."

"What? No, I'm not. I can handle myself just fine."

"Clearly you cannot."

"Hey, he tricked me, plus he had insider information."

"You're lucky he got to you first." Maetha turns her attentions to me. "Calli, you will return to your dormitory and continue with your Spring Break plans."

Brand struts in the direction of the door. "I'm leaving with her." Before he can reach the door, Maetha is instantly blocking his way. Brand's hair blows into his eyes. He freezes in place and freaks out. "Whoa! How . . . I thought you were just a Seer."

Maetha smiles. "Brand, your world is about to become larger. Over the next few weeks I'll teach you more about the world of powers and introduce you to your half-siblings. You need to understand, though. I'm deadly serious when I say your life is in danger."

"What about school? What about my family?"

"Don't worry. It will all be taken care of," Maetha says.

Brand angles his head and says, "Did you just say half-siblings?"

"Yes."

Brand's body visibly relaxes and I realize Maetha is using her diamond powers on him, like an instant sedative.

Calli, Maetha speaks to my mind, *you need to go now before you're missed. I will come to you at a later time.*
What about being followed? I ask.
I don't see any danger for you in the near future.

I leave the hotel room feeling a bit more secure, knowing Brand has settled down and is in good hands. Two hours later I arrive back at my dorm and grab my already-packed bags. I change out of my Runner's suit and then drive my car home to my parents' house. I get there at 2:00 in the morning. After checking in with my parents, I snuggle into my comfortable bed and try to forget the eventful day before drifting off to sleep.

The last few days played out rather boringly. The pile of boxes my mother and I are working on is shrinking. We've found a few significant items of memorabilia, but mostly items to donate to second-hand stores. My mind is preoccupied and I don't share the same enthusiasm as she does over small trinkets and documents.

At one point, my mother asked me about Brand and Suz. I didn't have much to tell her because I haven't heard anything about Suz, and there isn't anything I can tell her about Brand.

I return to school following the break, prepared for negative remarks or speculations concerning Brand, but find no one really misses him. I scan the minds in the cafeteria and can't find a single person who is wondering about his absence. Then, just as I am about to feel sorry for Brand for not being missed, I realize this is Maetha's doing.

She did the same thing when I returned from Montana. *How does she do it?*

Even though Maetha said my future didn't show any danger, I still keep a vigilant eye open for suspicious people. And I've been practicing my meditation. A lot.

The last few weeks leading up to finals were un-eventful, almost boring—well, except for receiving the box of Pulse-Emitters, which I didn't even open. There really wasn't any point in it because I didn't have anyone to test them for me. I've watched closely for signs of Freedom or any other Unaltereds. Nothing.

Suz's friends no longer give me the time of day, and the occupants of the entire building seem to have calmed down to the point of seriousness—and it's really strange to see serious freshmen.

I haven't even heard from Beth, but then again, I haven't contacted her, either.

The semester is almost finished and I've found a job at the public library for the summer. The job is tedious and boring, but it pays me money and constitutes as my very first job. I give it my best effort with the goal of becoming a model employee.

In the middle of July, I took a week off to go to Hawaii with my parents. Two things to note while in Honolulu: one, I came across an older female Seer who was a street vendor selling seashell jewelry. I looked into her mind and found she was of Hawaiian descent, and, when her powers emerged in her adolescent years, Curtis

Schultz personally taught her about the Demons. Her family embraced her ability and praised her for it; they also helped protect her through the years.

The second noteworthy occurrence happened on the beach down from our condo. I saw a man who looked strikingly similar to Chris: blond hair, deep blue eyes, toned muscular body and a smile to melt every girl's heart. The guy was with a poofy-blonde-haired, bikini-clad girl with unnaturally large breasts that her tiny bikini top struggled to hold. When she turned her backside in my direction, I came to the conclusion she must be extremely proud of her buttocks because she wore a thong bottom.

When I saw that couple, I recalled the vision I'd seen of Chris on my last night at the Runners' compound. Through his eyes I saw myself enter his hospital room, although at first I didn't recognize myself because of my mature appearance. I was older looking, filled out, and I even dressed differently than I normally dress . . . almost like how one would dress for an office job.

The man and the nearly-naked female I saw on the beach helped me understand better that my body still needed to change dramatically before the events in the vision could take place. I certainly don't own any dressy clothing, or thongs—not that I'd have to own a thong for the vision to happen.

I guess my mind was a little preoccupied with thongs when I watched the busty blonde readjust her butt-floss.

Oh no . . . thongs are not for me.

Once we returned from Hawaii, my day-to-day activities have become quite limited and mundane. I work, I eat, I sleep, and I live on my laptop in the evenings researching DNA, medical advancements, and medications. This goes on for three weeks until August seventh rolls around again: my birthday.

My parents are coming to take me to dinner at a fancy restaurant, and I know I'd better go shopping because nothing in my closet can be even remotely considered fancy.

I call Pamela. "Hey, Pamela. You know how you said you'd love to take me shopping to jazz up my wardrobe?"

"Yeah."

"I'd like to take you up on your offer. Do you have time?"

"Calli, there is *never* a time to not go shopping! When do you want to go?"

"Today, if you can. We could meet at the mall."

"Sounds great. Give me an hour and I'll meet you in the courtyard by the Cookie Shoppe."

I get ready and head over to the mall, arriving a half hour before Pamela. I order a cheeseburger and fries and find an empty table.

A million thoughts run through my mind—the thoughts of all the people in the courtyard. I take a moment to close my eyes and concentrate on controlling my ability, shutting out the noise and placing a barrier in my mind so I won't be assaulted by the flying thoughts. Then I open my eyes and take a bite of my cheeseburger. I have to wonder what it will be like when I have the whole diamond in my heart.

I remember back to when Suz and I spied on Brand in the mall soon after I received the diamond shard. I don't recall hearing everyone's thoughts like I am now. I guess I'm better at harnessing the powers of the diamond.

Across the courtyard by the pizza vendor, a group of rowdy teens laugh and throw food at each other. A quick look into their minds reveals their ages range from thirteen to sixteen and overall they're good kids just out having a fun time.

I think about when I was thirteen. My day was usually spent doing my chores, reading books, helping with the yard work, or helping at either of my parents' offices. I wasn't allowed to "go to the mall" at thirteen without my parents. In fact, I didn't start doing that until I was fifteen and I had to beg my parents to let me go with Suz. Even then, I found that shopping was not my thing. I've always preferred to sit and observe people.

Back then, I would read lips to determine what people were talking about. Now, I don't even have to do that.

The table of teens all laugh in unison at a joke one of the guys tells. I find it interesting how each of the kids at the table has their different "crushes" on each other. My matchmaking instincts kick in as I mentally match the pairs that are compatible. Then I stop. *What am I thinking? These are just kids.*

I finish my food and clear my trash. Before I sit back down, I see Pamela coming my direction.

"Calli, is that you?" Pamela asks.

"Hey, Pamela."

"Whoa! You've changed!"

"Huh?"

"Haven't you looked in the mirror lately? Sheez, how long has it been since I saw you last?" Pamela walks a full circle around me, which makes me feel embarrassed. "We need to dress that bod of yours in something stunning. Come on."

She grabs my arm and drags me to the most expensive store in the mall, naturally.

Pamela asks, "So, what's the occasion? Got a hot date?"

"No, my parents are taking me to dinner tonight for my birthday."

"It's your birthday?" She hugs me tight. "Happy

Birthday! You are the most modest person I've ever met. If I hadn't asked, you wouldn't have told me. Am I right?"

I nod.

Three hours and a maxed-out credit card later, I have a new wardrobe. The outfit I'll be wearing for the birthday dinner is a dark green, short-sleeved, silk dress that stops just above my knees. It has a belted-waist and a v-neckline, which Pamela says really accentuates my shape.

Pamela holds up a pair of green and brown heels that I feel sure I'll break an ankle in. "Oh, these are the *pièce de résistance*," she fans her face dramatically with one of her hands.

I take the shoes and look at the price tag. "They'd *better* be the highlight of the outfit. They cost more than all my other shoes put together!"

"Try them on, Calli."

I have to admit, they *are* great looking shoes.

"Make sure you wear your hair up and put on a pair of dangly earrings. You'll be a show-stopper for sure."

"You should be a personal shopper, Pamela."

I arrive at the restaurant and am escorted to my parents, who are already waiting at the table. As I approach, I notice a third person, a female, sitting with them. Maetha.

Chapter 11 - Missing Persons

"Calli," my mother exclaims as she puts her hands to her mouth in shock.

My father stands as I approach and embraces me in a warm hug. "Here's the birthday girl. You look spectacular, Calli."

"Thanks, Dad."

"Calli, I want to introduce you to Dr. Janice Johnson. She's a neurologist who studies the brain function of proclaimed psychics, and she has a job offer for you."

My mother motions toward Maetha. "I hope it's all right if Dr. Johnson joins us for your birthday dinner."

Maetha stands and extends her hand for me to shake. I stare at her in confusion. My parents have already met Maetha, so why is my father referring to her as Janice Johnson?

Maetha's voice fills my head. *Calli, to them I appear to be a different person. Just play along. You look great, by the way.*

I want to ask her how she's able to "look different" to my parents, but instead I reach forward and shake her hand and say, "Nice to meet you, Dr. Johnson." I turn to my mom, issuing a reassurance. "It's just fine for her to join us."

We sit down, and the waiter arrives with the menus. His nametag says "Cody," but his mind reveals his name is actually "Sven." His eyes are on me as he introduces himself and asks for our beverage choices, all the while he seems skittish and uncomfortable. My mother orders a glass of wine and the rest of us ask for water. He writes our choices down, then looks at me again before turning to leave.

My mother nods her head in Sven's direction as he walks away. "I think he's smitten with you, Calli."

An unladylike scoffing sound escapes my throat. "I don't think so, Mom."

My father leans forward and says, "Calli, Dr. Johnson was talking about the research she does and how she could use your help for the next few weeks till classes begin."

Maetha's voice fills my head, drowning out my father's voice. *It's time to take Brand to meet the clans. He needs you, Calli. His progress is stunted without your influence. He's actually waiting nearby in a secure location, and once we are finished here, you will leave with him. I want your parents to believe you're working an internship with me. That way they won't worry, and we don't have to reveal your abilities yet. Your parents aren't ready to accept them.*

Sven arrives with our drinks. He places each corresponding glass with each person and waits to serve me last. As he reaches forward with the glass of water his upper body jolts as though he just got shocked. The glass slips from his fingers and crashes to the floor.

"I'm so sorry," he says, flustered.

Another waiter comes over to our table with a towel to help mop up the water.

I place my thoughts on the front of my mind for Maetha. *Something's up with this waiter, but I can't quite put my finger on it.*

He's an enemy, Calli. Your water was tampered with, so I made him drop it.

What? My stomach knots up, fearing for my parents' safety and my own.

Relax, Calli. I won't let anything happen to you or your parents.

The floor supervisor brings me a fresh glass of water and says, "Please accept my complete apology. Cody is new to our establishment. Would you like me to have another server help you?"

"No, not at all," my father says. "It was an accident."

I pick up my glass of water and smell it. I can't detect anything wrong. I glance over at Maetha and she gives me a nod of approval, indicating the water is safe.

After the restaurant staff leave, my father asks, "So, what do you think about Dr. Johnson's internship offer?"

I smile. "I'm interested."

My mother begins talking animatedly about one of her internships. I pretend to listen while asking Maetha with my mind, *Who is Sven working for? How did they know I'd be at this restaurant, seated at this table? I don't understand.*

Maetha looks across the restaurant at Sven, then at my father. Sven reaches up and scratches the top of his head. Maetha says, *Your father made these reservations a while ago, providing those tracking you with enough time for Sven to be hired as a waiter. Sven wasn't scheduled to work this section of the restaurant tonight, but the other employee called in sick.*

Well, that's convenient.

Exactly.

How long have they been tracking me?

Since you left Montana.

What? Are they the same ones who were following me when you took me to help Hans?

No. They're a different group. I've kept an eye on your future to see when they would interfere with your safety. This is another reason I'm here tonight interrupting your personal time with your parents.

I notice my mother looking at me with question in her eyes. She asks, "Did you hear anything I just said?"

"Uh, sorry, Mom. My mind is a bit preoccupied."

"With the waiter?"

Instead of trying to convince my mom of Sven's real intentions, I simply say, "Yeah."

All things considered, the evening plays out nicely . . . and a bit on the entertaining side. Sven tries again to meddle with my food, but this time I detect the smell of poison in my garlic mashed potatoes. The rest of the food is untainted, so I eat everything except for the potatoes. Sven behaves in an over-accommodating manner, trying to refill my water, asking if there is anything wrong with the potatoes, and pressuring me to order a dessert. My mother insists he's flirting. I know otherwise. I have to admit though, it's kind of fun to watch Sven become frustrated with his inability to complete his assignment.

The evening wraps up, and I hug my parents and tell them how much I love them, maybe overdoing it a bit because, honestly, I can't tell how long it will be before I'll see them again. The thought frightens me a little, but at the same time I feel reassured that everything will work out well in the end.

Maetha accompanies me back to my dorm. On the way, we discuss Sven.

I ask, "Do you think he works for Freedom?"

"I don't think so. I didn't see any evidence of Freedom in his mind. However, I did see he and his group became aware of you after the Sanguine Diamond delivery. I couldn't get a fix on details. Sven's mind was rather difficult to navigate."

"Maybe you should have extracted his thoughts."

"Absolutely not. That would give away my ability to

do so. I don't know who he's working with, but they clearly have more power than most people. I need to know more before I expose myself. You should hold off on using powers as well."

"I agree."

We arrive at the dormitory and she follows me inside.

"Calli, pack enough clothing and basic necessities to last you a week. Try to keep it minimal. You're going to be on the road with Brand for a little while."

I start loading some of my freshly purchased outfits into a suitcase. It's hard to believe that just this afternoon I was trying on these clothes with Pamela at the mall. After packing, I change out of my birthday dress and into some more comfortable clothes.

"What's this?" Maetha asks, holding the unopened box of new Pulse-Emitters.

"They're my new devices. I haven't tested them out yet, you know, because I haven't been around Brand."

She tears into the box and hands me one of the small units. "Take one for him to try. I'll repackage the box and send it to Indiana for safe keeping. We need to go now."

I snap my case shut after stuffing in a few bathroom items. Then Maetha follows me outside to our vehicles. She opens her trunk and pulls out a large bag. As she does so, I scrutinize the shadows, looking for Sven or anyone else. Not finding anyone, I turn to Maetha. "Should I be on the lookout for Sven?"

"No, he's forgotten all about you." She smiles as she approaches.

I open my car and shove my suitcase in the back seat. "When I have the complete diamond, will I be able to do what you do?"

"We'll see. Here, hold this." She hands me the bag, then she walks a circle around me similar to when she spoke with me after the Death Clan's destruction. "Our conversation is now private. Listen closely. You are to take Brand to visit the clans of the Healers, Readers, Seers, and Runners, in that order." She emphasizes the directive strongly. I figure we are to visit the Runners last because Chris is an instructor at the compound. She continues. "Refrain from showing Brand any other powers or abilities other than healing unless absolutely necessary. I've put together some supplies you'll need on this journey," she says, pointing to the bag she gave me, "including cash and directions to four different locations where you'll be exchanging vehicles along the way. You are to drive straight through and not stop at any hotels. Knowing the government is working with Freedom, we can't risk leaving a trail of credit card breadcrumbs."

"Can I take my cell phone to call my parents?"

"No. Give it to me and I'll hold it for you."

I hesitantly hand over my phone, feeling naked and vulnerable. "What about a prepaid phone in case of emergencies?"

Maetha pauses for a moment and closes her eyes. I assume she's looking to the future. "No. Bringing any kind of phone will cause complications. It makes you much easier to track. Besides, I don't foresee any life-threatening events in your near future. On that note, I want to remind you to avoid looking into your own future. Small incidents create larger situations which precipitate the overall outcome of you attaining the diamond. Do not look to your own future lest you be tempted to behave a certain way or attempt to alter a situation, as you've already done."

"What? I've already done that?"

"Calli, you altered your physical appearance. You've unconsciously caused your body to change to match the vision you saw concerning Chris. The changes you've already made will help in one way, but they'll be a detriment in others."

"A detriment?"

"Calli, I choose to look the age of fifty because I was the happiest at this age long ago. By looking older, it reduces the number of suitors I have to deal with, as well as allowing me to pass by less-noticed wherever I go. You have willed your looks to an extreme level, and this change will bring about new difficulties as you will soon discover."

"So, I'm too beautiful?"

"There's no such thing. Beauty is in the eye of the beholder, and not everyone will see you as beautiful. In fact, many will see you as a threat. People can be funny that way. Others may feel compelled to protect and guard you, hoping to ensure your loyalty to them. Be careful with your beauty, do not use it to open long-term opportunities, for such things always come with strings attached, and do not use it to achieve what you believe to be your future."

"What?"

"I'm sorry, Calli. That's all the time we have to discuss it. You must go now and pick up Brand." She hands me a card with an address. "He's waiting for you."

As I drive to the address Maetha gave me, I think about her comments about beauty and the difficulties she mentioned. My mind fills with memories of the Runners' compound. Is it possible their mistreatment of me was out of jealousy because I looked ordinary? Do extremely good looking people wish they could for one day be treated for their accomplishment and smarts instead of being ogled and lied to? This is definitely news to me.

I pull into the parking lot of a diner called Spunky's on the outskirts of town. My first thought is: *this is considered to be a secure location?* Brand sits in a booth by the large window. He looks different even though it's only been a couple months since I saw him last. He's seems older, a bit defeated, and tired.

From the moment I walk in the door until I stand in front of him at his table, his eyes are on me. I say, "Hi, Brand."

"Calli?"

"Yeah."

"Wow!" He stands and hugs me tightly. "I leave you alone for a couple months, and you go and turn all beautiful on me."

"Good to see you too, Brand."

He releases me from his embrace and motions for me to sit down at the booth.

I glance around the diner, examining each of the occupants, still feeling a little unsettled over the whole Sven deal. "I don't think we should stay here."

"Well, it's not like I can go very many places after dark."

I reach in my purse and pull out the one-inch-by-one-inch square electronic device. Brand lets out an appreciative sigh and takes it as I say, "I haven't been able to test them yet. Are you up for it right now?"

His eyes perk up and he smiles, exposing his dimples. "You bet, beautiful."

I'm beginning to see what Maetha just warned me about.

He grabs his suitcase from the floor and drops a twenty-dollar bill on the table to cover his expenses. We walk out of the diner into the warm summer air. Brand sets his suitcase down and clips the device on his shirt, turns it on. The lights from the parking lot illuminate a great distance, but we eventually reach the shadows where the Demons hover. He walks into the shadows and the Demons float away from him. He extends his arms out from his body and spins around joyfully.

"Finally! It's about damn time!" he shouts to the star-lit sky.

"There's a small LED light on it, too." I point to the power button, and he pushes it, turning the light on.

"This is perfect, Calli. How long will the battery last?"

"It's supposed to be good for sixty days of continuous use, and will start beeping when it has one day left."

He grabs my hands and spins me around in the dark. "Thank you! I've missed you, Calli."

Oh boy. I must direct his attention away from me. I stop him and begin to pull him toward my car. "We've got to get moving, Brand. We're not safe here."

"Oh, all right. But can I ask, why California?"

I don't think it would be wise to tell Brand all the details. Instead, I say, "Because the government goons who were chasing after you in the spring are now after me. So, you're my protector while I take you to meet with other clans.

As per Maetha's instructions, Brand and I stop at a Zippy Lube car shop just outside of town to make the first car swap. An old man stands inside the Zippy Lube, watching us through the window. A two-door hybrid car is parked nearby.

Brand turns to me and says, "This guy knows Maetha."

"How do you know?"

"Seriously, Calli. Have you forgotten what I can do? Come on, let's go." He opens his door and gets out. "Pop the trunk so I can grab our luggage."

I'm amazed with the level of connections Maetha has, and I trust her judgment, but I'm worried about my

Cooper. I don't want to leave it with a stranger. I get out of the car and approach the building. Brand joins me at the door, a suitcase in each hand.

The man opens the door but doesn't move aside. "She's full of gas," he grumbles in a hoarse voice, "new tires and such. Treat her nice and she'll be good to you." He extends his hand holding the keys. I take them carefully.

"Thank you. My keys are in the ignition. Where will you, I mean, what will happen to—"

He cuts me off. "Maetha said she'll pick it up tomorrow."

"Oh, all right." I'm relieved to hear this.

We load the luggage and settle into the new car. At least we won't have to fill it with gas very often, being a hybrid. We drive through the night, switching places every couple of hours. Brand keeps his Pulse-Emitter clipped to his shirt and turned on just in case. I don't blame him one bit.

As the sun peeks up eight hours later, we cross the border of Illinois. We've reached the next vehicle exchange location. This time the car—another hybrid—is found in a parking garage, unlocked, and keys under the seat. Our instructions are to leave the keys of our current car in the nearby garbage receptacle. We do so and get back on the road.

At the western border of Oklahoma, we swap vehicles again at the home of a retired Runner. The man, Wendell, is quiet and frail looking. I can tell he's dying a slow death from cancer, but I can also tell that Maetha has not healed him when she very well could have done so. There is probably a good reason. We don't stay long at Wendell's home.

As evening approaches, we enter New Mexico and

find a truck stop for food and gasoline. Brand fills the tank after I prepay the cashier, and then we head into the restaurant and take a seat.

"I feel so gross," Brand says as he looks the menu over.

"What do you mean?"

"I stink . . . I'm tired . . . I'm stinking tired. I want to take a shower and sleep longer than thirty minutes at a time." He lays his menu down and rubs his face with his hands and scratches at his beard stubble.

The waitress comes to our table to take our order. I ask for a grilled chicken salad and water. Brand orders the fajita special.

After she leaves, Brand says in a defeated exhale, "What's the point of all this, Calli?"

"What do you mean?"

"How long are we going to have to run?"

"I really don't know."

Brand says, "Too bad Maetha isn't here. She could look at the future and give us an answer."

"She already did. That's why we're doing what we're doing." I take a sip of my water and say, "Tell me about your time with Maetha. Did you get to meet the other Repeaters?"

"Yeah. I got to meet five others," he says. "They're all my half brothers and sisters, just like Suz, and we all kind of look the same." He points to his dimples.

"Suz doesn't have dimples, Brand, and she doesn't look like you. Did anyone look more like Suz than you?"

"I don't think so. It's not uncommon for some recessive gene to surface somewhere along the way."

"That's true. So what happens when two Repeaters come face-to-face?"

"To anyone watching, it seems like nothing's happening. However, to me or the other person, the meeting drags on *for-eh-ver.* We started with greeting each other by name and then listing a few random facts about each other. I would ask them a few questions, then repeat back to when we first met to tell them the answers. We went back and forth like this for quite a while. We were both repeating, trying to control the conversation, and always trying to one-up each other on what kind of dirt we could dig up through our repeated conversations.

"At first it was fun, but then it started getting creepy when our deepest, darkest secrets started coming out. One of the guys named Billy tried to attack me. We went back and forth, on and on, over and over again, never landing a hit on each other, always blocking, dodging, and countering every move the other made. Then, the last time I repeated, he didn't try to attack me at all. He just sat there with a huge grin on his face, flashing his dimples at me. Then he started laughing." Brand looks at me with wide eyes. "Calli, it was the creepiest thing I've ever seen! Maetha was quite frustrated with the whole deal to say the least."

"I imagine."

"Oh, and that's not the worst of it. Every one of them is some kind of lunatic, criminal, or psycho. Billy bragged over and over about the stores, houses, and people he's robbed. There was no guilt or shame in his voice, and I think he was *proud* of his crimes. Then I called him a psychopath, and he attacked me. The other four were a lot like him, violent and sadistic. One of the girls was pure evil. She admitted to being a serial killer, with a tally of over *twenty* victims! I will never forget that cold, dead stare in her eyes, and that horrible smirk on her face when she told me about how many of her murders were framed on innocent people." Brand takes a deep breath. "Oh, and the worst part? The five Repeaters I met with were not *all* the

Repeaters on the list. Two others were wanted criminals with bounties on their heads. As far as we could tell, none of them were in prison. Obviously, they didn't want to be found."

"Well, that isn't good news. Were *any* of them good?"

He laughs out loud with a forced 'are-you-crazy?' tone in his voice. "Define 'good.' Calli. The only one of them that I would trust *not* to murder me in my sleep was a kleptomaniac who successfully stole my wallet *nine times*. She gave it back each time I asked. I figured out pretty quick that I had to keep checking all my pockets every thirty seconds, or else things would mysteriously end up in her purse."

"So, all your half-siblings are criminals." I give him a playful smile. "I suppose being a perverted womanizer is not the worst thing you could be."

He chuckles. "Oh, shut up."

Our food is delivered a few minutes later, and we eat in silence. Before we hit the road again, we both change our clothes in an effort to feel a little better in our own skin. It's possible we'll make it to California tomorrow afternoon and will be able to find a location to shower and rest.

Last night, we pulled over at a rest area in Arizona and slept for three hours straight. Because of that delay, we are behind schedule. We're presently in California at a truck stop, awaiting our turns for the showers.

Once my turn arrives, I welcome the invigorating spray of hot water as it washes away days of sweat and grime. I don't like going so long between showers. I've selected a nice outfit to change into: indigo blue jeans, a sleeveless v-neck shirt and a classy cream-colored cotton blazer with contours that nicely accentuate my shape. The fact that I don't have a hair dryer means I'll have to let my hair air dry, which will cause it to go frizzy in this humidity. I can at least apply some makeup to blend away the fatigue under my eyes. I figure I should at least try to look nice when meeting with the Healers.

I leave the shower room and find Brand waiting for me in the lounge area. He has cleaned up nicely. He's shaved and is wearing a nice designer dress shirt and jeans . . . and he smells really good.

I have to shake my head and clear the cobwebs out. I need to think logically. We are about to meet with the only individuals besides Maetha and Clara Winter who know I have a diamond piece in my heart, and I need to be on my toes mentally. I can't communicate telepathically to alert them to the fact Brand doesn't know. I hope they'll keep that information confidential. More than anything, I hope they don't refer to me as a Runner, since Brand believes I'm a Healer.

The temptation to view my own future is over-whelming, especially since I can't view Brand's to see what will happen when we meet with the Healers. Maetha advised me not to look into my own future, so I don't. However, I'm having a hard time trusting her advice at the moment. "All will be well" is not much of a comfort, nor does it tell me what I can expect.

Maybe this is how Justin and Chris felt whenever I'd give them a vague answer for what the future held? The thought of *why* I didn't tell them the details doesn't bring me any comfort for what lies ahead. However, I do understand the future will most likely change if I view it, and if Maetha is telling the truth then I may put myself in danger if I try to look ahead.

I'm starting to doubt Maetha's intentions. Aside from recruiting me into a life of immortality against my will, she also used me as bait more than once. Although I'm still alive and now possess superpowers, I would be lying if I said I've been safe all this time. I don't know anything else about Maetha, other than she claims to be unbelievably old and has a habit of withholding important information. She never denied Freedom's accusations that she's deceptive. She also has more abilities, skills, and allies than she lets on.

What else isn't she telling me?

I try to shake off the suspicion that I'm being used as bait again. However, here I am, on the run from a rogue Diamond Bearer who apparently has friends in the CIA. I'm traveling with a guy whose superpower was created in a government lab, on our way to visit a clan of Healers for the first time—as per Maetha's vague instructions, but someday, after I get the full diamond, she and I are going to have a much longer chat about all this.

We travel north from Los Angeles to the Los Padres National Forest and follow the instructions Maetha gave to find the Healers' location. It comes as no surprise to find the large headquarters operating under the guise of a "spa for mind and body."

Brand parks the car and takes off his seatbelt. "How long are we going to stay here?"

"I'm not sure."

He unpins his Pulse Emitter and sets it in the cup between the seats. He says, "When it gets closer to sunset, if we're still here, I'll come get this. The lady at the desk is overly curious about it."

I point to the building. "The lady at the desk?"

"Yeah. Let's go."

"You repeated?"

"Duh."

I clear my throat and take off my seatbelt. We both get out of the car.

We approach the building, stepping aside as two people exit the front doors. I feel inside their minds and determine they aren't Healers, but regular humans who just attended their spa appointments.

Inside the foyer, a young woman greets us at the reception desk. "Hello. Are you here for an appointment?" She must be the one who took an interest in Brand's Pulse Emitter . . . or would have taken an interest.

"No," I say. "I'd like to visit with Andrew Stuart if he's available."

The woman stares motionlessly for a moment, then walks to a door behind the desk and opens it. She stands half-way in the doorframe, with her face out of view, talking to someone else. I listen with my intensified hearing.

"Someone is here to see Andrew. I think she's the girl who carried the diamond to the Death Clan. What was her name?"

Another female voice says, "Calli Courtnae? Are you certain?"

"Yes."

The door opens more and a short older woman with a round waist and warm, caring eyes steps out with the receptionist. "Calli Courtnae. So good to see you again. Do you remember me?"

"Sorry, no."

"I'm Maria Madrid. I helped you when you were injured—"

I cut her off so she won't mention the diamond in

front of Brand. I pretend to recognize her. "Oh, hello! How are you, Maria?"

"Good, good."

Her eyes travel to my chest and her thoughts reveal she's about to ask about the diamond. I hurry and say before she speaks, "I want to thank you for your discretion about my injury. I'd like to see Andrew Stuart, please."

"He's under heavy security. Excuse me while I call him." She picks up the phone on the desk and presses a button.

Brand thumbs through a services flyer while we wait. "Hey, I think I'd like this vetiver and quillaja body soak." He shows me the picture.

"Right. Like you'd actually sit in a tub of oily juice for more than two minutes."

Maria hangs up the phone. "Andrew would like you both to join us for dinner, after which he'll see you, Calli."

"Excellent. We look forward to meeting him," I say.

"My apologies, but only you will be allowed to see him. Your friend will have to wait."

"That won't do. My *bodyguard* doesn't leave my side, not since the abductions. If that's unacceptable, then I will have to decline Mr. Stuart's invitation."

She nods. "I see. Come with me and I'll get you seated for dinner. Then I'll talk with Andrew again."

"Bodyguard?" Brand whispers in my ear. "I like that."

We follow her through the door behind the desk, leading to the "staff" area of the building. The hallway is not unlike the Runners' compound. I assume the different doors on each side of the hall lead to private rooms.

"How many Healers live here, Maria?"

"Several dozen. We operate the spa as an income source. As long as we provide our customers with an enjoyable, de-stressing environment, they keep coming back."

We enter a large dining room with a buffet table full of food—real food. Not many other people are in the room. Maria introduces us to a couple nearby Healers. Brand is referred to as "Calli Courtnae's friend." I can tell that bugs him a little because he corrects Maria each time with the title of bodyguard.

After we dish up plates of food, we sit with the Healers. Brand leans close to me and asks, "Everyone knows you, it seems. But that only makes sense because you're one of them."

"Uh, yeah."

"What is the injury they all talk about?"

They all? Has he repeated again after having conversations about me? I say, "I'll tell you later in private."

Maria excuses herself. Her mind reveals she is going to talk to Andrew about my wishes to have Brand accompany me. I feel a little unsettled deep in my gut. Maetha has referred to her "gut instinct" leading her many times, and I have to wonder if my gut is trying to tell me something. The other Healers at the table are engaged in polite conversation with Brand. No one asks about his powers, and no one questions our visit. Then I realize Brand is controlling the conversation by steering it away from his abilities. I chuckle and shake my head a little.

Brand sends one of his trademark dimpled smiles my way in acknowledgement of my suspicions.

Maria returns hastily to the table, but instead of talking to us, she walks to the oldest member and whispers something in his ear. He quickly stands and motions to two other men to follow him. They move to the doorway and have a hushed conversation. I read their lips and minds and gather that a trio of Runners is headed our way to offer further protection to the Healers' amulet wearer, due to the fact that the Runners' leader was abducted yesterday.

Clara's been abducted too? How this could have happened when Runners are able to evade capture?

The Healers discuss the topic as old news, obviously having heard about it yesterday. One Healer mocks the offer, saying, "The Runners were unsuccessful in protecting their own amulet. What do they think they'll be able to do here?" Maria relays a message from Andrew Stuart that involves Brand and I being brought to him. A couple of Healers protest the action, but in the end the decision is made to allow us entrance.

Brand and I are ushered by Maria to a well-fortified section of the building protected by a large, steel door similar to a bank vault. Two armed guards wearing body armor stand on either side, and each one has a holstered handgun. Their minds reveal they are Healers who train new recruits for violent encounters, but have been repurposed to guard Mr. Stuart since the abductions.

One of them looks at me and speaks in a smooth, low tone. "You may want to be careful with how you use your powers, Ms. Courtnae. Some of us know how to tell when we're being *observed*." He turns to Brand next, looks him up and down, and raises an eyebrow. "What kind of bodyguard carries no weapons?"

"Are you doubting the firepower of *these* guns?" Brand flexes his muscles in a dramatic pose. Brand has definitely packed on mass since high school—mass that he's now showing off. He points to his temple. "My protection comes from here."

The guard suppresses a laugh, and drops the subject. The other guard opens the massive door to Andrew's windowless private office. Andrew sits behind his desk, flanked by Robert Yates on one side, and another Healer I haven't met before on the other. Maria leads us to the desk.

"Welcome, Calli." Andrew reaches forward and shakes

my hand, then turns his head to Brand.

I say, "Mr. Stewart, this is Brand Safferson. He's a new person with powers, and the best bodyguard money can buy. Brand, this is Andrew Stewart, the leader of the Healers' Clan."

Andrew interrupts. "I apologize, Calli. We have a situation that must be addressed first before simple conversation can take place. Are you aware the Runners' amulet wearer was abducted yesterday?"

"Oh no! Ms. Winter has been taken?" I try to act distressed.

Andrew continues. "A trio of Runners is on the way here to give further protection to our clan, however, I cannot discern what the future holds. Truth be told, I'm not very good at looking into the future with this thing." He points to the amulet around his neck. "I think you should wear the amulet, Calli. With your combined powers and prior experience, perhaps you can shed some light on the future."

"You want me to wear your amulet?" *Can I even do that? Will it break from its casing if it gets too close to my shard? Another thought enters my mind: what if this is how I will end up with all the shards, by having them enter my heart one piece at a time?*

Andrew grasps the leather cord that holds the amulet and pulls it up over his head. "I relinquish my amulet to you," he says. He extends his hand forward, and I take his offering. The diamond shard begins spinning wildly within the glass as I slowly pull it closer and closer to my body. My chest begins to pain me greatly as the diamond shifts within me, and I pull the leather cord over my head and wait for the fireworks to begin. Immediately the amulet clamps onto my skin and the spinning diamond halts within the glass. I feel pressure inside my chest, probably due to the diamond shards pulling on each other.

Brand's gaze is glued to the free-floating diamond. "What is that, Calli?"

I have to remind myself that he knows nothing about the diamond. I keep waiting for something to happen with the diamond shard, but the longer I wait, the more I realize nothing spectacular is going to occur.

Robert Yates says, "Well, what do you see?"

Admittedly let down, I say, "Nothing yet."

He continues. "I believe the Hunters are responsible for this. They are systematically kidnapping the amulet wearers. It was a mistake for the witch to give the Hunters an amulet because it enhanced their senses to a point that no one can hide from them, plus it gave them all the other powers too. They are most likely trying to reassemble the whole diamond, and they won't stop until they have *all* the pieces."

I think Robert is implying that because I have a shard within me, they'll be after me too. I look for the future of the diamond shards and find Justin Macintyre's face filling my mind. Of course! I'd had the vision of Justin heading up a group and being the next evil force to be reckoned with. I choose my words carefully. "Robert, the Hunters aren't the ones stealing the amulets."

Robert pauses and puts his hand up to his forehead. He leans back in his seat and shakes his head. He looks like he's having a hard time keeping focused.

"Ms. Courtnae," Maria says, "If the Hunters aren't doing this, then who is? Are you able to see the future clearer than Andrew?" She turns her head toward the men just in time to see Robert lean forward, putting his elbows on his knees with his head in his hands. She says, "Robert. You're unwell?"

"Just a little dizzy, Maria."

Andrew puts his hand to his head, too. "I'm dizzy as well."

"I will heal you." Maria moves closer to the men and places a hand on each forehead. "Did you take some medication, Robert? A sedative?"

"No. Why would I take anything?"

"I detect similar substances in your blood, Andrew." Maria says, alarm is evident in her voice.

Robert passes out and begins sliding from his chair. I rush over and catch him before he hits his head. I look up at Andrew, who is struggling to keep his eyes open, and I notice Maria is wobbling back and forth.

Brand speaks through short, quick breaths. "I think we've been drugged. I'm dizzy too."

I search Brand's body with my mind and find some sort of sedative coursing through his veins. A quick scan of my own body reveals I've also been drugged. *But how? Why didn't I detect it?* The room spins around and around. I hear Maria call for the guards, but her voice dims into nothingness. I'm not sure if I'm dizzy like everyone else or if Brand is repeating.

The room stops whirling around after Brand repeats us back to the point where I've just accepted the amulet and have put it on. Brand is staring, slack-jawed, at the amulet. His eyes meet mine and I expect him to ask me about it. Instead he grabs my shoulders and says, "What do we do? I can't repeat far enough to prevent the drugging. I don't want to pass out here!"

Andrew steps forward. "What is he talking about?" Perhaps Andrew is second guessing his decision to give me the amulet.

Brand's voice squeaks as he says, "We have to leave now, Calli."

Chapter 12 – The Amulet Thief

"You're not leaving with our amulet." Robert lunges forward from his chair. He's apparently not dizzy yet.

"Guards!" Maria shouts.

I turn to Brand. "Repeat."

We spin back to where I've just accepted the amulet from Andrew. The others in the room have no idea what's about to hit them. They're waiting to hear my assessment of the future.

Brand moves back and forth in his spot as if he desperately needs to use the bathroom. "Calli, come on. We can't stay here. The clock is ticking."

The three Healers look at us curiously. I rest my hand on Brand's arm. "Hang on a moment. I want to try to help." Then I announce to the others, "We've all been drugged. You need to heal one another before you pass out."

"What are you talking about?" Maria asks.

I point to Robert who already has his hand up to his head. "The drug is taking effect. You must hurry and heal each other before you all pass out in two minutes."

"She's right." Andrew says, rubbing his head. "I'm dizzy too."

Maria moves to the men and places a hand on each forehead. "It's only a sedative, not poison. At worst, we'll have to sleep it off." Maria continues to administer her power to the two men, who then use their power on her to remove the drug.

I turn to Brand. "Hold still for a second." I place my hand on his stomach, feel for the sedative leaking into his blood, and will the substance to travel back the way it came. I follow it along with my hand, traveling up his chest and throat, until a tiny drop of clear liquid floats out of his mouth and drops to the ground. As I focus on reversing the course of the sedative in my own body, I notice the Healers are still working on each other. I realize their power works much slower than mine does.

Brand says, "We've passed the two minute mark."

"Who did this?" Andrew asks.

Robert follows up with, "Why did this happen now?"

Maria looks my body over and says, "Why can't I feel your body, Calli? Were you even drugged like the rest of us?"

I don't like her accusatory tone and what she's implying. "You asked me to look to the future. I did and saw you three were about to pass out. While you healed them, I healed myself and Brand."

Maria points her finger my direction. "It's all too coincidental that you two arrive and everyone gets sick. Guards!" The heavy door creeks open and Justin Macintyre storms into the room with a gun in his hand. I see the two guards lying unconscious on the ground outside. The whole room falls silent.

He looks at me and does a double take. "Calli? What are you doing here?" I don't answer him. He turns to the Healers. "I'm only here for the amulet wearer. Surrender and no one gets hurt."

I step forward. "I'm wearing their amulet. Take me."

"Easy enough," Justin says, grabbing my arm. He pulls the trigger three times, shooting all of the Healers in a single effort. Then he points the gun at Brand.

"Repeat!" I yell at Brand.

The room stops spinning this time just after I tell the Healers they have been drugged and to heal each other. It's clear that if we remain here, these three people will definitely die. Brand and I will have to run away with the amulet and hopefully Justin won't kill them. I don't take the time to look to their futures. I turn to Brand, who seems to be awaiting my order. "Hold my hand and run with me as fast as you can."

"Gotcha." He takes my hand and we turn toward the door.

Maria shouts behind us, "Guards!" The door opens and one of the guards falls through, landing flat on his face. I pause expecting to see Justin. Instead I see the other guard struggling to remain upright, fumbling on the grip of his gun. Justin is nowhere in sight . . . yet. The guard slurs for me to stop, but stumbles backward into the wall and slides down.

I tighten my hold on Brand's hand and run as fast as we can through the building to the nearest exit. The halls and doors fly past us in a blur, and I have to yell for everyone to get out of the way as we run past them. At one point I think I see Justin across a room, but I don't slow down to confirm. We exit the building and I pour on the speed, unleashing as much Runner's power as I think poor Brand can withstand. We run for only about a minute, then stop somewhere in the surrounding forest.

I let go of Brand's hand, and he takes a step away from me in shock, struggling to keep his balance.

"What was that, Calli? How did you run so fast? How did I?" Brand's total confusion is compounded by the sedative taking effect. He stumbles over an exposed root and lands on his backside.

I point to the amulet. "All the cosmic powers are in this diamond."

"Even healing?"

"Yes."

Sitting on the ground, he rubs his head. "Heal yourself, Calli. Then me."

I feel inside his body and find the foreign substance. He tries to get up but falls to his knees as I try to extract the drug from his bloodstream. My own body begins to slow down as the drug takes effect.

Everything begins to spin. Brand pulls me with him as he repeats back to when we stopped running in the forest.

"Dammit, Calli, heal yourself first, not me!" he barks, before the drug takes full effect again. He sits on the ground, arms wrapped around his knees.

I feel inside my body and find the substance placed in the food we ate for dinner. I will it out in the same manner as I did in Andrew Stuart's office a few minutes ago, before we repeated and ran away. As I finish pulling the sedative out of my body, Brand passes out and crumples to the ground.

Justin arrives in a whoosh of air. He aims the gun he used—or would have used—on the Healers at me. I can smell his unwashed body and see his beard growth of several days, both of which reveal his exhaustion. "Well, well, well. Calli Courtnae. I thought that was you I saw fly through the building. You grew up. Not a little teenie-bopper anymore, are you? No, you're a grown woman."

"Likewise, Justin. You grew up, too—into an even bigger jackass."

"You're mouth hasn't changed a bit."

"Neither has your intellect."

"You're pretty daring to talk to me like that." He waves his gun slightly. "You might want to watch your tongue." Justin walks to me and stands close. "It's so kind of the clans to let you have an honorary place. What with losing all your powers after the diamond exploded, you must envy everyone instead of the other way around." His eyes travel down to my neck and focus on the amulet. "Well, isn't that nice, they let you wear the shard. This must be the source of your bravery. How does it feel to have its power once again?"

"It's almost as if I never lost it." My snide remark makes his eyebrows lower. Despite my powers, my heart still thumps with anticipation, and I stand at the ready to deflect or cause injury in order to protect myself and Brand.

As luck would have it, I'm now Brand's bodyguard.

Justin reaches forward and longingly strokes the leather cord near my collarbone, twisting it between his fingers. His eyes focus on the floating diamond within the bulb, resting against the exposed skin on my chest. Now would be a good opportunity to disarm him with a snap kick, but Justin is an experienced Runner, the *fastest* of the clan. I don't dare make a move unless I can take him by surprise. His voice drops to a throaty, wolf-like growl. "You *will* give me the amulet, Calli."

"Why don't you just take it?"

He steps back and launches into an accusatory tone. "You're trying to trick me the way Maetha tricked the Death Clan. If I take it from you I'll die. That's why the Death Clan died. She didn't tell them everything."

"You sound as if you know someone who knows more than Maetha."

"What's the matter? Can't you read my mind?" he pokes at his temple.

As a matter of fact I *can* read his mind with the amulet and he knows it. I just can't see who gave him the misinformation about the amulets, and he seems to know that too. His mind is locked up tight, and not even my diamond shard can pierce through his mental barriers concerning the subject. I wonder why Justin's informant didn't tell him all he has to do is kill the Bearer and the amulet will be his.

Perhaps Justin's puppeteer doesn't want him to kill anyone, or maybe they don't want him to hold any of the amulets. Perhaps his future will show me why.

An impish grin spreads over his face. "What's wrong, muck? I heard you could read *anyone's* mind while wearing an amulet. I can feel you inside my head, but *you*—the all-powerful Calli Courtnae—can't get through my blocking ability. How pathetic!" He forces a mocking laugh.

His future shows a pretty clear image: the amulet shards sticking out of a bloody hole in his chest, his lifeless body lying on a dark, dirty, cement floor, and a puddle of crimson blood oozing out of his chest wound. Without an amulet he cannot see his own future, or else he would know that he's being played like the gullible fool he is—but by whom?

I match his grin with an evil smile of my own. "You're right, I can't read *all* minds. The future, however, is *very* clear to me."

His grin returns to a scowl as he raises one eyebrow. "What do you see?"

"As if you'd believe anything I have to say."

"Humor me."

"You're going to die."

"Mmm hmm."

I add, "You're obviously meant to be the gatherer so your master can steal them from you at the last minute."

"Now I *know* you're lying! The amulets will kill him if he tries to take them away from me."

"So your master is a man. Does he have a name? Is it

Freedom?"

Justin's eyebrows scrunch together. "What are you babbling about? You'll have to get past my mind blocks to learn his name, and, as we both know, you're just a muck with a magical amulet." As he speaks, the name of his master slips through his mind block and into the front of his thoughts: *Agent Alpha.* The name is not familiar to me. He turns and looks at Brand, keeping the gun trained on me. He asks, "What's this guy's deal? Is he a new Healer?"

"No, he's with me. We were visiting the clan." Justin points the gun at Brand. I shout, "Wait, don't kill him!"

"He's a witness, and I don't need him."

"If you kill him, I will *never* give you the amulet."

A creepy grin spreads across his face. "Is he your *boyfriend?"*

"No, but he's my friend. Please don't kill him." Thinking back on Maetha's words about trying to lure out a bigger threat, I decide I'll go peacefully with Justin in an effort to help further Maetha's plans. Who knows? Maybe I can help free the other three kidnapped victims. I put on my best "scared-to-death" face and let out a defeated sigh. "Look, I will come with you, just *please* don't hurt him. He means a lot to me."

"Well, then. He's coming with us. If you try to harm me, Calli, the boyfriend gets it." Justin hoists Brand's bulky body over his shoulder, then retrains the gun on me.

I haven't seen Brand fight a Runner yet, but watching Justin clutch his family jewels after meeting Brand's signature "nutcracker-kick" is something I would like to see.

Justin says, "There's a black van two miles down the road. Let's go."

We run to the van, and Justin dumps Brand in the back. He then ties a blindfold on my head and cuffs my hands behind my back.

"You know, Justin, I already know where you're taking me. Is the blindfold really necessary?"

"Yep. If you can't see me, you can't read my mind or harm me." Justin directs me into the back of the van and then he closes the door.

Years ago in the hotel room when I tortured him by making his stomach revolt, I discovered I didn't need to be looking at a person to continue feeling their body. I only needed eye contact once, and then I could maintain the link to the body. This situation isn't any different. I remember a few months ago when I was learning about brain disorders that epileptic seizures occur when both halves of the brain fire off at the same time. Feeling into his body, I realize that I could easily cause one right here, right now, and if I hold on to it long enough I could kill him. However, I'm not going to harm Justin. I know there's more behind this situation, the man named Agent Alpha is feeding Justin misinformation, trying to reunite the shards by taking advantage of his stupidity, and I need to find out why.

A young, stern, female voice sounds from outside. "Where's my payment?"

"We're not done yet."

"I delivered you the amulet wearer, and now you pay me. That was the contract *you* agreed to when you hired me."

"Technically, you didn't capture this amulet."

"What the—what do you mean?" Her voice rises to an aggravated shout. "If I hadn't put that powder in the food, you wouldn't have been able to get the amulet!"

"Yeah, I got this amulet, not you." Justin sounds irritated.

I hear a scuffle and someone's body slam against the van, probably Justin's. The female speaks in a quieter voice.

I imagine her face is close to Justin's. "Your job was *easy* because of me, and if you can't appreciate that," I hear what sounds like a switchblade opening, "then I'll take my payment out of your *skin*, strip by pale strip! So what's it gonna be?"

Justin's quivering voice mumbles, "Fine." I feel the van rock back as Justin's body pulls away. I hear more fumbling and the sound of rumpled paper. Justin clears his throat and says, "Bring the next one to my facility."

She huffs and says, "Moron." Her footsteps walk away from the car, and then stop. She shouts back at Justin, "Oh, and if you *dare* try to change the terms of my contract again," something metallic hits the van and Justin lets out a high-pitched squeal laced with curse words, "I'll do to you what I did to the Runner." She laughs a spine-tingling cackle as she walks away.

A long, tense silence follows as the mysterious woman's footsteps fade away into the distance. My Hunter's abilities sense Justin standing beside the van, and a pungent smell of sweat mixed with some other odor enters my nose. My intuition tells me it's the smell of fear, or so I'd like to think. He lets out a slow, deep, shaky breath, and yanks out a metallic object stuck in the van's exterior wall. I realize the object is the switchblade. She must have thrown it at him with such force that it *stuck* in the side of the van!

Who is this woman?

I hear him fumbling through some sort of box containing glass jars. He's quiet for a second, then he climbs in the van, starts the engine, and begins driving.

I lean back against the wall and decide now would be a good time to practice the meditation that Maetha insisted I learn and make routine. It's a good call too, because we drive for what seems like an eternity. I manage to calm and empty my mind during this time, trying to focus on staying cool and letting the future play out as Maetha foresaw. I remember what she told me about the diamond shards coming back together through a series of coincidences. Being in the same place and time as Justin is more than just a coincidence.

It must be fate.

When the door finally opens, I listen to several male voices as they discuss who will carry Brand's body inside and which cell to put him in. Justin orders two men to help me out of the van and then instructs them to take me to my cell.

Still blindfolded, I stumble a bit even though the guards hold onto my elbows. I hear a rusty metal door screech open, and we enter a building with a heavy musty smell. We walk for a little while, turn a couple of corners, and then they let go of my elbows and push me into a room.

My blindfold is removed by one of the guards right before they shut the metal door.

The room is mostly dark, with a concrete floor and stony-grey brick walls. A medium-sized wire-mesh window on the western wall allows a beam of orange light from the setting sun to illuminate the room. Aside from a decrepit, rusty, sorry excuse for a bed below the window, there is nothing else of interest in this room.

Justin speaks through an intercom. "A key to your handcuffs is on the bed. Remove your cuffs and set them down on the floor by the door's pass-through slot."

"Where's Brand?" I ask as I fumble awkwardly with the key, trying to unlock my cuffs behind my back. I set the cuffs and key down on the floor by the little sliding door. I figure my food will be pushed through this door as well, just like a prisoner's food would be in jail.

"Who?"

"The guy you carried to the van."

"He's safe, as you asked."

"You'll have to prove it, or I won't give you the amulet."

"I'm not in a rush to get that off you just yet. I still need the Hunters' shard and the final piece. Tell me, where can I find Maetha the witch?"

"I don't know. She doesn't really have a location if you know what I mean."

"No, I don't know what you mean."

"Why don't you have that ornery girl find Maetha for you?"

Justin slides the small door to the side and grabs my cuffs and key while muttering curse words under his breath, then slams the door closed. I notice other aspects of the main door: the hinges are on the outside, the door handle locks on the outside, and a dead-bolt has been installed for added security. The shiny metal of the door indicates it was installed recently, and intended to prevent anyone from kicking it down.

I listen as Justin's footsteps fade away from my door and down the hall. The sound of the ocean outside my window draws me in its direction. I walk to the window and find I'm able to open it two inches before the blocking mechanism stops it—fresh air, at least. The vantage point out the window is limited, mainly I just see ocean about a hundred feet directly below, and I conclude the prison is built on a sheer cliff. Escaping from the window is not an option.

I sit on my rock-hard bed and ponder my situation. I

wish I had a way to communicate with Maetha. I cross my legs and relax, taking deep, calming breaths, and clearing my mind of any intrusive thoughts. Perhaps I can contact Maetha through the diamond's power, like the day I fell into the river and Chris rescued me. I have no idea if this would work, but it's worth a try.

I hear a gentle tapping outside the window. I open my eyes and realize I fell asleep against the cold, hard, brick wall. I get up on the bed to look out the window and I can't believe what I see: Brand is clinging to the exterior of the building, a smile on his face.

"Brand!"

"Yeah."

"How did you . . . what are you holding onto out there?"

"Well, not much, to be honest. It took me a long time to find the weak bricks around my window that would allow me to escape. I can tell you there's no way into your cell from out here."

"Be careful, Brand. Go back to your room and figure out some other way to get Justin to open your door."

"You talk as if I'm the cleverest guy on earth, yet I still can't figure out how to get you to go out with me."

"Brand!"

"All right. It's not like I have anything else to do," he mutters as he moves along the wall to his window. "Go wait in your cell, *Brand*. Go save the world, *Brand*."

I sit back and wait for him to come to my door, knowing he'll manage somehow.

I hear Justin talking outside my door as he walks down the hall. Justin starts shouting at Brand, but I can't tell what's being said. Then I hear footsteps near my door and Justin's voice on my intercom. He sounds irritated.

"Calli, I know I told you I'd keep your friend alive, but he's trying to jump to his death from his window. I really don't care if he does or not, but—"

I can hear background yelling over the intercom as Justin speaks. Brand is yelling, quite convincingly, "Don't come any closer or I'll jump!"

A light bulb clicks on in my head. Brand is putting his Performing Arts major to good use. I decide to play along. "No! Don't let him jump!" I plead, faking a catch in my throat to sound like I'm crying. "I've worked *so* hard to convince him that suicide is not the answer, until *you* kidnapped us! I swear if he dies because of the stress you are putting him through, you'll *never* get the amulet from me. Do you hear me?"

"Hey, it's not my fault if he jumps."

I plead some more. "Let me go talk to him. Come on, Justin. He'll listen to me."

"No way. I'm not bringing you out until I absolutely have to. I'll tell him you want to talk to him. Maybe that will get him back inside."

I hear some noise and what sounds like pleading, then footsteps outside my door. I can hear Brand saying through tears aplenty, "You said I could see Calli! Where's Calli? I need to see my *Cal-Cal!*"

I resist the urge to laugh at his improvised pet name.

Justin answers, "Shut up you big baby! Keep walking."

Their footsteps and Brand's weeping fade out of earshot. A couple of long, silent minutes go by. I pace my floor in fear and frustration, feeling helpless, worried about Brand. Then the lock on my door clicks and the door slowly opens. I hold my breath, not knowing who is entering until I see Brand's head poke around the door. He enters my cell, sans shirt.

I let out a relieved burst of air, rush forward, and give him a hug. He wraps his arms around me and hugs me back. He says, "Hey there, Cal-Cal. Miss me?"

I push him back and regain my composure. "Like the plague. Where's Justin?"

"He's a little tied up at the moment."

"What happened to your shirt?"

"It's a little tied up at the moment."

"What did you do?"

"Does it really matter? Let's get out of here while we can."

"Not yet. We have to rescue the others."

"Who? What are you talking about?"

"The other amulet wearers from the other clans are here too. We have to find them."

"They're in the other locked rooms down this hall. Come on! We need to hurry before the guards show up." Brand pulls on my hand, leading me down the hallway.

My Hunter's smell detects the unique scent of Charles Rhondell from the Readers' Clan behind one of the doors. "I found one," I whisper. Brand pulls out a set of keys, which I assume were stolen from Justin, and hands me one key. He hurries forward toward another door. I unlock the door in front of me and find Charles sitting on his bed, looking surprised to see me. I motion with my hand for him to follow, and he immediately stands and joins us in silence.

Brand opens the next door down the hall, and Curtis Shultz from the Seers' Clan exits the cell. Curtis walks briskly toward Charles about to embrace him in a hug.

I raise my hands to signal them to stop moving while keeping my voice low. "No. Don't. If your amulets touch, you might die." I turn to Brand and say, "There's got to be one more person: Clara Winter, the Runners' leader."

"Over there." Brand points to the last door at the end of the hall.

Brand opens the door and I rush past him into the room, expecting to smell Clara's scent. The room is much smaller than the others, and the bed looks more like a hospital bed than the uncomfortable cots in the other rooms. The scent that reaches my nose confuses me because it's familiar—and definitely not Clara's.

I can't believe my eyes! Chris Harding, *not Clara Winter,* lies in the bed with his wrists tied to the bed rails. I stand still, frozen in awe of the moment. I step into the light and walk to his bedside. Both of his legs are angled in unnatural directions, obviously broken. He looks extremely weak as he opens his eyes and blinks to clear his vision. I figure he must have arrived here only a few hours ago.

He sees me and his lips move, but no sound comes out. His lips form the words "my legs" as his eyes look down the bed toward his feet. He lays his head back, taking a deep, painful breath and a weak smile spreads across his face.

I place my hands on his legs as gently as possible and send numbing energy to help with the pain before I begin the healing process. A buzzing sensation, originating from the shard in my heart and the amulet around my neck, races through my whole body. I slide my hands up and down his legs, one at a time, channeling my energy into them. I feel the tiny bone shards and fragments under my fingertips as they slide out of the surrounding skin and muscle tissue and go back into place. Piece by piece, his legs straighten back into their natural form.

My own physical energy drains from my body as I send more healing energy into him. By the time his legs are fully repaired, my own legs are feeling wobbly and my head is starting to spin. I recall after healing Brand's Demon attack how my body wasn't as drained as it is now. *Why is this so different?*

I bring my attention to his face and behold his astonished expression. He is now wide awake, his eyes focused on mine. I carefully lean down, hold my amulet to my chest with my right hand, and press my cheek against his as I wrap my left arm across his body. I inhale his unique scent. I'd forgotten how good he smells.

"I knew you'd come, Calli," Chris whispers in my ear.

My whole body shivers. The vision has come true.

"You're very weak," I say, pulling my head back and meeting his delirious gaze.

"I feel much better now." He smiles up at me.

"How long have you been here?"

"I'm not sure. They knocked me out with drugs. I knew you'd come, Calli, but I still don't believe you're here or that you healed me. I feel like I'm in a dream." His eyes wander to my neck. "You're wearing an amulet, I see. That's how you were able to fix my legs." He touches his amulet. "I tried to heal myself, but all I could do was dull the pain. I don't know how to use all the powers."

I slide my arm behind his neck and shoulders to help him sit up. "Come on, I've got you." I help him sit up and turn my head to the doorway where Brand waits, amazement etched across his face. He must have witnessed the healing abilities I just used on Chris. I ask, "Can you help me, Brand?"

Brand nods and comes around to Chris's other side. Chris, still weak from the drugs, wraps his arms over our shoulders and stands. He catches his balance and turns to look at me. A warm smile spreads over his face as he looks down at his now-functional legs. I sense infinite gratitude on the surface of his thoughts, and his feelings for me now blaze in his mind like a forest fire.

Once we're out in the hall, I notice the others are also a little worse for wear. Charles and Curtis are weakened from the lack of food, the continual drugging, and the inexperience with healing themselves. I used all my excess energy to heal Chris's legs, so I don't feel it's wise to weaken myself any further by increasing their strength. Charles and Curtis will have to hang onto each other, while I hold onto Chris.

"We have to hurry," Brand says, rather frazzled. "It's not easy getting past the guards. Follow my lead, and don't make a sound."

I figure he must be repeating and knows we are about to be discovered. Brand takes point, and we follow close behind him. We hurry down the hall and Brand holds his arm up for us to stop just before the corner. He motions for us to stand against the wall. I assume there must be a guard approaching, and I strain my hearing for any sound of footsteps.

My back is toward a closed door, and through my increased senses I can hear a muffled voice on the other side. At first I wonder if it's the Hunter's amulet wearer, but the more I listen to the person's voice the more I realize Justin is behind the door. He sounds as if he's gagged. I think I figured out what happened to Brand's missing shirt.

We hear footsteps coming closer from around the corner, and I watch Brand bob his head in time with each step, counting and plotting his attack. The moment the tip of the guard's boot comes into view, Brand leaps forward and punches his fist directly into the unsuspecting guard's temple, taking him down with one single and quite impressive hit. In a swift motion, Brand wraps his arms around the guard before he falls and slowly lowers him to the floor without making a sound.

Charles' weary eyes pop open as he mumbles beneath his breath. "Whoa . . . That was *perfect.*" I wonder how many repeats Brand had to do to achieve perfection.

We round the corner and proceed down the next hall, taking care not to make any noise with our footsteps. Brand puts his hand up again to bring us to a halt and motions us up against the wall again. As we stand in silence, I listen to the surrounding sounds: the buzzing of the fluorescent light above our heads, the flush of a toilet in a nearby room, and the casual whistling of a man who's just finished his business.

The door beside Brand opens, revealing a guard wearing body armor and a handgun. In a swift and flawless attack Brand delivers a groin kick followed by an uppercut to the jaw that knocks the guard out cold. Again, his arms move fast to catch the guard's body before it falls to the ground. This guard is fully equipped with body armor and a handgun. We wait in tense silence while Brand drags the guard back into the bathroom and comes out a minute later tying on the guard's belt, containing the handgun and two extra magazines of ammo.

Charles says to Brand, "Wait, why didn't you put the armor on?"

Brand shakes his head. "I don't need it."

Charles raises an eyebrow and whispers, "Can you dodge bullets or something?"

"Or something." Brand starts walking with the gun tight in his grip, aimed at the floor.

Chris whispers in my ear, "Where did you find this guy?"

I quickly glance up at Chris while squeezing his hand that's draped over my shoulder, hoping he doesn't expect an answer right at the moment.

Brand points down the hall to the exit and says, "There's one more outside the door. Let's go."

The solid door at the end of the hallway has no windows. I know the others must be wondering how Brand can tell what's on the other side, but no one speaks up. We approach the door, come to a halt, and watch as Brand pulls out the handgun and bobs his head in rhythm again. Without looking, he kicks open the door and rams the butt of the gun out around the doorframe, dropping the last guard with a lightning-fast pistol-whip.

Curtis can't contain his curiosity any longer. "All right, young man, what kind of power do you possess?"

"No time right now. We have to get to a safer place." Brand bends down and removes the guard's jacket and long rifle. After putting on the jacket, Brand looks like a military man with his AK-47 and all. He says, "We only have about an hour before the Demons will be out, and we need to find a safe place to hide."

I look over at Brand. "Too bad you don't have your Pulse Emitter?"

"I really wish I'd left it on, believe me." He starts walking and motions for us to follow.

I glance into the future to see if I'll be able to determine where we should hide, but all I can foresee is the interior of a building and the five of us huddled around the dim embers of a fire. I suppose that's better than watching everyone get mauled by Shadow Demons.

The sun hangs low on the horizon, just above the ocean, casting an amazing array of orange, red, and yellow colors on the cloudless sky and the calm waters below it. The scene fills me with a sense of victory and hope.

We appear to be at an abandoned wharf or dock of a closed-up factory of some kind. We hurry as fast as our weakened legs will take us, running toward other buildings.

We stay in the shadows as we move along looking for a place to hide for the night. The Demons have not yet come out, and I can't smell them yet, either. Charles and Curtis are able to move quicker thanks to the power of the amulets, but they are still weak from the sedatives in their bodies and have difficulty maintaining their balance.

As the others talk about potential solutions of where to hide, I try to determine where we are. We are definitely on the west coast, judging by the fact that the sun is setting over the ocean, and probably still in California. Oregon would be more forested, I think.

We arrive outside of a smaller building with shattered windows. I leave Chris and follow Charles inside. I can tell right away this will be our hideout—it's the room I've already seen.

The others enter the building, and as a team we use old cardboard we find in one of the rooms to cover the windows. Curtis finds a bag of grilling charcoal that we can use as a heat source, but we have nothing to light it with. I decide I will need to leave and find some matches, food, and water for everyone.

Chapter 13 - Revelations

"I'm going to go find us some food and water," I announce. Chris is about to object, but I cut him off. "You and I know I'm the only one who can do this. I'll hurry back. Don't worry about the Demons. They won't enter the building, even if there's no light." I turn to Brand and say, "Will you tell everyone about our experiments with the Demons while I'm gone?"

"Yeah, but please hurry."

Curtis adds, "Matches. Don't forget matches."

I nod and leave the building.

The clothing I chose to wear today is not good running attire. I'll have to slow my pace. As I run toward the lights on the horizon, toward civilization, I realize I'll have to shoplift because I don't have any money, and this bothers me. I'm not a thief, yet my companions need nourishment, and I have no other way of providing it for them.

The first store I come upon is a small gas station and convenience store. I enter the busy store and pull a small shopping basket from the stack, then stroll through the aisles looking for the best nutrition choices. I settle on sports drinks, water, beef jerky, and assorted nuts and chocolate bars. I also grab a lighter, flashlight, and some batteries.

When a customer enters the store to pay for his gas, I

run out of the open door. I wonder what it will look like on the surveillance cameras—probably like a streak or a blur.

I pass a payphone as I run through the small town. Oh how I wish Maetha had a phone, I could sure use some support right now. Beth's mobile phone number pops into my head. She was right when she said it's easy to remember with all the sevens. Perhaps she can come and help. I place a collect call to her number. The phone rings long, agonizing tones, then Beth answers and is asked if she'll accept the call. She agrees.

"Beth, it's Calli. I need your help."

"Calli, where are you? Why did you steal the Healers' amulet?"

"Steal? Come on, Beth, you know me better than that. It's not what you think, but I don't have time to explain right now. I found the missing amulet wearers. Justin had them locked up, but Brand helped me break them out. Can you come help get them to safe place?"

"How can I believe that? The Healers said you took their amulet and ran."

"That's true, but their lives were in danger. Justin was about to kill them."

"I don't understand what you're trying to tell me, Calli. Tell me where you are so I can come with some council members and get this all sorted out. They want their leaders and amulets back."

"Council? I didn't know the clans had such a thing."

"A council was formed when the amulets started disappearing. The Healers alerted us about your abduction of their amulet. I'm here at their compound and I've been assigned to bring you in, along with Brand. Now, tell me where you are and I'll come first thing in the morning."

"No, I won't be doing that. I thought you were my friend, Beth."

"Let me come get you so we can get this all straightened out."

"I'll straighten it out on my own. Bye, Beth."

I end the call and begin my journey back to the others. I try to convince myself that Beth is only being a responsible leader. She's embracing life and justice, and right now the evidence shows I am on the wrong side of right. Besides, I'd already seen this day in her future when she would be chasing me.

Running with groceries isn't easy. The basket is heavy because of the drinks. If I stop too quickly, the contents of the basket fly out just like seatbelt-less crash test dummies.

It's a confirmation of the laws of physics.

Before returning to the others, I stop by Justin's compound and see him through a window talking to his injured guards. Now that I can see the guards, I sense they are Unaltered men. I wonder if Justin understands the advantage of having these men in his employ or if it's just a fluke. I'm betting Justin knows exactly why it's important to have Unaltered guards taking care of people with powers. And who's the one person who has access to "a dime a dozen" Unaltereds? Freedom.

I resist the urge to read Justin's mind to see if he's associated with Freedom. The last thing I need is Justin scratching his head realizing he's not alone. Using my increased hearing, I hear Justin say, "They won't move till morning. We'll capture them tomorrow."

"Why not now?" one of the guards asks.

"Because I said we'll do it tomorrow!" Justin's raised voice ends the conversation. I glance into his mind for a second and see he's concerned the guards might try to drag the amulet wearers out into the dark, accidentally killing them before they can relinquish their amulets.

I hurry back to the group.

The moment I close the door behind me, Chris is right there, waiting to embrace me tightly. Having his strong arms wrapped around me feels so good, but is short lived. A sharp pain rips through my chest. I push him away, drop the basket of groceries and clutch my chest. Did his amulet break? My eyes search his neck for the amulet. I can't see it.

"What is it, Calli?"

"Where's your amulet?"

He reaches around his neck and rotates the leather cord to the front. He'd twisted his amulet to his back for protection. "Charles and Curtis told me about your warning about the amulets touching. You don't look too good. Are you sick?"

"I'll be fine. Would you take the food to the others while I rest a moment?"

When he leaves, I slide down the wall and sit on the floor, willing my heart to heal. My mind replays Maetha's words that someday all the shards will reunite within me. But if this is the kind of pain I can expect, then no thanks.

Brand comes over to me and kneels down. "Calli, you and I need to talk."

I sense his brewing anger, and can tell something happened while I was gone—something that disturbs him greatly.

"What do you want to know?"

He points at my amulet. "Why didn't you ever tell me about your adventure with the diamond?"

"Ah, they told you about that, huh?"

"I thought you trusted me?"

"Brand, look, there's plenty I didn't tell you and there's plenty I'm not going to tell you. It doesn't mean I don't trust you. Now you know as much as everyone else concerning me and the diamond."

"Yeah," —he wrings his hands together— "and how

Maetha fits into all this. I just can't believe you kept that experience a secret from me after revealing you're a Healer."

"Um, I have some more explaining to do. But not yet."

Brand lets out a huff. "Of course not." He blows air out in exasperation. "So, the little diamond inside the necklace holds all five powers. What would happen if I wore one?"

I think about that intensely and come to the conclusion that if he wore an amulet he might be able to use his powers to manipulate outcomes on a much grander scale. Unfortunately, Brand is just beginning to use his power for better purposes, and until his heart is focused in the right direction, the power would most likely be misused.

"I don't know, Brand. The powers of the amulet are limited, and there's no lesson manual on how to access and use them. That's the reason why everyone else was caught so easily, despite having the ability to see the future or run away from danger. If a Seer isn't looking for that part of the future, then they will never see it coming. A Runner cannot see behind them, and a Reader's power can be blocked. Hunters have their weaknesses, and it won't be long until one of them is captured. Even you saw how the Healers didn't detect the sedatives in their food simply because they didn't bother to check. In fact, it was *you* who pointed it out, remember?"

"Yep."

"You don't need to see the future, read minds, run fast, heal your body, or smell your surroundings like everyone else. Your power is much stronger than all of ours combined, and far more useful. For now we need to help the others."

Chris is in the center of the large room, trying to light the charcoal. He uses crumpled paper and torn cardboard placed under the mound of briquettes in the hopes of them igniting. Good thing the floor is cement, and there's plenty of cross draft due to the broken windows to carry most of the smoke out of the building.

I walk over to Curtis and Charles who sit with their backs against the wall as they drink their sports drinks. "I can help heal you both if you like," I tell them. "I know you're both very weak, and I don't suppose you have enough energy to spare to heal each other."

"We don't want to drain yours, Calli," Charles says.

"I'll only give you what I can spare." I feel into Charles's body and rejuvenate his blood by increasing the oxygen. The drug Justin used is one that slows the body's natural system, so I cleanse Charles's body of the residue. Right away his energy increases. I do the same for Curtis and remove the drug from his body.

"Thank you, Calli," they both say in unison.

I smile and look across the room at Chris and Brand talking quietly as Chris feeds the growing flame with more cardboard. I read their lips and listen with my increased hearing.

Chris asks Brand, "Are you and Calli dating?"

Brand replies, "What? No. I can't say I haven't tried to win her over, but dude, her heart belongs to someone else."

A pleased smile spreads across Chris's face.

Curtis notices I'm watching Brand and Chris and asks, "Why is Brand's future so muddled?"

"What do you see?" I ask.

"Not much. Only enough to know he has a future. When someone is on their deathbed I see endings or nothing at all, so I know he's not going to die in the next month. With him, I see snippets and swirls. That's the best way to describe his future."

Charles adds, "Yes. I've never seen a mind like his before. There is nothing to read and everything to read. His mind shows possibilities as near as I can tell. Not necessarily specific actions."

"Brand's power is confusing, I know. I caution you to avoid looking too long into his mind. You'll get a serious headache."

I stand and walk over to Chris and Brand. I kneel next to Chris and take one of his hands in mine to feel inside his body for the invasive drug. I look into his blue eyes and he looks into mine.

Brand's mouth gapes open as he realizes what's going on. "*He's* your guy. He's Chris, isn't he? That explains your reaction when you found him."

I smile. "Yeah, and you better give us a moment before he kicks your ass." I hope he remembers the last time I said this to him. Brand jumps up and walks away, leaving us alone. My eyes meet Chris's. "I need to remove the last of the drug from your system. Just relax."

Chris closes his eyes, relaxing his whole body, allowing me access to his entire being. Frankly, I am caught off guard that he opens himself up so completely, with absolute trust. The intimate moment brings tears to my eyes: tears of joy and love. I pause for a moment to appreciate the circumstances of our reunion before I begin to extract the drug from his body.

The first thing I see in his mind is the vision Maetha had shown him concerning me. It's the exact same vision I saw when I peeked through the Healer's cabin window, looking for my own future, following the Death Clan's destruction.

Maetha told me future visions cannot be fabricated,

and with that knowledge I sit in awe of my new realization: Maetha also foresaw that Chris and I would end up together. By giving me the diamond, she saw to it the events would play out as needed to destroy the Death Clan. I imagine Maetha experimented with the future the same way I did when I tried to figure out how to save Chris. She must have tried over and over with different people, trying to discover who would be affected enough by seeing me in a vision as their "one and only," to help bring about the Death Clan's demise. Chris's mind was primed with the desire to find a companion to share his life with, so naturally when Maetha looked to see what his future would hold if I was given the diamond, she saw success.

Chris's memory of our vision ends, and I am thrown into his past, and he allows me to see his deepest secret, the one he guarded intensely when we transported the diamond—he's a spy, or at least he was. I see new memories that took place after we parted. Chris's resignation wasn't taken well. His father insulted and threatened him, ordering he remain with the government or else. Chris held firm to his decision to quit, feeling that his life had never been his own.

After resigning, Chris had to go into hiding while his father calmed down. I feel the intense depression he suffered during that time, a depression arising because he felt his future had been ripped away from him. Even if he wanted to pursue a relationship with me, he would have to wait until I aged a few years and hope I didn't fall in love with another man in the meantime.

His memories continue. Chris went back to the Runners compound, after many months of seclusion, and reentered the familiar lifestyle as an instructor. Deep down he hoped somehow, some way, his vision of me would come true, but in the meantime he would stay close to the clans in case any word of me came along. Much to the dismay of the female population at the compound, Chris remained single, vowing to allow enough time for me to grow up.

Moments ago, Brand told him how we met and how I had shown him the example of healing the knife-wound at Cedar Point. I feel his emotions and confusion. I recognize he's putting his thoughts forward for me to read.

Calli, how did you heal Brand? I thought you lost your powers once the diamond was destroyed. I thought you were only human and never a person with powers.

I look at his face, at his partially opened eyes, and whisper, "I couldn't tell you or else the future might not have worked out the way it did." I reach forward with my other hand and stroke his cheek. "There," I whisper, "the drug is gone now. You're as good as new."

"You have no idea." He wraps an arm behind me and pulls me close to his body, his mouth descending to mine, but before our lips can touch the shard in my heart shifts. I cry out in pain and shrink back from him.

He releases his hold. "Calli, what's wrong?"

Charles, Curtis, and Brand come over and sit down. Brand asks, "Are you all right, Calli?"

I rub my chest between my breasts and will the pain to subside. "Yes, I'm fine. Our shards got a little too close, that's all."

Chris reaches forward and places his hand over mine. "Calli, why does it hurt down here when your amulet is near your throat?"

I'm embarrassed that I've actually slipped up, and that he caught me. I look into the faces of the four men in front of me, who are all thinking the same question, and try to come up with an excuse or explanation. I think I can try to explain why my heart hurts, and if they don't buy my explanation then Brand can repeat time and undo it—but Brand will still remember. I decide to follow my gut and go ahead and tell why my heart hurts.

I say, "As you already know, Justin is rounding up the amulet wearers in the hopes of reuniting the shards and extracting the powers from the reassembled stone. So far he has four of the six pieces. He told me a Hunter was about to be captured and delivered to his little fortress, but he still needs to find one last piece. He thinks Maetha has it, probably because she's the one who orchestrated the delivery and then assembled the amulets for the clans, but he's wrong. She doesn't have it . . . I do."

Chris lets out a gasp.

Charles says, "I don't understand. Do you have two amulets?"

"No, only one amulet. The sixth shard is inside me. I have a diamond piece lodged in my heart." I pause while the four men try to comprehend what I've just said. Their collective expressions tell me that won't happen any time soon.

I continue. "When the Death Clan tried to extract the powers of the diamond and it exploded, a shard entered my heart, killing me. Maetha healed my body around the shard and then restarted my heart. She told me the shard would remain there for safe keeping. Now Justin is trying to extract the power of the diamond, like the Death Clan tried to do. His attempt will result in his death."

Chris stares at the ground. I resist the urge to read his mind.

Brand says, "So let me get this straight. This Justin kid is collecting all the pieces of the diamond, trying to reassemble the thing, so he can become some all-powerful guy. How does he get the piece that, according to you, lies in your heart?"

"That's the catch," I say. "He can't. He'll die in his attempt."

Curtis speaks up, "I don't foresee Justin's death."

I ask Curtis, "What do you see happening when all the amulets break open and the shards slam together?"

"I don't see that happening. I see five amulets being handed to Justin at the same time, and then everything goes dark. But not the kind of dark associated with death."

Charles and Chris agreed.

Charles adds, "It's more like a fog or mist obscuring the future."

"You would have relinquished your shard to Justin at that point. Therefore, your vision concerning it ends. The shard in my heart allows me to see beyond the relinquishing."

Brand blurts out, "Wait a minute! So, that's what the Healers meant when they said 'use your combined power.' They knew about your diamond."

Chris rubs the back of his neck and asks in a barely audible whisper, "You've had powers all this time because of the shard inside you?"

"Yes," I answer, casting my eyes to the ground. I want to explain more to him, but Curtis interrupts.

Curtis asks, "How are you able to live with a . . . a foreign object inside your heart, let alone a sharp diamond?"

Charles points out the bigger issue. "Forget that, why isn't the diamond deadly to you? You told us if our amulets break we would die. Why are you able to live?"

Everyone focuses even more intently on me. I realize there's no way out around it. I have to tell them more.

"My DNA was unaffected by the cosmic energy rays when I was in the womb; therefore, I'm what is called an 'Unaltered.' Because the Sanguine Diamond contains all the cosmic powers, anyone with an alteration cannot physically hold the stone—not even a tiny piece. However, because I'm an Unaltered, I can touch the stone and not be harmed. That's how I was able to carry the whole diamond before."

"So," Brand says, "you have a piece of diamond inside you? Do you have a scar?"

"Yes, I have a small scar, and *no*, you can't see it, Brand."

"Well, are they ever going to remove the diamond piece from your heart?"

"I don't know exactly what will happen concerning the diamond."

Charles asks what I was hoping no one would. "How did Maetha come into possession of the diamond?"

"It's not my place to say. I hope you understand."

Curtis says, "After the Death Clan was destroyed, Maetha didn't tell us you ended up with a piece inside your heart."

"No, she didn't." Chris agrees. He points to my amulet and says, "Why are you able to have two shards so close together?"

"The piece in my heart holds the amulet to my skin. The two are drawn together like magnets, but my body protects the amulet from breaking. When you hugged me after I returned with the food, the diamond shard inside me moved, probably because of your amulet being so close. That's why I dropped the basket. It happened again just now when you hugged me. The same thing happened a couple years ago when Charles came to my mother's clinic."

Charles nods his head. "Ah yes, I remember. I distinctly felt my amulet move when I stood by you. I figured it was because you had held the diamond recently. I certainly wouldn't have thought you had a shard of your own."

"Make no mistake, if two amulets get too close together, they will break," I warn the group.

Brand clears his throat. "So, what do we do now? I mean, everyone will give the amulets over to kill Justin, but when will that be?"

Curtis answers, "Young man, not one of us wishes for his death. He will die by his own hand and not by ours. Greed has a way of doing that."

Charles states, "I foresee the amulet hand-off happening tomorrow."

Curtis, Chris, and I nod simultaneously.

Brand eyes the shard around my neck. "I'm the only one without an amulet." I figure he must be thinking that I already have a piece of diamond in my body and I don't need two.

Chris takes the conversation in a different direction. "So do we try to escape in the morning, or do we surrender?"

I answer. "We will be captured by Justin's thugs and taken back to the main building. Justin already knows where we're hiding. I eavesdropped when I left for the food. He knows we aren't going anywhere till morning."

Curtis says, "Why did we bother with escaping then?"

"Because I'd hoped there would be a vehicle we could take. Besides, you wouldn't have known as much going into the amulet hand-off as you do now."

Chris turns to me and says, "I, for one, am happy to be out of Justin's imprisonment, even if it's just for one night." He doesn't break eye contact. My heart begins to race as I imagine spending a whole night with him.

Charles stands and says, "Curtis and I will round up more cardboard to use as insulation to lie down on while sleeping. The idea of sleeping on bare concrete doesn't appeal to me."

Curtis joins Charles and takes the flashlight and inserts the new batteries. They begin searching the other smaller rooms off of the main room.

Brand stays with us. He still has questions. "I don't understand this, Calli. All this time you had superpowers and you didn't use them, well, except for healing, and then running when we fled the Healers. I feel like an idiot for thinking I was one up on you, when all along it was the other way around."

I know Maetha hasn't told Brand about his ties to the government T19 program, and I feel strongly I shouldn't either. I haven't had a chance to explain to Chris the intricate nature of my relationship with Brand, and I know it must be confusing to him. I try to answer in such a way that I give Chris information too.

"Brand, listen, I don't understand your powers or why you're able to repeat around me, and neither does Maetha. That's why she asked me to teach you about the different clans and abilities. Through understanding comes knowledge. The most important thing you can learn from me is the advantage of observing a situation instead of trying to control it. Take our upcoming capture, for example. Try observing rather than manipulating the outcome. Your true power will come in the form of choosing wisely: when to intervene and when not to. Sometimes people need to die for the will of nature to be satisfied, and sometimes a person must be saved for the same reason. The trick to figuring out which outcome is natural is found through observation."

"You make it sound like I might have to let people die even if I can save them."

"I'm sure you'll find yourself in that very situation many times in your life, but if you learn to look at the situation, look for the cause and effect, the good or bad choices leading to the moment, you'll be able to come to a conclusion about whether or not you should help."

I throw a quick glance at Chris and find his jaw clenched and deep creases running across his forehead.

I continue talking to Brand. "The day a diamond shard entered my heart was the day a group of Healers who called themselves the Death Clan was wiped out. They had taken nature's will out of the equation when they decided who lived and who died, and when that happens, nature finds a way to eliminate the impediment. An unaltered human needed to be used in order for the Death Clan to destroy themselves. It didn't have to be me, but I was chosen to attempt the mission. If I'd failed, someone else would have been used, and the diamond shard would now be embedded in their heart instead of mine."

Chris blurts out, "Yeah, and in order for the mission to succeed, lies were told and false impressions were made. Sometimes nature is not so kind. Sometimes she's a manipulative bitch!"

The room grows uncomfortably silent. I sense Chris regrets his outburst but can't seem to control his anger toward Maetha. I ask, "How far off base was your vision, Chris? You misinterpreted it from the beginning. I was never a Healer, only a girl with a powerful piece of rock in my body. Maetha chose me because of your desire to find love. Of all the powers floating around in the universe, love is the strongest. Without it, heroes would cease to exist. There'd be no one to risk our lives for, and no one to protect. Your need to protect me, and my need to protect you, is what brought the Death Clan down. Without that variable, without that passion, or the immense power of love . . . well, there wouldn't be much to fight for. The vision you were shown wasn't fabricated to toy with your head or emotions. You were not played, Chris. Maetha introduced an idea into your future to see what you'd do with it, and she found you'd help the whole plan succeed. Without your desire to find love, the rest wouldn't have been possible."

Brand muses, "That's deep."

The previously angered heat radiating off Chris changes to the pure warmth of romantic desire. His eyes have a way of looking deep into my soul and tugging on my pinky toes. I don't divert my eyes from his, and actually cherish being able to stare unabashedly at him.

Brand clears his throat. "Well, I can tell when I'm a third wheel. I'll just go help the other guys find cardboard." He stands and leaves me and Chris alone.

Chris speaks quietly. "I've missed you. I've spent too much of my time being bitter and hurt." He places his palm on my cheek and rubs his thumb across my bottom lip. His touch feels so good that I can't help but press my cheek into his hand. "I want nothing more than to hold you close to me, but I can't because of this thing." He grasps his amulet with his other hand.

I reach up and cup his hand that still cradles my cheek. "I've missed you, too. Why were you wearing the amulet instead of Clara?"

"Beth called for her assistance in the investigation of Charles' and Curtis' disappearance. We discussed the possibility that it might be a trick to get the Runners' amulet wearer out of the compound, so she relinquished it to me for the duration of her trip. I was taken the next day. I have to say, when I watched Brand take each and every guard down flawlessly during our escape, it reminded me of the girl who took me hostage."

"How was she able to get you out of the compound? Were you drugged?"

"She had me at gunpoint and told me that if we didn't reach the checkpoint by a certain time *you* would be killed." Chris takes my hands in his. "I figured Justin was behind the kidnappings, because who else would know to use my fear of you dying to force me to do something? Anyway, I also had decided I would not give over the amulet if you were, in fact, dead. It would do Justin no good to kill you, and I really felt he knew that."

I say, "Unless Justin has more than one female working with him, I think I overheard her talking with Justin when I was blindfolded in the van." I pause and squeeze his hands. "Chris, there's more concerning the diamond shards: all Justin needs to do is kill the amulet wearers, and the shards can be taken. Justin doesn't know this. Wherever he's getting his information from, it's not complete, and I don't quite know why. I have my own suspicions about this whole deal and who's really behind it . . . using Justin as a puppet. For now, we need to rest. I can tell you honestly that there's nothing I want more than to be held in your arms tonight, but—"

Chris smiles and leans forward to kiss my lips carefully, taking care not to get our amulets too close. His warm lips feel heavenly against mine, but they leave too soon. Chris positions a couple large pieces of cardboard next to the charcoal fire and lies down on his side and pats the floor in front of him.

I lie down on my back near him, but not too close.

He places his hand on my arm and says, "These necklaces might as well be chastity belts. I can't wait to get mine off . . . wait a minute. I could give mine to Brand just for the night."

"Not a good idea, Chris. We don't need to make him anymore powerful than he already is."

"What is his power exactly?"

"He can rewind small stretches of time."

"He's a time traveler?"

"Something like that. It's confusing to think about, but terribly powerful. He used his power on you earlier. I could tell."

"What?"

"Don't worry about it, Chris. He only used it to manipulate an answer out of you. Didn't you find it suspicious that he figured things out a bit too quickly?"

"I just figured he's a smart guy."

"He is, and that's part of the problem. You can't give him the amulet, Chris."

"All right."

The others rejoin us with their piles of cardboard, which they position around the glowing embers just like I saw in my vision. We eventually drift off to sleep on the hard floor. I awake several times in the night, and each time I realize Chris hasn't removed his hand from my arm. It's as if he's afraid that if he breaks contact with me, I might not be there in the morning, that perhaps this is all a dream. I feel the same way and find comfort and joy in his need for contact.

Chapter 14 - Relinquishment

The guards break our door down at dawn, flooding our room with sunlight. With guns pointed at the ready, they yell for us to raise our hands and freeze.

Justin walks in behind them, laughing. "You're pathetic, all of you! Get up."

The guards encourage us to move with the tips of their guns. One guard kicks Brand in the gut, doubling him over in pain.

I shout to Justin, "He gets hurt, and I won't give you my amulet!"

Justin glares at his guard, giving him an unspoken message to take it easy, and then turns on his heel and leaves the building.

We are ushered back to where we fled from the evening before. It seems we are going backward, not progressing forward, and yet I know better. Our hands are held behind our heads while the guards hold their rifles to our backs. We walk in pairs, with Brand beside me, Curtis and Charles behind me, and Chris walking beside Justin at the front of the pack. Verbal silence amplifies the sound of crunching gravel under our feet. I sense the fear among my comrades and wish I could reassure them everything will be fine, but I can't see the future beyond the black fog either.

I take a moment to take in the disarming beauty of the sunrise to the east and the sound of the crashing waves to the west. This provides a strange comfort to the stress of the moment, being surrounded by nature. Is nature's will about to be followed? Or is nature's will about to be ignored? I've wondered if Maetha is behind Justin's lack of knowledge concerning the amulets. Perhaps she's manipulating things with the intention of helping the shards rejoin within me. Maybe she's not manipulating anything.

I'll find out soon enough.

We are taken to a large room inside the building we escaped last night. Old machinery and tables are piled up in the far corner abandoned and forgotten. One wall has large dusty windows and an exterior door.

"Stand right here," Justin says to Chris, pointing to an exact spot on the floor. Chris does as he's told. One by one, Justin positions us in a semi-circle. I'm in the middle with Charles and Curtis to my left and Chris and Brand to my right. The guards stand behind each of us with guns to our heads. No one utters a word while Justin paces the floor, looking at his watch. He continues to pace, becoming more and more agitated. Minute after minute passes by.

Brakes whine and squeal as a large-sounding vehicle comes to a halt outside the windows. Justin rushes over to the door and opens it, letting in a male and female.

"It's about time," Justin growls.

As the two near our semi-circle, I'm able to get a better look at them. The female has a handgun pressed into the back of the male, directing him with the barrel. She's close to my age, shorter than me, with a round face, tan skin, and long, dark-brown hair tied in a ponytail. She wears a tactical vest like the guards that shows her toned, muscular arms. Around her waist is a belt with two pistol holsters holding up black, baggy cargo pants. I notice a knife strapped to the outside of one of her combat boots. I have a hard time understanding how this petite girl could overpower her male captive.

The male is obviously the Hunter with the diamond shard around his neck. He's at least a foot taller than the female and muscular, yet he's the captive. I feel into his mind and learn his name is Dominic. I recognize him from the diamond delivery. He was one of the Hunters who came to talk with me. I also see his capture through his memories. He was on his way to the Healers' compound, traveling with a convoy and sitting in the back of an armored truck for safety. A couple miles from his destination, his convoy nearly ran over a young lady on the road. Stopping to help, Dominic watched helplessly from the back of the truck as his team of trained killers was taken down systematically and effortlessly by the girl. Then she slid in behind the steering wheel and drove away with her captive.

I try to feel inside the female's mind for a name but have to stop. I find the exact same mess as in Brand's mind. She's a Repeater! I look at Chris, and he brings his thoughts to the front of his mind, confirming this girl is the one who abducted him.

After positioning Dominic in the semi-circle by Charles and Curtis, the girl walks over to Justin and says, "I think I deserve a little extra for this one. He was hard to catch."

I find it interesting that from Dominic's point of view, there was nothing hard or difficult about catching him. He was pre-packaged, locked in the back of the truck. All she had to do was incapacitate his crew which appeared to have been effortless as well.

But I know what Repeaters have to go through to get the final outcome.

"You're late." Justin says, looking at his watch. "You'll get what we agreed upon, and nothing more."

"No, I want a bonus."

"No. Take your money and go." He points to a briefcase by the door.

She steps close to him, looks up to his face, places both her hands on his chest and slides them down the front of his jacket. One hand enters his side jacket pocket and pulls out an envelope and waves it at him. "This will do just fine." She turns and leaves the building with both the briefcase and her bonus.

Justin releases his held breath, once the door closes and she drives the truck away. He returns to the group. "Here's how this is gonna work. If you want to live, you'll each remove your amulet and reassign its ownership to me. Then you'll extend your arm toward me with the amulet."

I have to at least act as if I care, so I say, "Justin, you don't have all the pieces yet."

"I don't need all of them, just most of the pieces."

"Who told you that? You will die."

"Shut up, Calli. I'll be able to heal myself with the powers of the stone."

"They won't work on you." I feel this is all I should say, so I don't try to engage him further.

Curtis, Charles, and Chris begin to remove their amulets. Dominic looks between us, shaking his head. Charles and Curtis encourage him to follow Justin's orders. Reluctantly, he does so. My amulet clings like a magnet to my skin, but I free it and begin reassigning ownership, verbally saying I'm giving the amulet to Justin. Then together we extend our arms toward Justin. The dangling amulets begin to shake on their strings, wobbling back and forth between each other, and Justin shouts, "Closer! Tighten the semi-circle! Bring them closer together!"

We inch forward, and in one fluid motion Justin cups his left hand in front of him, palm up, while with his right hand he gathers the leather cords in a sweeping motion, catching all the clinking amulets in his left hand. He pulls his hands to his body, toward his chest.

The glass pieces explode with a loud crack, flinging broken glass in all directions; blinding rays of light shoot out from between Justin's fingers as he screams in pain. His hands tremble and then seem to move uncontrollably, slamming into his chest. The impact knocks him off his feet and causes his body to crumple to the ground. He lies face up, motionless, with a large gaping wound in the center of his chest that oozes blood where the diamond blasted into him.

I can see the merged shards deep in the bloody crater of his chest, and it sickens me to think that if Justin hadn't been so bent on having ultimate power, he'd still be alive. Yet, like Maetha had said, it's the way the human mind works in so many cases. I can't believe how calm I am feeling. Perhaps it's because I knew this would happen. I'd seen it already.

Brand breaks the silence. "Should I repeat, Calli?"

I look at Chris, who says to me, "It's nature's way."

I agree, but my senses alert me to something else, an oddity I can't quite wrap my mind around concerning the guards. They still have their guns on us even though their leader is lying in a growing pool of blood. None of us dare move for fear of being shot, and yet the guards stand their ground as if they are waiting for something or someone else: the puppet master—Agent Alpha, as Justin revealed.

The door opens, and Freedom walks in with an open pocket watch in his hand. Before I can process much thought into why Freedom is here, or when Agent Alpha will appear, I lose my breath as my powers rush out of my body. I don't know what's happening. My powers have vanished. They are completely gone! I can't do anything!

Brand looks at me, clearly confused as well. Maetha appears across the room, seemingly from out of nowhere, looking confused. Her presence causes Freedom to do a double-take.

"Well, good of you to join us, Maetha. I didn't know you were here." Freedom nods to one of the guards to indicate she needs to be watched. A guard quickly positions himself by Maetha.

Freedom then looks at me through his squinty eyes and says, "Calli, I'd hoped you would be with me at this point, but I guess we all have our choices."

My eyes connect with Brand's. "Okay, this would be a good time to repeat." I know my statement holds a little too much emotion, but for the first time since I was sixteen I have absolutely no powers radiating through my body and it scares me to death.

"I'd love to, Calli, but I can't."

"Disturbing, isn't it?" Freedom says in his low, oily voice as he bends over Justin's body and digs into his chest, pulling out the bloody stone. He stands and walks over to me and says, "I believe you have something I need, Calli."

He holds up the bloody diamond so I can see the vacant notch where the shard from my heart should go. He turns and issues an order to the guards: "Except for these two," he points to Brand and me, "kill everyone else."

I watch in absolute horror as the guards open fire on Maetha, Chris, Charles, Curtis, and Dominic. Brand rushes toward Freedom, whose back is turned, and knocks him to the ground. I'm completely stunned and in shock at the carnage all around me. Charles, Curtis, and Dominic are moaning from their injuries, and Chris and Maetha lay face down, completely still. Dead!

I scream without even realizing I am doing so. This can't be happening. Chris is supposed to live. He was in my vision.

Brand shouts my name. I look over and see he has Freedom on the ground, using him as a human shield.

Freedom yells to the guards, "Don't shoot!"

Brand exclaims, "It's the pocket watch, Calli! It kills our powers when it's open."

I look at his hand and find he's holding the watch Freedom had in his hand. It's open.

Brand continues. "I'm taking you back with me this time. I can't save everybody on my own. Look to see who gets shot first and see if there's a way to take out a few guards or get hold of a gun."

This time?

I watch as Brand snaps the pocket watch shut. I immediately feel my powers return, like blood rushing back into my body and giving me new life. The whole world feels like it rotates a hundred times in only two seconds, and I find myself in the same place I'd been just a few seconds earlier with the guard's gun to my head and Freedom walking to Justin's body. Freedom pulls the stone out of Justin's chest and says, "I believe you have something I need, Calli." He turns away and gives the order, "Except for these two, kill everyone else."

I listen for the sound of guns firing, trying to determine which one went off first. Brand rushes Freedom, and the three on my left are shot almost simultaneously. The gun to my right fires into Chris, and I look over to see Chris and Maetha falling down.

Instinctively my hands reach forward for Chris.

"Again!" Brand yells, and I hear the pocket watch snap shut and everything spins wildly right back to the same starting point.

"Kill everyone else." Freedom turns away from me.

I immediately turn and fight with my guard for his

gun, but the strap is over his head, and I fail. The five shots go off, marking my friends' demise. I look back at Brand on the ground with Freedom and hear Freedom shout, "Don't shoot!" and feel the ground spin as we repeat back again.

"Kill everyone else." Freedom says, and I quickly spin around and grab the strap and yank it over the guard's head. He fires his gun into the opposite wall while the other guards shoot their prisoners and then turn their guns on me. Freedom's yell to stop is evenly timed with the butt of the gun ramming into my nose, breaking the bridge with a nauseating crunch. The pain is all-consuming, causing my knees to give out, and as I fall backward the ground begins to spin wildly.

I find myself back in time, wiggling my unbroken nose, remembering the pain, while looking at Justin's body as Freedom crosses the room. I look at Brand, who mouths, "No guns this time."

"Can't you go back further?" I whisper.

"No."

I look over at the three people to my left, marveling at how a moment ago they were dead, and now they are alive. We need to figure out a way to keep it that way. I glance over at Chris and Maetha as Freedom says, "Kill everyone else."

Brand rushes Freedom in a slightly different way this time, jumping up at a sideways angle and planting his feet on Chris's chest, pushing off toward Maetha and knocking Chris down. Brand's hands push her shoulders back, knocking her into her guard, and then Brand cart-wheels into Freedom, taking him down to the ground in the same fashion as before. I note the surprised look on Freedom's face never lessens with each time Brand takes him down, particularly with this latest sudden display of acrobatics.

I stand in shock as the three to my left are already lying on the ground bleeding. Chris and Maetha have been shot as well.

Freedom shouts to his guards, "Don't shoot!"

Brand grunts, "Oh shut up already, you piece of—"

Freedom, struggling against the disabling hold Brand has on him, chokes out, "You'll never escape. Look outside."

I look out the window and see multiple military vehicles screeching to a halt, the dust clouds behind them. My jaw drops open, and I turn my head back to Brand.

With a dizzying whoosh, we repeat again. Freedom walks in with the pocket watch extended in front of him and Brand says to me, "Go for Maetha's guard. Follow my lead."

I look to my right at Chris, who repeatedly ends up dead in every scenario, and wonder if I should attack *his guard* instead of Maetha's. Next time. I face forward and watch as Freedom bends down to pull the diamond out of Justin's chest. The gruesome image has lessened in strength with the many replays, the same as it has watching Chris, Maetha, and the others get gunned down. It's almost as if it isn't real because all Brand has to do is repeat and the injuries will be gone.

As Freedom begins straightening himself up with the bloody diamond in his hand, I see Brand move toward him. I take the cue to rush Maetha's guard. The guard isn't even looking in my direction when the brunt of my shoulder rams into his gut. The tip of his gun points upward, and when he pulls the trigger, the bullets hit the ceiling, making plaster fall down.

More guns are fired. Then I hear the familiar snap of the pocket watch closing. My powers rush into my body and a split second later Maetha commands loudly,

"Freeze!"

Everyone halts, literally frozen in place. I'm able to move my eyes to see that Charles, Curtis, and Dominic are already down. Unconscious, but alive. Chris is unharmed, as am I, and Maetha appears unharmed as well. Brand is under Freedom, with his arms and legs wrapped around him like a pretzel. He doesn't look like he's been shot. The guards are still armed and ready to fire, but are frozen in place.

So much confusion inundates my mind. I've never felt like this before—with powers, yet unable to use them.

Multiple military vehicles skid to a halt in front of the building.

Freedom's strangled voice chokes out, "Well hell, Maetha, how long have you had it?"

"A while."

"Yet you held off using it all this time."

I look at Freedom and Maetha, confused by their conversation.

"I will not allow you to do this, Freedom. The diamond belongs to Calli."

"Where did you find it, Maetha?"

"Two pieces of the twenty-one will not double your powers."

"But a piece of the Grecian Blue Diamond will, as it does with you. You're even able to control the use of my diamond's powers. Now that's strength."

Maetha's voice sounds in my head. *Calli, I can't hold everyone for much longer, nor can I release individuals. I have to release everyone at once. When I do, Freedom's abilities will be released as well. Prepare to grab the diamond and run with Chris on my word.*

"What?" I can't keep myself from speaking aloud. I look around for the diamond and see it lying on the floor a short distance away, next to Justin's body. "But Freedom already touched it—"

Brand grunts and says, "Just do it, Calli. I can keep him pinned down long enough for you three to escape."

Had he heard Maetha's telepathy? "What about you?" I ask Brand frantically.

"If I let go, he will catch us all, and no one will get away. Now go!"

The door busts open, providing the way for a dozen or more soldiers to enter. A tall, older man marches in after the soldiers.

Chris gasps out, "Dad?"

Freedom tries to yell, "Shut the door," but it comes out as a raspy whisper.

"Now!" Maetha shouts.

I feel my legs run—but not on my own power. I'm being controlled. My body bends forward, and my hand snatches the diamond off the floor. As I straighten myself up, I notice Maetha catching a flying object. It's Freedom's pocket watch that Brand has tossed her. Maetha takes my hand. Chris is by my side, and the room, its occupants, and intruders become a blur of colors as we run as fast as lightning out the open door.

Once we've run a few miles, I sense the release of control over my body and I'm able to use my diamond's powers once again.

As we run, I can't help but worry about Brand. He clearly tried to escape with us. He'd repeated at least once without me to determine the dismal outcome of Freedom catching us, and then he sacrificed himself so we could get away.

What of the three injured companions, Charles, Curtis, and Dominic? I look to the future and see that I can't read their futures. At least I don't see the black fog in the immediate future like last night. I try to view Brand's future, but I'm met with bombardment and frustration, typical for him. I try looking for what will happen next, but my mind fills with Maetha's voice.

Calli, stop using those powers! You're holding Freedom's property, and we can't risk any connection to him.

What about my running?

Only focus on running, no other power. Don't drop the diamond. I need to take Chris's hand so we can go faster.

She runs near him and grabs his hand with her other one and I feel a jolt of energy electrify my muscles and supercharge my speed. The new sensation is coming from the diamond in my heart.

With Freedom's diamond clutched tightly in my free hand, we run through mountain passes, over surfaces of lakes, around major cities, over farmlands, and beneath roaring thunderstorms. We have to slow down for forests, hills, and other troublesome obstacles, but every time we enter flat land we accelerate to speeds that no Runner could dream of. My legs run on their own will, faster than nature intended them to go, perhaps even faster than the laws of physics should allow. Hours of running pass by with no stop for rest, and our eastward movement causes the sun to move across the sky at a faster rate.

We move southeast, into the desert and plains of Texas to avoid slowing down for rough terrain. Eventually, we enter the Great Plains region where we are able to use the full diamond-strength running power which Maetha passes on to Chris. The land around us becomes a blur of pure speed. Maetha leads us this way and that, avoiding the large obstacles, landmarks, cliffs, and highways that get in our way.

The intense focus required for the journey is welcome, as it takes my mind off of what I saw this morning. Time itself seems to be passing by in a blur as well, and every time I glance at the sky the sun has moved further west.

We reach Maetha's lakeside resort in Indiana during the early evening as the sun is flirting with the western horizon. Now that we've stopped, I feel a heavy fatigue saturating my muscles, making me feel dizzy and worn out.

Maetha says, "Don't use your healing power, Calli."

"Where are we?" Chris asks breathing heavily.

"Indiana," Maetha answers calmly as she leads us to a side door. After typing in a key code, we enter the well-lit hallway and walk to her room.

Now that we've finally stopped running, I notice the tattered condition of my clothing. I glance over to Chris and find he's just realizing how poorly his clothing held up during the all-day run. Maetha's clothing, on the other hand, is in perfect condition. She's not wearing a Runner's suit, but I can tell the material is similar.

Hans Lindlbauer comes out of the bedroom looking more than a little shocked. "Maetha. I didn't know you were coming back so soon." He glances at Chris and me. "Oh my God, what happened to you two?"

Maetha speaks for us. "We've been running all day, Hans. Please bring juices from the refrigerator for them. Then go get the box of clothing from the other room. Please." She looks us both up and down. The she says to me, "I think we should address your wounds and get you changed into new clothes before we do anything else. I will heal you instead of you using your diamond's powers."

Wounds? I look down and realize my upper-inner thighs are horribly chaffed from running. The pain hadn't registered in my mind yet. Now I understand why a Runner's suit is essential. My shoes lost their soles somewhere in Texas. My slacks and blazer are worn completely away where my clothes rubbed together, leaving little to the imagination. Chris's clothing is in the same condition. However, after what we went through this morning, the decency of our outfits feels minor and insignificant.

Maetha places her hands on our shoulders, and sends a wave of healing energy into our bodies. My sore, chaffed skin heals up and the pain fades away.

Maetha walks into the other room and sits on the bed in the lotus position, closing her eyes and relaxing her body.

Hans brings two juice bottles to Chris and me and says, "Calli, your devices have arrived. I'll go get them."

"Thank you, Hans."

Chris asks me, "Your what?"

"The Pulse Emitters I designed. They sure would have been useful last night."

"Oh, right. Brand told us about the testing you two did with the Demons, and the device you designed to protect people with powers, while you were out getting supplies."

I set my juice on the table, along with the blood-encrusted diamond. The juxtaposition of the white tabletop and the brownish-black diamond is a stark reminder of the deaths that occurred only a few hours before. My mind replays the horrible sight of seeing Chris shot over and over again, followed with the relief of seeing him alive in the next second. I guess I didn't realize I was seeing potential outcomes, well, until Maetha somehow froze the process of repeating. The last scene I saw was Brand holding Freedom down on the blood-soaked floor, a few feet away from Justin's gruesome corpse. Dominic, Curtis, and Charles were lying on the ground completely still, soon to die if not already. I feel terrible that I couldn't save them. Tears well up in my eyes and my throat clenches.

Hans returns with the box of clothing and the Pulse Emitters and sets them down on the table. He points to the diamond. "What is that?" Then he reaches out to touch the bloodied stone. I quickly grab the diamond, and Chris launches his body into Hans to stop him from touching it. The two of them fall to the floor with a thud.

"What was that all about?" Hans asks as he sits up on the floor, rubbing his shoulder.

Chris answers, "Sorry, but you can't touch it or you'll die."

"If it's so deadly, why can she hold it? What is it anyway?"

"A diamond," Chris says.

I look through the doorway at Maetha. The scuffle hasn't pulled her out of her meditation.

I loosen the grip on the diamond and hold it out for Hans to see. The stone no longer looks like a polished cut diamond, but a huge cloudy crystal—a diamond in the rough—with an obvious missing section.

"Where did you get it?"

I say, "It's a long story, Hans, one that Maetha should tell if she wants you to know." I try not to sound rude. I walk over to the kitchen sink and set the diamond down in the bottom of the basin. Chris continues talking to Hans about the recent events, including the fact that three clan leaders were shot and our friend taken captive, but I don't focus on their words. I wash my hands, taking extra time to clean the dried blood under my nails. As the blood residue goes down the drain, I imagine a deeper meaning to everything. I feel as though Justin's journey had been predestined to end tragically, that his purpose in life was to further the process of nature. Freedom used him as a tool to round up the shards. Justin's lust for power resulted in his death.

I use my Seer ability against Maetha's wishes and determine Charles Rhondell, Curtis Schultz, and the Hunter named Dominic have definitely died. Tears spring up in my eyes and begin falling into the basin, joining everything else going down the drain. I didn't know Dominic on a personal level, like Charles and Curtis, but I'm sure he didn't deserve to die either. I'm angered how the consequences of one person's choices have affected so many lives.

My thoughts retrace the final moments of Justin's life and the events that took place after his death. What happened exactly? I thought Agent Alpha would appear, whoever that is, but instead Freedom walked in. What was in Freedom's pocket watch that rendered us powerless? How did Maetha appear in the middle of the room? Why did she look shocked, as if her cover was blown? What had Freedom meant with his cryptic questions? What will happen to Brand? He sacrificed himself so we could escape. My eyes water with fresh tears at the thought of never seeing Brand again. He's my friend and I'm afraid for him.

I take a deep breath, blink back my tears and refocus on the diamond in the bottom of the sink. I pick it up and rub the remaining blood residue off, admiring the defined lines within the stone that signify the separate sections, and am amazed at how the diamond merged back together on its own.

I think about Maetha's story of the last time this stone

had been bloodied, when my relative, Gustave, willingly removed it from his own heart, thus ending his life. Had he gone through a similar experience like what I went through when he received the diamond? I'm curious to find out. I dry my hands and the diamond, wipe my eyes, and place the cleaned stone on the table top once again.

Chris has already changed into a spare Runner's suit. He's set aside a suit for me. I take it and change in the bathroom. When I come out, I sit down on the sofa next to Chris. He hands me my juice from the table and puts his arm around me. Together we sip the replenishing fluid and try to relax.

He says, "I hope the others are all right."

I turn my head to look at him. "Chris, they're dead."

"What?" His voice shakes.

I tell him what I've seen concerning the clan leaders.

"How did all this go wrong? Couldn't we have prevented it?" he asks.

I shake my head. "I couldn't see the future past the point of Justin's death."

"What about Brand? Did he use his powers? Did he try to help at all?"

Chris is obviously trying to work out a better outcome than what we witnessed. I say, "Brand repeated many times, Chris. Believe me, he tried to save everyone. It just wasn't possible."

Maetha comes out of her room and whispers something to Hans concerning Chris. She turns to me and says with her mind, *It's time, Calli. Come with me.*

I stand from the couch, and Chris does as well.

"You need to stay here with Hans, Chris," says Maetha. "Calli and I have some business to attend to."

"What are you going to do?"

"Calli," Maetha says, pointing to the diamond, "bring

the diamond."

He looks gut-shot as he turns to face me. I open my mouth to tell him I'll be back, but he grabs my head and pulls my face to his before I can speak. He kisses me feverishly for a moment, then pulls me into his trembling arms. My arms instinctively wrap around his body, absorbing his anxious energy. I press my cheek to his chest and hear his racing heart.

"I don't want to let you go," he whispers in my ear. "I've waited so long to see you again."

"I know," I say, my body ablaze from head to toe.

Maetha interrupts, "It's time, Calli."

He releases me from his arms. His scent lingers on my skin. I have always loved his aroma. I look into his eyes and smile, then turn to Maetha. Together, we leave the room. I catch one last glimpse of Chris over my shoulder before the door closes.

Chapter 15 - The Diamond Bearers

Maetha and I walk down the hall to the door we'd entered through. I'm pretty sure I know what's about to happen. It's time for me to join the Diamond Bearers officially.

"Calli, don't worry. We'll find a way to rescue Brand. I know you're concerned. I am too. Did you notice the female bounty hunter Justin hired was a Repeater?"

"Yes, I picked up on that. Wait a minute. You weren't there . . . were you? You didn't show up till Freedom arrived."

"I was in the room the whole time, out of sight. I read Justin's mind and found he wasn't even aware of her immense power." Maetha opens the door for me, and I walk out into the evening air. "Imagine if Justin had known what she could do . . . imagine the possible devastation. I will need to find her, since I can see that any hope of rescuing Brand is dependent upon her involvement."

We walk across the parking lot and into the trees. The cool night air rustles the leaves and sends a shiver down my back. The sun has set and the Demons are on the prowl.

Maetha must have noticed my shiver, because she says, "There's nothing to be afraid of, Calli. It only hurts for a second, then you'll feel the intense power of the stone emanate through you. You already know how to use the healing power, and it will be second nature for you to immediately heal yourself. Besides, I'll be right beside you if for some reason you're not able to heal yourself quickly enough."

My heart starts to race with anticipation. I wasn't afraid before, but this explanation has amped up my nervousness. "Maetha, if you're worried I won't be able to heal myself, why don't you look into the future to see if there will be problems?"

"The future is unclear at this point. Instead of debating and speculating what I or any other Diamond Bearer foresees, we need to get this diamond reassigned and out of Freedom's control."

We emerge from the line of trees at a clearing by the lake. A woman stands by the water's edge wearing a long, light-colored gown. She turns in our direction as we enter the clearing. Several other individuals enter the clearing as if they are literally coming out of the hearts of the trees. A couple more materialize out of thin air—similar to how Maetha appeared at Justin's compound—each wearing a gown or robe of some kind, even the men.

Most of the Diamond Bearers look to be about the same age as Maetha. Some are younger looking and a couple are much older in appearance. The male-to-female ratio is fairly equal. My nervousness overwhelms my desire to analyze the group of Bearers further.

Maetha motions to bring the circle of Diamond Bearers closer and proceeds to converse with the group through telepathy. *Calli Courtnae, of the ancient bloodline, failed to receive the shards during the attempted merging of the diamond. Henry was behind the failed attempt. He goes by the name of Freedom now, and also Agent Alpha. He used a young man to round up the amulets. Henry withheld information, bringing about the young man's death.*

My mind cramps with the new knowledge about Freedom: Agent Alpha is Freedom who is also Henry, or was Henry in the beginning.

A male Diamond Bearer with a British accent asks, *Did you find out how Henry has been hiding from us?* As his question fills my mind, his name also becomes known to me . . . Merlin.

Maetha responds, *Not exactly. He entered the room with this pocket watch.* She shows Freedom's pocket watch to everyone and then opens it. Instantly the group of eighteen disappears, vanishing into the night. My powers rush out of my body once again, and the darkness of the night closes in thick, reminding me that my Hunter's vision is almost always active.

Maetha looks at me and says aloud, "The black stone in the watch negated their bi-locating abilities, causing them to disappear."

She closes the watch and one-by-one everyone reappears. Gasps and audible shock fill the clearing as the Immortals have obviously never experienced the loss of their powers. The telepathic melee of confusion fills my mind. I'm still trying to catch my breath—having my powers restored takes it away.

Maetha opens the watch again. I brace for the unfavorable sensation of losing my powers, but this time my powers are not affected. However, the other Bearers vanish again. After a few moments, I notice a strange sensation in my heart. Not so much as a feeling but rather an awareness.

One of the male Diamond Bearers, named Amenemhet, bi-locates and says, "I no longer feel you, Maetha. I had to connect to Calli's diamond to return. It's as if you're visibly invisible."

Several other Bearers appear, all reporting the same thing. Soon, all the Bearers are bi-located back to the group.

With the pocket watch still opened, Maetha responds, "I noticed two hinges on the watch, two compartments, each holding a black stone, one significantly larger than the other. It seems the smaller stone blocks only my own power, whereas the larger stone blocks everyone nearby, including me. We must learn what these stones are and how Henry, um," she pauses and corrects herself, "Freedom came to have them in his possession. I have to assume he has more of these stones because he's once again gone dark." She closes the watch and resumes speaking telepathically. *Freedom waited until the pieces merged before taking the stone. He was about to remove Calli's shard to complete the diamond, but he was thwarted by Calli's Repeater friend, Brand Safferson. We were able to escape with the diamond and the watch, but only because Brand held Freedom at bay. General Harding arrived as we fled, and I have no doubt they will imprison Brand on Freedom's orders.*

A beautiful Bearer who looks like the female images on the walls of an Egyptian tomb steps forward and points to the diamond I hold. She says, "The stone is vexed. It belongs to both Calli and Henry, er, Freedom. It's drawn to the remaining piece, but its loyalty is to Freedom. Calli doesn't stand a chance."

"True," Maetha says, "the stone is split, but I believe once it's reunited with its last shard, loyalty will reassign to Calli."

"What if you're wrong? I cannot foresee her future," Neema adds.

"As this exact situation has never presented itself before, we shall all learn at once what the consequences will be. However, there's a pressing issue at hand: the Grecian Blue Diamond. The need has arisen to let each Bearer know I am in possession of the Blue Diamond."

A male Bearer speaks up. "I thought it was lost to natural forces." He has a heavy Spanish accent and his name enters my mind: Fabian.

Maetha says, "A convenient misdirect, Fabian. One directed by Crimson."

Several Bearers talk to each other in hushed, reverent tones. I look around the circle to see which Bearer is Crimson. I can't tell.

Maetha continues. "Freedom now knows I am in possession of the mind-control stone. I was left with no choice, and in a situation that caught me off guard. I used the mind-control ability in his presence after the pocket watch was closed. Freedom recognized the Blue power immediately and began asking questions. The Repeater and I tried many different approaches to try to bring about different results in an effort to save everyone in the room, but it simply wasn't possible. The only way we could escape was by the Repeater holding Freedom for a few crucial seconds."

I am beside myself. Maetha and Brand repeated too? I guess the more I think about it, the more I realize I already knew that had happened.

Neema says, "We all know what this means. Freedom will not stop until he has the Grecian Blue; therefore, he must die. He must have his heart removed and his diamond reclaimed. I propose a vote on the matter."

I'm surprised to see the Diamond Bearers work as a unit, with no discrimination based on rank or seniority. Why doesn't Maetha have the last word on a decision? She is the first Diamond Bearer. She's certainly earned the right to be the leader. Apparently she has more power than the rest with the Grecian Blue diamond.

Maetha's voice comes into my mind, answering my inquisitive questions. *Calli, the woman who brought me back to life when I first received my diamond is named Crimson. She instructed me to never take full leadership regarding decisions concerning the diamond. Every decision is voted on, and every Diamond Bearer has the opportunity to voice their opinion. All major decisions are put to a vote. What is your opinion concerning Freedom? What should happen to him?*

I don't hesitate and say with cold finality, "Cut his heart out."

Maetha addresses the group. "The vote is unanimous. Freedom will lose his stone."

Mary, the woman standing by the lake when we first arrived, steps forward. "Maetha, my protector tells me Calli is now the prime suspect in the murders of the missing amulet wearers. The word is she stole the Healers' amulet and fled. Now the Hunters, Readers, and Seers are mourning the deaths of their leaders, and all eyes are on Calli and the Runners' amulet wearer. They are being hunted as we speak."

Maetha reaches out to me. "Calli, give me the diamond."

I place it in her hand. She takes me by the elbow and leads me out into the center of the circle of gown-wearing, ethereal-looking people. She raises the diamond high over her head, and with her right hand extended above her body she lets go of my elbow, placing her left hand on my back between my shoulder blades. In one swift movement, she brings her hand down and rams the diamond between my breasts and into my chest.

The pain is excruciating! It feels like my entire chest is exploding, and the air compresses from my lungs. My legs give out. Maetha gently lays me on the ground, and I become aware I no longer have a heartbeat. I want to inhale, but can't. The pain, which seems already un- bearable, intensifies more, and I recall the agony I felt on the stone altar in the clearing with the Death Clan.

I focus my mind on my heart, willing it to heal. All the while my lungs burn with the need for oxygen and my brain begs for the same need.

"You can do it, Calli," Maetha's quiet, shaky voice urges me onward. I look up in her eyes and find her eyebrows are scrunched together.

Is she afraid or worried?

Some of the Diamond Bearers speak with concern.

"She's not strong enough."

"Give her time."

"She doesn't have much time left."

"It's not working, Maetha."

"Even if they merge, the diamond will behave erratically."

"You must remove it or she'll die."

"Help her!" Chris shouts from a distance.

My mind is fuzzy, and my hearing feels like it's fading, but I hear his desperate plea and wonder if I'm hallucinating. I stare up at the dark night sky, realizing rays of bright light are shooting upward from my body. The concerned voices around me fade away, and I cease to care about anything. Is this what it's like to die? Am I already dead?

Feeling begins to return to my brain as I sense the mending of tissue and the re-growth of bone. Life floods back into my body. The pain has subsided, and my body buzzes with a strange new energy. I open my eyes to find Maetha kneeling beside me, her hands covered in blood and holding the diamond.

"It didn't work?" I ask.

Maetha shakes her head. She smiles slightly, her lips quiver as she does so. I hear footsteps and turn my head to find Chris approaching with a jacket in his hands. He hands it to Maetha.

"Thank you, Chris." Maetha helps me into the jacket and zips it closed. She helps me stand, then turns to Chris and says, "Take her back to the room. She's weak."

Turns out I'm *very* weak. Chris wraps his arm around my back to give me support as I walk.

"I heard your voice, Chris, but I thought I was imagining it." I stumble over a rock and Chris readjusts his hold around my body. I hear the subtle sound of a heartbeat, but it's not his. I turn my head and see he's wearing a Pulse Emitter. I smile and lose my footing again over the uneven terrain.

Chris stops walking and scoops me into his arms, pulling me close to his chest. I wrap my arms around his neck and settle my head against him. He says, "I was so afraid you were going to die, Calli. You lost so much blood. I couldn't bear it."

"I know how you feel. I watched you die many times earlier today before we escaped with Maetha."

"What?"

"This has been a really long day, Chris. Let's get inside first, and then I'll tell you all about it."

After a few hours of being in-and-out of sleep, and many bottles of Ms. Winter's magical juice, I feel a little better. Chris has cared for me diligently, staying by my side, holding me in his arms—what a wonderful place to be. I find myself feeling happy we don't have the amulets around our necks to prevent close contact. However, thinking about the amulets brings the events of Justin's compound back to the front of my mind. Then I feel guilty for feeling happy because if I still had an amulet, Curtis,

Charles, and Dominic would still have theirs too and they'd be alive.

I've replayed the events at Justin's compound over and over in my mind. The point when General Harding entered the room and Chris nearly choked with surprise has me wondering what was going through Chris's mind.

I twist my neck a little so I can see his face. He removes his arm from under my head and we both reposition ourselves so that were facing each other on the bed. I ask, "Chris, were you shocked to see your father enter the room right before we fled?"

"Yes. But no more so than hearing Agent Alpha call you by name."

"Agent Alpha?" *Wait, what? Chris knows him as Agent Alpha?*

"Yeah. The guy Brand took down."

"You mean Freedom?"

"What?" Chris rises up on his elbow.

"That's the name he gave me. Freedom. But Justin called him Agent Alpha too."

Chris asks, "How does he know you?"

"He's a Diamond Bearer, like Maetha. How do you know him?"

"He works with my father. I've always known him as Agent Alpha. Wait. He's a Diamond Bearer?"

"Yes. I first met him just after returning home from Montana. He's been after Brand and the other Repeaters. But he also wants my diamond shard."

"Well, now he has Brand."

"Yeah," I say, feeling as though I've failed. "I hope Brand is all right."

He reaches forward and takes my hand into his. I can tell he has a lot on his mind, so I give him time to formulate his thoughts. His eyes meet mine and he says,

"So much happened tonight, Calli. One thing I'm still confused about is the significance of the pocket watch."

"Well," I say, "did you lose your Running power when he walked into the room?"

"Yes."

"The watch contains some kind of stone that removes our powers when it's exposed—even Diamond Bearers. No one knows what it is."

"My uncle is a rock-hound. He'd know what it is— that is, if it's a stone found in nature. He doesn't know anything about the world of the clans, but he knows everything about geology."

"Calli," Maetha speaks, making me jump because I didn't know she was nearby. "You and Chris will take the pocket watch to him and find out more about it. I have placed Freedom's diamond in this pouch," —she holds up a leather pouch that looks similar to the one I had when I first carried the stone— "to help protect both you and the stone. You will once again be this diamond's Bearer, but I'm afraid you will need to avoid using your powers, as this stone is clearly loyal to Freedom . . . or Agent Alpha as Chris knows him."

"What do you mean, 'loyal?' " I ask, sitting upright on the bed. Chris does as well.

"The diamond didn't merge with your piece, Calli, and I do not know why. A splintered diamond always merges together with its other parts, and I believed it would in this case as well, although I didn't know whether or not it would become loyal to you. I was prepared to remove the entire stone the moment I ascertained where its loyalty belonged, only the stone didn't merge. I couldn't heal your heart until I removed his stone and . . . I tried to remove your shard, but it's already living within your heart."

My confused expression must tell her everything I'm

thinking.

She continues. "I thought that if the stone wasn't going to merge, I could at least remove your piece, you could relinquish it to Freedom, and the stone would then be whole again. At that point, Freedom would have full ownership and would have no reason to kill you. Now it seems in order to get the remaining piece, he'll have to cut it out of you."

"Cut it out?"

She softens her voice. "Calli, the plan is to end Freedom's life, releasing his hold on the diamond. Then your shard will merge flawlessly with the diamond."

"But how do you kill a Diamond Bearer, Maetha, when they can see their own futures?"

"How indeed? The need has never existed."

I say, "Maybe he could be shot with a gun. I saw you get shot and die multiple times at Justin's hideout."

"A simple bullet wouldn't have killed me. I would have healed myself after a few minutes. My head or heart would have to be removed from my body for me to die. Freedom's life will have to be ended in a similar fashion."

I think for a moment and then say, "Would you still be able to heal yourself if the black rock was nearby?"

"I don't know."

"What if you had been decapitated after being shot but before you healed yourself? Would that would have killed you."

"Possibly, Calli." Maetha pauses momentarily, then says, "It will be a good idea to always avoid situations where the future shows the black fog. Life threatening situations could occur. As we are coming to this conclusion we can bet Freedom has already figured this out and won't put himself in a dangerous position where we could remove his diamond."

Chris says, "This doesn't help us at all. You're sending us into those exact kinds of situations where we could be harmed."

"If you have the black stone power activated, I don't think Freedom will come near it."

Maetha says, "I'm going in search of the female Repeater as she possesses the skills necessary to break into the government facility. Our other Repeaters are less than qualified to try to rescue Brand."

Chris cringes. "Are you kidding me? Isn't there another way to help Brand, one that doesn't involve her?"

"Not one I can detect," Maetha says.

"That girl is a complete psycho and you want to have her join our team?"

"Chris," Maetha lowers her voice, "Brand is the only one who can effectively protect Calli from Freedom. Not you, not me. Only Brand. Freedom will kill Calli if he gets the chance, especially now that he has Brand. I think that was the only reason he didn't kill her earlier and take the shard. He wanted Brand. Now there's nothing preventing him from doing away with her just to get her shard."

Chris dips his chin and grimaces.

I say, "I think you're right, Maetha." My mind reflects back on the fight by the river with the swarm of Unaltered boys and Brand. Freedom knew Brand and I were friends. He must have figured he could collect us both at the same time at Justin's hideout, which he almost did.

Maetha continues. "Calli, you will need to use the pocket watch to travel undetected with Chris until we can rescue Brand."

Chris jumps up in defense and raises his hands. "Whoa, wait. Are you saying we must purposefully suppress our powers?"

"She must. It's the only way to hide from Freedom.

Using whatever the substance is inside the pocket watch has worked for Freedom for decades. Now we have his method and Calli is going to use it to hide from him while you travel to your uncle."

I look at Chris. "Where does your uncle live?"

"Miami. I'll get us plane tickets."

Maetha interrupts. "No, you cannot use any form of public transportation. Because of Freedom's connections with the government, I fear he'll have Homeland Security searching for you. You don't want your face captured on any camera. No cell phones or anything the government can track. In fact, I'd be surprised if your faces don't end up on the FBI's most wanted list, which will put state and local law enforcement after you as well. I have a vehicle here you can use for as far as it will take you. I cannot see the future concerning how far that will be. The use of Freedom's black stone prevents it."

I take a deep cleansing breath. "Let me guess. All you can see is a black fog."

"Correct."

Chris scoots closer to me and puts his arm around my back, squeezing my shoulder with reassurance. "No problem. We have a lot of friends who will help us. We'll just keep our noses clean and not rob any banks."

I appreciate his attempt to try to lighten the mood. However, his touch causes my pulse to increase and the diamond shard within my heart shifts painfully. I quickly heal my heart with the diamond shard's power.

Maetha's eyes narrow and I wonder if she can tell I just used the Healing power. She doesn't address it. Instead, she says, "You won't be able to contact any friends or family. The clans are up in arms because their amulet wearers—their leaders—were kidnapped and then murdered. They think Calli has their amulets in her possession. They want them back, and they want justice to be served."

"You mean they want me dead," I say quietly.

Chris says, "But I can testify that Calli wasn't behind it. She wasn't working with Justin."

Maetha speaks with finality, "You must stay by Calli's side for this very reason. You are the only one who can tell the clans what really happened, since you were kidnapped yourself. Freedom's pocket watch is your cloaking device, and with Calli's cleverly-designed Pulse-Emitters you'll be able to travel at night, giving you the advantage over the Hunters."

"Why don't we have my uncle come to us instead?" Chris asks.

"No, you two need to stay on the move, or you risk being found. Freedom knows about this place, and it's only a matter of time before he looks here. Also, when you meet with your uncle, be on your guard. He is your father's brother and it's not too farfetched to think your father might suspect you'll go to his house instead of your mother's home."

Chris half-chuckles. "Except for the fact that my dad and uncle haven't spoken to each other in years."

"Regardless, be on high alert. Now, it's time for you two to leave. I don't want you here when Freedom arrives."

After packing a few more items into a backpack including extra emitters—besides the one Chris is already wearing—Ms. Winter's granola bars, juice, and an exceptionally large amount of cash, Maetha leads us outside to the parking lot and to her car.

Maetha hands me the pouch with Freedom's diamond inside and says to both of us, "Calli, when you carried the diamond before, it infused your body with powers and abilities. As long as the pocket watch is open, that won't happen. However, if the watch is closed or you move too far away from it, the diamond might act erratically. Be careful and only close the pocket watch in extreme emergencies."

I nod my head, realizing it means I will need to have the diamond and the pocket watch on my person at all times.

Chris asks Maetha, "What do we do once my uncle identifies the stone?"

"Find a safe place and close the pocket watch. I'll come to you." Maetha tosses the car keys to Chris, who catches them with ease.

The open watch rests inside my jacket pocket, emanating its eerie anti-power, both protecting us and making us vulnerable. The diamond in the pouch warms my hand, and I tuck it inside my front pocket as well. The pouch protected the diamond once before, but at that time it had been relinquished to me. Now the diamond's loyalty is divided, and the pouch may not be enough to disguise it properly.

Freedom undoubtedly understands the precarious situation, and the ease of which he can take possession of my shard by ending my life. If he had been given the chance, he would have killed me already. Nothing will stop him from ending my life to reclaim my shard . . . well, except for Chris. He would die protecting me, I am sure.

Hopefully, it won't come to that.

Thanks for reading!

Did you enjoy the book? Please consider leaving a review on Amazon to let other readers know what intrigued you most about the story. Reviews really matter to independent writers like me, as they help the books rise in visibility so more people can see them and, hopefully, purchase them. That's huge, as it allows me to make enough money to write full time and get more books on the market for readers like you!

Don't know how to leave a review? Send me a message using my Contact Me form on my website and I'll give you instructions.

http://lorenaangell.com/contact-me.html

The Unaltered Series adventure continues in Book Three:

The Diamond of Freedom

Calli Courtnae and Chris Harding race against the clock to identify the mysterious power-neutralizing stone that will help them hide from their enemy, but that will also prevent Calli from healing her life-threatening injuries. Their challenge is not simply to identify the stone; they must also learn how to counter its effects so they can fight against the rogue Diamond Bearer named Freedom.

General Harding, Chris's father, has made it his life's mission to eradicate all people with powers. Believing Freedom's lies, and misusing his position with the U.S. government, General Harding nears completion of a weapon designed to locate and destroy cosmic-energy individuals.

Calli meets Brand Safferson's half-sister, Deus Ex, who is a proclaimed mercenary, working for Freedom. Her repeating abilities are necessary to attempt the rescue of Brand from General Harding's compound, but the risks of recruiting her to join Maetha may be deadly.

In the epic battle between extreme cosmic-power holders, weaknesses are exploited and lifetime relationships shattered to gain the upper-hand, all in the quest to fulfill nature's will.

The Diamond of Freedom is available on Amazon and Barnes&Noble.com

or

As an audiobook on Audible

ABOUT THE AUTHOR

Lorena Angell is the internationally bestselling author of the YA fantasy series, *The Unaltered*. Inspired by an interview from J.K. Rowling, Lorena began to write and published her first book in 2011. Since then, she's earned over 4,200 reviews (average of 4.5 stars), has been a #1 bestseller in over 11 countries and wants nothing more than to write more books for her readers.

Connect with Lorena Angell at:

www.LorenaAngell.com
Twitter: @LorenaAngell1
Facebook: The Unaltered Diamond Series
Instagram: the.unaltered.series

www.ingramcontent.com/pod-product-compliance
Lightning Source LLC
Chambersburg PA
CBHW072357110726
47909CB00003B/729